You Can't See the Snow

Rokudo Ningen

YEN ON

New York

You Can't See the Snow

Rokudo Ningen

Translation by Taylor Engel
Cover photo by Shiori Iwakura

KIMI WA YUKI O MIRUKOTO GA DEKINAI
©Rokudo Ningen 2022
First published in Japan in 2022 by KADOKAWA CORPORATION, Tokyo.
English translation rights arranged with KADOKAWA CORPORATION, Tokyo through TUTTLE-MORI AGENCY, INC., Tokyo.

English translation © 2024 by Yen Press, LLC

Yen On
150 West 30th Street, 19th Floor
New York, NY 10001

Visit us at yenpress.com ❊ facebook.com/yenpress ❊ twitter.com/yenpress
yenpress.tumblr.com ❊ instagram.com/yenpress

First Yen On Edition: April 2024
Edited by Yen On Editorial: Emma McClain
Designed by Yen Press Design: Wendy Chan

Yen On is an imprint of Yen Press, LLC.
The Yen On name and logo are trademarks of Yen Press, LLC.

Library of Congress Cataloging-in-Publication Data
Names: Ningen, Rokudo, author. | Engel, Taylor, translator.
Title: You can't see the snow / Rokudo Ningen ; translation by
    Taylor Engel.
Other titles: Kimi wa yuki o mirukoto ga dekinai. English
Description: New York, NY : Yen On, 2024.
Identifiers: LCCN 2023053704 | ISBN 9781975379582 (hardcover)
Subjects: CYAC: Love—Fiction. | Sleep—Fiction. | Sick—Fiction. |
    College students—Fiction. | LCGFT: Romance fiction. | Light novels.
Classification: LCC PZ7.1.N576 Yo 2024 | DDC [Fic]—dc23
LC record available at https://lccn.loc.gov/2023053704

ISBNs: 978-1-9753-7958-2 (paperback)
        978-1-9753-7959-9 (ebook)

10 9 8 7 6 5 4 3 2 1

LSC-C

Printed in the United States of America

CONTENTS

Every year on October 31, I tell you good-bye.

Laying my head on top of the blanket that cocoons you, I pick up a gentle scent and the sound of your slowly beating heart. *Badmp*—...... *Badmp*—...... It's much, much too slow for a human heartbeat.

Even so, Yuki Iwato, you're alive. Even if the sofa we're sitting on were cut off from the rest of the world, that wouldn't change.

When I raise my head again, you softly rest your hand on it and smile. Your senses always fade to the point of vanishing before you fall asleep, but not the sensation in your fingertips. That stays clear until the very end. My "job" is to hold your hand.

It's already past eleven PM. In the dining room, your mother, Touko, is bustling around getting everything ready. The fresh, clean table holds an impressive array of medical equipment; it looks like a trade-fair display.

Your father, Reiji, has just gone to get the rubber tubing for the catheter.

Fuyumi's sitting on a chair in the blazer she always wears around the house, hugging her knees, watching TV. It's a Marvel movie; gunshots and the sound of breaking glass reach us faintly, and with every burst of noise, she steals a glance at us.

Light flashes across the gap in the curtains. Just as I register it, the sky rumbles.

You pinch my finger—or rather, you gently hold the skin between your fingertips. I hastily shift my focus back to you. Your face is so pale that you look like you're wearing a performer's white face powder, and your lips are drained of color. You trail your fingertips down my neck. They're cool; it feels nice.

"Can I ask you to do this bit?" Touko hands me a thermometer.

I put my hand through the front of your button-down pajama top and stick the thermometer under your arm. The mouth of the vase-shaped humidifier glows blue and starts to give off white mist. Around it sit string-bound stacks of cookbooks and fashion magazines for high schoolers. When I withdraw the thermometer, it simply reads *Error*.

You grimace as if this is a nuisance. Cheering you on, I try again. This time it beeps properly, and a faint *31* shows in the little gray window. There we go.

Confidently, I relay your temperature to Touko without taking another reading.

"Yes, good. It's almost time, then." Touko nods. You tap the back of my hand with your finger three times. After shifting you to lean against the back of the sofa so you won't fall over, I get up.

"Is there any water?"

"In the fridge. It should be right there when you open the door. Oh—," Touko says. "Be careful not to give her too much at once, though."

"Fifty milliliters at a time, right?"

"That's right. She can't swallow as well right now, and we can't risk her choking."

I open the refrigerator. It's packed with Tupperware containers of potato salad and Ziploc bags of marinating meat. Just as I extract a plastic bottle of water, Reiji comes downstairs, carrying a thin length of brown tubing that forks in two.

Behind me, there's a clatter. I whip around, all my hairs standing on end. You're on your hands and knees on the floor: You tried to get up on your own, and your knees buckled under you.

"Sis!" Fuyumi screams. By the time I start to move, she's already run to you and has her arm around your shoulders, supporting you. I hustle over to give her a hand, and we pull you up onto the sofa together.

Fuyumi shoots me a harsh glare.

I grit my teeth and nod several times.

The Iwato family has done this for a long time. When this season comes around, you prepare to fall asleep. It's a serious affair that happens once a year, every year, and your whole family has always supported you through it. Technically, as an outsider, I shouldn't be here. The family system that's grown up around you shouldn't have any room for me.

However, right now, they're letting me hold your hand.

"Seriously, for the love of— Do this right, would you?"

Fuyumi's voice is trembling. She's two years younger than me, but there's enough pressure in her sharp eyes to make a full-grown adult flinch.

"I'm sorry."

"My sister is your one and only girlfriend. Can't you look after her properly?"

"I'll be more careful."

"Obviously. That's your job," Fuyumi mutters.

You squeeze my fingers again. There's about as much force behind it as a bug bite, but I know that's the very best you can do right now.

I'll keep the promise I made you that day. The one thing I can do. The reason they're letting me stay by your side.

Reiji comes over and puts a hand on Fuyumi's shoulder. "It's all right. Fuyumi, you shouldn't be so prickly." His warm eyes shift from her to me. "I'm sorry to ask for your help with this every year. You're a third-year in college now, aren't you? You must already have your hands full with job hunting."

"No, it's no trouble at all. Job hunting is… I mean, I wouldn't say it's going smoothly, but I'll get it figured out."

"We really should be doing this by ourselves. I'm glad you've started to join us for it, though."

Touko takes a pouch filled with clear liquid out of a blue cardboard box. Loading it and the other medical equipment into a sanitized laundry basket, she starts up to the second floor.

"Well, let's all see Yuki off together," Reiji says, putting an arm under your right shoulder. I support your left shoulder, and we hoist you to your feet as if we're assisting a wounded soldier on the battlefield.

"We're about to go upstairs. We'll help support you," I whisper in your ear, and you nod slightly. Then we walk you along, one step at a time. Next to us, Fuyumi watches my every move like a hawk.

We go all the way up the stairs and down the hall, to a room warmed by two oil heaters. There, Touko has attached a catheter drainage bag to your medical bed.

A clear infusion pack with blue writing on it hangs from the IV stand that's part of the bed frame. Next to it, there's an electrocardiograph with lots of cords attached.

Reiji and I have gotten you onto the bed. Beneath half-closed lids, your eyes are drowsy. Touko scrubs your left forearm with an alcohol pad until it's faintly flushed, then deftly sticks in a needle and stabilizes it with a piece of clear tape. She connects a tube to the needle, then looks at me and asks if I'd turn the other way for a moment. She's holding the brown tubing that Reiji brought.

"Um, I'll step outside."

She's about to insert indwelling catheters into your rectum and bladder. If my mom were putting tubes up my butt and my privates, I wouldn't want anybody but family around.

"If you wouldn't mind, that would probably be best."

Fuyumi looks triumphant. Shooting her a sidelong glance, I leave the room.

The Good Night Ritual—that's what the Iwato family calls this. At the end of October, when you fall into a deep sleep, everyone sees you off.

On the balcony, a bath towel swims in the lashing rain like a manta ray that's strayed from its squadron. In the hall of this unfamiliar house, the ceiling feels higher somehow.

I knock, then go back inside. You're all tucked in, your head sinking into the pillow, and you look happy. Three tubes stretch from the bed, each connected to different things; it reminds me a bit of a freeway interchange. The EKG emits a soft, regular double beep as waves run across its square green screen.

Touko leaves the room, taking the dubious-looking Fuyumi with her. As they pass me, I bow slightly. The door closes, and then we're alone.

I look at the clock. Seventeen minutes until the date changes. I lean against the wall farthest from the bed, then slide down it into a crouch.

It feels like I need to watch from here.

If I get too close, it'll be the end of me. I'll start thinking about what the days are going to be like from tomorrow on. I have to avoid that, no matter what.

"What kind of dreams are you going to have?"

The EKG's rhythm is getting slower and slower. It occurs to me that you might die, but I pull that idea back into the depths of my heart and fasten it there.

"Aren't you lonely?"

The monitor shows a heart icon and jagged lines. Below them, there's a number that keeps falling: sixty-seven, fifty-four, fifty-two. I can't take it; I get to my feet, cross to the bed, and kneel right by the safety rail.

You look comfortable. Your eyes are closed.

I slip a hand under the covers and squeeze your fingers.

Fifty-one, fifty, forty-four... The number falls to twenty, then finally stabilizes.

Your half-asleep life echoes at the speed of water dripping from a faucet.

Your pallid lips seem to move slightly.

Startled, I stare. I search the air for the remnants of a sound, but your weak breathing doesn't even stir a speck of dust.

I bend forward again, head bowed, and gaze down into your face.

"Okay. I'll see you next spring," I tell you, as if I'm chasing after you. It's a good-bye that won't reach anybody.

Still, those words are the only reason I am here.

If you didn't sleep all winter, if your life were perfectly normal, would we even have met? Could I have entered your family home with you, held your hand as it grew colder?

The next day, on November 1, 2020, the Meteorological Agency records the year's first snow in Nagano.

Once again, alone, I walk into another winter.

I hear your breathing.
I feel your warmth.
I wave.
I shout, quietly, that I'll be back soon.
When the world around me grows cold, my body starts down a
dusky street. Traveling as I'm led, I'll dance with the streetlights
and play with the night wind. In this solitary, isolated place, until
morning comes, I'll offer a ceaseless prayer shaped like my breath.
I'm waiting to wake up.
In order to wake up, I leave on a little journey,
taking only myself.

1

When I was a kid, I believed in the sort of nocturnal monsters that inhabited fairy tales. I knew ghosts didn't exist, and yet I saw monsters again and again, in the dingy AC condenser unit on the balcony or between pieces of swaying laundry. I made peace with them long ago, and I'd assumed they had simply gone back to Monster Land. I never dreamed I'd see them again at university.

An upperclassman with an athletic build reached with his thick arm for a pitcher, his face flushed red as an ogre's. Whenever he found an empty cup, he'd slosh lukewarm beer into it with the force of an air raid. Keeping about three centimeters of the flat liquid in the bottom of my cup, I munched on raw cabbage dressed with something that tasted like black vinegar.

From time to time, I'd smile politely and nod to show I was listening, although I didn't really get what the conversation was about. If I butted in partway through with my opinion like a know-it-all, I'd tick people off, and it wasn't as if I could just stay silent and blank-faced the whole time. It was almost funny how little anyone cared to help me when I got to the conversation late.

That year, 2018, I'd met Atsushi and Tomomi at the new student orientation, but at the moment, they were both enmeshed in conversations at separate tables. I'd joined this club on their invitation, in fact.

I watched them out of the corner of my eye. They looked like they were having fun. They were the type of people who got through life with no problems. They managed to laugh at the senior members' idiotic bragging, and even if nobody asked them, they could express their own opinions while making the other person look good.

In this room filled with smoke and carbon dioxide, they seemed able to breathe without even a hint of trouble.

Only capable people like them lasted here. All the rest of us could do was force smiles and go along with them, toughing it out until the time was up.

"Why're you leaving? Got something you need to do?"

The conversation around me was all agreement and falling in line, so that alien note of dubious irritation really stood out.

When I looked over, the sober guy in charge of taking attendees' money—that drinking party staple—was loudly calling out to a woman as she tried to leave.

"No, it's nothing like that."

The woman was just stepping down into her high heels from the raised tatami flooring.

"Do you feel sick, then? Should I get you some water?"

"No, I'm fine. I just want to go home," she said flatly.

The man seemed a little taken aback. "Um, were you not having fun?"

"That's not it."

"Huh? Then why are you leaving?"

I felt as if a ray of light had broken through. As if I'd seen the end of the tunnel.

Without a word, I got to my feet and went over to where we'd all piled our stuff. Several people glanced my way, but I kept my eyes down and shouldered my backpack. *If somebody stops me now…* The thought sent a shudder through my body. My heart throbbed at the base of my throat.

Atsushi glanced up and noticed me. I looked away quickly, but not fast enough.

"Hey. Natsuki. You're leaving, too?"

I nodded as indifferently as I could.

"We're hitting two more places after this one," he continued. "Or hey, no way… Are you walking Ms. Iwato home?" he asked, intentionally gathering the group's attention. He probably didn't mean any harm. He was drunk, and there was no way he could know what was going through my head.

Half the people there were looking at me. A shiver ran down my spine, and I stood paralyzed. My throat closed up; I felt hot, and a suffocating sensation swept over me.

Out of the corner of my eye, I looked at the woman. She had both feet in her heels now, and she straightened up resolutely. Her dignified stance seemed to lay low all of creation. When I saw her, a mysterious strength welled up inside me, and my paralysis lifted.

"Yeah, that's right. I'm walking her home," I shot back.

The woman left the pub. Now was my only chance.

I walked briskly over the tatami, jammed my feet into the sneakers I'd left in the dirt-floored entryway, and headed for the door at a trot, the heel of my foot stomping down the back of one shoe. I heard what sounded like an angry yell behind me, but I plugged my ears.

I did it! I did it, and I'm gonna wish I hadn't!

That club had forty members, and more than half were in my department. I shared classes with a dozen of them. How was I supposed to face them at school the next day? Until now, I'd done my best not to stick out. I'd worked hard so that things wouldn't end up this way... And now I'd gone and blown it.

Regret crawled up my spine, making me feel itchy all over. Wanting to get out of there as fast as possible, I smacked the shop curtain away from my head and stepped outside.

Strangely, my feet stopped there. It was early summer, and the night air was still a little chilly.

"Thank you," a voice said.

The woman from earlier was standing flush against the sign of the pasta place two doors down, just pulling on her cardigan.

"Um... Why?"

"What do you mean, 'why'? You bought me time to leave."

My face froze, mouth open slightly. I thought hard, searching for the right thing to say as hot air from a huge, shuddering AC condenser blew on my cheek. "...You were the one who helped me. You were already leaving, so I grabbed the opportunity to go."

She looked blank for a moment. Then, as suddenly as a bursting balloon, she broke into a grin. "Oh really? You didn't have to go out of your way to set the record straight."

"Why not?"

"It's more convenient to have people be grateful to you, isn't it?"

"It would feel sort of unpleasant, though. Lying, I mean."

"Oh? Then what about lying to avoid hurting somebody? You know what they say: 'Lies can ease suffering.'"

I was flustered, and my eyes focused on one random thing after another: the charcoal brazier outside the eel restaurant, the rainbow-colored lights of the karaoke place, the scalloped shop curtain outside the fishermen's pub. My nose caught the aroma of yakitori and savory hotcakes, and to my chagrin, my stomach growled.

"Well, um, the thing is, I'm not religious. That's a Buddhist phrase, isn't it? I'd feel bad about borrowing the ethics of something I don't believe in…"

At my earnest answer, her mouth fell open for a second, but then she smiled even more vibrantly. "Um, excuse me? Aren't you being a little picky?"

I thought she was making fun of me. I almost took offense, but she kept laughing for so long that it started to seem ridiculous, and finally, I ended up laughing, too.

"You're funny," she said, wiping her eyes with her index finger.

At this point, I took a good, long look at her for the first time. She was wearing a floral lace see-through top and a checkered calf-length skirt. Her glossy black bob hung perfectly straight. The clean line of her jaw, her prominent nose, and her clear, deep-set eyes reminded me of a European princess.

Catching myself with a jolt, I glanced away.

She smiled, then turned around and took a few languid steps.

Well, of course: It wasn't like I was actually going to walk her home.

"Aren't you coming?" she called.

Those were the words I'd been waiting for.

As her back dissolved into the vivid neon night of Shinjuku's Kabukicho, I followed her as if my life depended on it.

Somebody with dreadlocks was sitting on the guardrail between the sidewalk and the street, talking rapidly in a foreign tongue. An office worker was fast asleep in front of a shuttered storefront. The woman breezed past both of them. The road was littered with cigarette butts and disintegrating, water-logged flyers, and yet somehow she seemed to be walking over her own personal red carpet.

"I'm Yuki. Yuki Iwato, a second-year."

Oh, good—she was an upperclassman. One year above me, at that. I'd been speaking politely for no reason in particular, but it had been the right call. "My name's Natsuki Uzume. I'm a brand-new first-year."

"Uzume…" She—or rather, Ms. Iwato—repeated the word, looking a bit troubled. "What characters do you write that with?"

"Just one. *Uzume*, as in 'burying something in the ground.'"

"Huh! That's one you don't see much."

"My grandfather on my father's side was from Fukui. I hear it's a pretty common family name over there."

"I see. And you're living by yourself now?"

"Yes. I live near here." Privately, I thanked my grandpa. Explaining my family name was always a winning move; I'd already used it several times since starting school. "Ms. Iwato, do you belong to that club?"

The woman grinned, flashing her white, even teeth. "I was just there to help out. They needed to fill out their numbers for the drinking party."

The club was called GTR, and I'd joined because I'd heard they made films. But they didn't actually do that—they were just a drinking club. Nobody even knew what GTR stood for.

"What department are you in, Natsuki?"

"Literature."

"Why did you mutter that like you're embarrassed about it?"

"Um, no real reason…"

When I was applying to universities, the Literature Department had been my first choice, but that wasn't true for most of the people around me. I'd heard quite a few of them say it was their fallback option, or that it was for rejects who couldn't get in anywhere else.

Having someone else point out my reticence made me ashamed of being spineless.

"What about you, Ms. Iwato?"

"I'm in the College of Art, majoring in oil painting."

"Isn't that program really hard to get into?"

We went to the same university, but there was a pretty big popularity difference between the general ed departments and the art departments. Of those, I'd heard that the Fine Arts Department, in particular, had extremely difficult entrance exams.

Ms. Iwato refuted my claim modestly. She didn't seem bashful or anything. "The oil painting professor is called Kanzaki…"

"I've heard that name somewhere before."

"Yes, he appears on TV sometimes." Ms. Iwato gave the names of a few late-night programs that Norihito Kanzaki had appeared on. "He's a lech, though. He makes us write down our addresses for him, even though his class isn't a seminar. And he only asks the girls."

"That's creepy."

"Isn't it?"

I gave an exaggerated nod.

"So I wrote down my parents' address. It's not even in Tokyo, so I got off without a scratch!" Ms. Iwato declared loudly, then laughed.

I told her she'd gotten him good.

"All universities are like that, though."

Apparently, all universities were like that.

After we'd walked for fifteen minutes or so, we started down some stairs leading underground. On the landing, there were jars of preserved cayenne peppers of various sizes and a dark-red sign with TANGIER written on it in flat white letters.

"I've wanted to try this place for a while," she said.

The excitement on Ms. Iwato's face was dazzling.

The door opened to reveal a stylish interior hung with unique fabrics. Warm light from teardrop-shaped lamps illuminated the room in a soft, subtle way. In sharp contrast to the gentle atmosphere, there was a pungent, tear-inducing aroma that flustered me. "What a smell…," I murmured.

We were near a padded bench built for three, and Ms. Iwato sat down a bit left of the middle. When I hesitated, she looked up at me through her lashes. "Not interested?"

I shook my head. The seat was soft and deep enough that my thighs sank into it.

We ordered, and when they brought us water, I gulped mine down. Ms. Iwato and I were sitting so close that our shoulders almost rubbed together. Didn't she mind? Feeling a little uneasy, I stole a glance at her face. She was already looking at me, and her eyes seemed to ask, *What's wrong?*

"I was wondering why you slipped out of the party," I said.

Ms. Iwato tilted her head to the side, thinking. "Spring is short, you know?" she said at last.

"Yes, it is."

"The thing is, summer's really short, too."

A dish of dressed vegetables promptly arrived: coarsely chopped cucumbers sprinkled with black flakes. Ms. Iwato dug in first. When I took a bite, a complex fragrance shot up through my nose. What was this stuff?

"I wish it could always be summer, though." Ms. Iwato smiled elegantly, covering her mouth with one hand.

My tongue finally picked up on something odd. Whatever they'd put on the food felt exactly like the anesthetic used at the dentist's before they drill one of your molars. I couldn't stop salivating, and my sense of taste started to go screwy.

Ms. Iwato seemed to be just fine. Not only that, but she called a server over and asked, "How hot can you make your mapo tofu?"

The server thought for a moment. "There's a ten-yen surcharge per level."

"Take the spiciness up to twelve, then."

The server gave her an awkward smile, disappeared into the kitchen, then came back with a gray clipboard and pen, which he held out for her to sign. It was a waiver.

She scribbled her signature, and the server promptly brought out a stocky cocotte pot and set it on the tabletop burner.

The red molten liquid bubbled, sending a shockingly pungent smell all the way over to where I was sitting. It irritated my eyes and nose. Just looking at it hurt.

"This isn't a hobby of mine or anything," Ms. Iwato said. She looked down slightly, as if she was embarrassed. "It's just how I'm wired."

I didn't know what sort of expression I should be wearing. My tear ducts were leaking without permission, and I wiped at my eyes.

Before long, they brought out my fried cutlet rice bowl, and we both dug in.

The breading on the cutlet was crispy, and the seasoning and the amount of fat were just right. The soft-boiled egg couldn't have been better, either. If I hadn't eaten this, I probably would have ended up hating pubs for the rest of my life.

"How is it, Ms. Iwato?"

She sipped one Chinese soupspoon full of sauce and beamed, flashing me a thumbs-up with her free left hand. Then, looking a little melancholy, she said: "There was someone I wanted to see, but they weren't there today. I asked, and it sounds like they quit the club. That meant there was no reason for me to be there." Then, for just a moment, her eyes went cold, and she murmured, "It's my fault."

Instantly, she seemed far away. She was right next to me, and yet the divide that ran between us made it feel as if she were in a completely different dimension.

"That was delicious, wasn't it?" she said.

I nodded silently.

"What should we do now?"

"……"

Ms. Iwato gave me a long, appraising look. "Hey. Do you know what time it is?"

Her smile was bewitching. It was a smile with implications.

Hastily, I glanced at my watch. It was 12:44. With a gasp, I looked up.

"Oh, drat. I've missed the last train," Ms. Iwato said deliberately.

Before I'd realized what was going on, she'd pulled me under. This woman wore the night like it was just another piece in her wardrobe, and I didn't think I could get away from her if I tried.

2

I spotted Tomomi Oujiro the moment I got to the cafeteria. She was wearing a leather jacket and a pleated skirt. I waved, then sat down across from her. "This place is packed."

"Pay up. You owe me for grabbing you a seat." Tomomi held out her right hand.

I clapped mine together in reverence. "Where's Atsushi?"

Tomomi pointed toward the food service counter, and I spotted Atsushi Aogiri standing impatiently in the long line, tray in hand.

"He said the B set meal was sold out, so he lined up again. Forget that. Listen, this is insane!" Tomomi set her sausage roll down across the rim of her teacup and launched into her story, gesticulating wildly. "I got a ticket!"

"A ticket to…?" I asked.

"The Baggages' dome concert!"

Tomomi was an enthusiastic band chaser, and she had a particular fondness for hard-core punk rock.

"It's all just noise," I said, a little weirded out.

"Look at this! Isn't it awesome?" Tomomi pulled a ticket out of her pass case and held it in front of my face. It was pitch-black, with some text in a violent-looking font.

"It's a little hard to read… Though this part looks like it says 'Nagoya Dome.'"

"Exactly. I reserved a night bus ticket, too. I splurged and got one of the 'extra room' seats."

"November's still quite a ways off. Aren't you jumping the gun a little?"

"Huh?! It's right around the corner! This is huge. It's gonna keep me alive for the next four months."

Smiling wryly, I gazed at Tomomi's profile. She looked unbelievably happy. That smile of hers had put down solid roots; you'd have to do an awful lot of shoving to knock it over.

Right at the beginning of my first college drinking party, we'd had the inevitable round of self-introductions. I'd written it off as dumb and childish, but unexpectedly, most of my year-mates had spoken proudly about the things they liked. Everyone had gotten really into it, but I hadn't had anything to tell people about. I'd felt daunted, and it had been even harder to talk than usual.

Actually, maybe that was when I'd started to hate drinking parties.

I took my lunch out of a paper bag. It was a prepackaged meal I'd bought at a fried chicken place on my way to school. I reached for the plastic lid, then went still.

"Aren't you going to eat?" Tomomi sounded puzzled.

"I'll wait for Atsushi."

"You're pretty conscientious, huh, Natsuki."

Was I? I thought about it. As she brought her sausage roll up for another bite, Tomomi smiled, the expression stretching out her pierced lower lip.

Abruptly, as if overwriting Tomomi's face, I had a flashback of Ms. Iwato.

"What's up?"

I knew it was in my best interests to stay quiet about this, but I couldn't keep my face from softening. "I think…I might have a girlfriend. Or something."

I'd said it as casually as possible, but Tomomi's elbow slipped off the edge of the table with a clatter. Her eyes widened inside their borders of heavy eyeliner; you'd have thought she was rubbernecking at an accident. "Are you for real? This isn't something from your novel, right?"

"Hey, that's mean. It's not that unbelievable."

"You can't be a writer if you're happy."

"Like I keep saying, I'm not going to be a writer. It's just a hobby."

I set my chopsticks down on the lid of my meal and thought for a moment. What was I to Ms. Iwato anyway?

"Hey, what's with that face?" Tomomi eyed me dubiously. "You're not serious, are you?"

At that point, I spotted Atsushi heading our way with his tray, weaving in between chairs. By the time he set everything down, the brimming bowl of watery miso soup had slopped over, getting the tray all wet.

"What's up? You two look like you just got done with midterms or something."

Tomomi glanced at me as if she wasn't sure what to do. Feeling conflicted, I looked from her to Atsushi and back. *Hmm, guess I shouldn't discriminate.*

"Um, we were talking about how I've maybe got a girlfriend."

"Hey, congrats." At Atsushi's casual tone, a weight lifted off my shoulders. I opened my lunch. "You don't sound too sure about it, though."

I took a bite of fried chicken and rice, then swallowed. "We spent the night together, but I haven't told her I like her."

Tomomi's shocked stare bore into me. Next to her, Atsushi yelled, leaning forward. "Dude! Way to go! So what's a college coed's place like, huh?!"

"Actually, she came to my place. We were drinking over by the station, and she missed the last train."

"Well, that's a classic."

"Is it?"

"Making her miss the last train and then inviting her back to your place is basically a pickup artist cliché."

I nodded noncommittally, my gaze wandering a little. What was Ms. Iwato doing now? The College of Art's campus was right next to ours, but even the cafeterias were separate. I knew looking for her was pointless, and yet...

"So what happened?"

"What do you mean, 'what happened'? ...I hadn't been expecting company, so I cleaned up in a hurry. I set a futon out on the floor, and we lay there and watched *Stranger Things* on TV, and then—"

I had a flashback of Ms. Iwato lying on my bed. Under the moonlight streaming through the window, her skin shone faintly. I could feel the warmth of her body from her irresistible limbs.

I really couldn't put that fever dream of a night into words.

"Haaah. Don't even bother; that expression's enough," said Atsushi. "So what's she like? Does she go here?"

Come to think of it, I'd just been saying *her* and *she*. For some reason, I'd been reluctant to mention her name. However, Ms. Iwato hadn't suggested we keep anything secret.

What was I embarrassed about? I swallowed and forced my tightly closed lips to move. "Iwato," I said, and then it got easier all at once. "Yuki Iwato, from the College of Art."

Feeling like I'd accomplished something, I looked up and saw that the other two had gone stiff.

"Iwato...," Tomomi echoed quietly. For a moment, she frowned.

Atsushi looked like he wasn't sure what to say. Then he stood up and thumped me on the shoulder, beaming. "Well, good for you! Don't blow this, man! And come to me for advice so I can get a play-by-play of how it's going!"

I was sure I hadn't been wrong to tell them. I did feel a little ticklish and uncomfortable, but I didn't want this to be the sort of relationship I couldn't talk to anybody about.

An image promptly rose behind my eyelids: that cold, raucous nighttime street, with the lithe-limbed Ms. Iwato standing boldly in the foreground.

"You can sleep if you want to."

Her voice whispered sweetly in my ear.

The swing Yuki Iwato sat on swayed back and forth, creaking softly.

"I'm fine," I told her. It was 4:11 AM.

"Liar. You've been fading in and out for a while now."

We were in a little park wedged into the space between two apartment buildings, the only things in it the swings and a sandbox. We were passing the night there, one of many such nights, our relationship still undefined.

"Aren't you tired?" I asked her, yawning. I couldn't blame her for suspecting I was sleepy.

She shook her head.

Embarrassing confession time: Being outside late at night scared me a little. Before starting college, I'd never gone out alone at a time like this. Until then, it had always been off-limits to me. Adults' skillful guidance and my own cowardice had walled it off.

Now that I'd taken that first step, though, I realized it was nothing but deserted streets stretching off in all directions.

Ms. Iwato smiled.

Strangely, even when liquor and drowsiness blurred my vision, I could make out her expression.

It was the bewitching lamp that had lit my path here.

I heard a light clatter. When I looked up, she was standing on the swing, gazing up at the sky, which had developed a faint blue cast.

"I love..."

Those words woke me up fast.

Immediately, though, I realized she wasn't talking about us.

"I love the sight of couples leaning close together in the light from convenience stores, and traffic signals working all by themselves in empty intersections, and the slightly damp asphalt of parking lots reflecting the light of those 'twenty-four hours for two thousand yen' signs."

Every word she spoke was like a picture. Speechless, I gazed at her streaming black hair.

Then she hopped down from the swing and turned back, peeking at my face. "I love the town at night as it waits, sleeplessly, for the people who'll wake again tomorrow."

Right then, I didn't care what we called this relationship. Just being with her was enough for me.

I felt sure this was that sort of summer.

3

Kita-Senju Station overflowed with people. Street stalls and houses that had been converted into shops jostled each other all the way down the road leading to the riverside embankment, and the red and yellow glow of paper and metal lanterns reminded me of runway lighting. This was usually just an ordinary street, but now it teemed with people in *yukatas* and traditional *jinbei* outfits. It looked like a river of humans. I stared.

"The fireworks haven't even started yet. It's too early to be overwhelmed." Ms. Iwato hid a smile behind her hand. She was wearing a breezy-looking iris-patterned *yukata* and her usual philosophical smile. That day, though, she'd put her hair up, and the nape of her neck lay exquisitely bare.

"Watching TV at home is fine, but this sort of thing is nice, too, isn't it?" She plunged down into the street, wooden geta clattering hollowly, drawstring purse dangling from her wrist. Pulling me by the hand, she joined the flow of people.

The heat of her palm soaked into my skin.

I hadn't been to a summer festival since my parents took me as a kid.

"Oh, I want one of those!"

Ms. Iwato had spotted something right off the bat, and we veered off in the direction she was pointing. A middle-aged man wearing a knit bellyband was selling candy apples. Just one cost a whole seven hundred yen.

"Are you getting one, too, Natsuki?"

"Um, I…" Impulsively, I looked around, then zeroed in on a frankfurter stall. "I'll go get one of those."

I slipped out of the line and bought a sausage. As I was squirting ketchup and mustard into the sticky container, Ms. Iwato came over with a red fist-sized lump speared on the end of a wooden chopstick. "Ta-daa!" Holding the candy apple out to me, she puffed out her chest proudly.

"Is it good…?"

"Mm, not really." She stuck out her tongue and gave the candy a subdued lick. "I wonder how long it's going to take to get through this to the apple."

"I think you'll probably have to bite it."

"Really? It looks pretty hard, though."

When she tried to sink her teeth into it, I heard a dull crunch. Ms. Iwato lowered the candy from her lips, pulling a face that made her look as if she'd just been to the dentist. "No good."

"Ha-ha. Okay, so…should we smash it open?"

I mimed swinging a hammer, and she laughed.

After rejoining the flow of people, we bought *yakisoba* with sauce, grilled squid, and shaved ice.

Deciding to find seats on the dry riverbed before our shaved ice turned into plain old sugar water, we climbed the embankment, but the sheer number of people we saw down below left us stunned. The riverbed was almost completely buried by onlookers and their stuff. We could barely even see the tarps they were sitting on.

Ms. Iwato and I exchanged looks.

"Let's give it a try anyway," she said.

I nodded, and we started hunting for an open space. However, the few times we did glimpse a patch of open blue tarp, it was scattered with some-one's things, or somebody was already sitting there waiting for their friends.

Ms. Iwato gave me a questioning look, and I shrugged helplessly. But just then, someone called out. A pudgy elderly woman was beckoning to us from the darkness.

"This is quite a crowd, isn't it?" I said, moving closer.

Vigorously flapping a paper fan to cool her face, the woman pointed to the open space beside her. "Here. It may be a bit of a squeeze, but it's open."

"You're sure you don't mind?"

"Mm-hmm. Someone else reserved this area; I'm borrowing my spot from him, too."

The woman pointed to a middle-aged man in a tracksuit nibbling on grilled squid, a bottle of sake in his other hand. When we both bowed to him, he sang out, "Sit yourselves down; have a seat." Then he stuck his liquor-flushed nose high in the air and gave us a thumbs-up. In response, the dozen or so people who were sitting on the tarp all waved their hands or saluted him with their kebabs.

Enveloped in a weird sense of unity, we sat down. We'd managed to get to our shaved ice just in time. When I stuck my spoon in, there was a light, pleasant crunch, and the chill worked wonders for my flushed body.

"Are you two dating?"

I'd gotten about halfway through my shaved ice and had just begun to settle in, and the woman's question caught me completely off guard. Flinching so hard I almost fumbled my spoon, I looked at Ms. Iwato for help.

What I saw was the face of a devil, faintly illuminated by the glow of the paper lanterns. Ms. Iwato's canines were bared, and her lips were open in the shape of a half-moon. "Yes, we are," she said quietly.

"Really?" I asked her in a low voice. When Ms. Iwato bent over, I saw the nape of her neck, which was beaded with sweat. The vaguely sweet smell of it made my head spin.

Ms. Iwato nodded, shoulders swaying. "For the summer," she said with a faint smile.

Bang! The sky flashed green. Then two bursts of yellow. These were test shots. Then the announcement that signaled the beginning of the fireworks played.

As I munched on *yakisoba* that was almost nothing but noodles, Ms. Iwato leaned in toward me. I could feel her feverish heat. "Let me have a little of that."

"Go ahead."

"Oh, that's good. Proper street-stall stuff."

Ms. Iwato stuffed her mouth full of *yakisoba*. Figuring I might as well, I took the candy apple she'd been holding and tried to take a bite.

I thought it was going to chip my front teeth. Even so, I managed to break through to the apple, chewed—it felt a lot like eating gravel—and swallowed. My mouth and the inside of my throat stung.

"Just throw it away."

Ignoring Ms. Iwato's suggestion, I kept eating.

"You have some real stamina, don't you?"

Getting a little desperate, I bit into the apple and chomped my way through the candy shell by turns. Ms. Iwato shifted away from me and looked down in the direction of the river. "I already gave up," she said.

The sky flashed as if it were exploding. The boom followed a moment later.

The intense silvery light made everyone catch their breath. I raised my head, gazing at the scattering remnants.

"Fireworks are great, aren't they?" Ms. Iwato said.

"They really are. They're much more impressive when you see them in person and can feel the crowd."

"No, they're good because they're gone so fast."

I cocked my head, puzzled.

"I think fireworks make good memories because they don't last, physically. They make you try hard. You think, 'I have to watch this. It's now or never.'"

A sequence of countless little lights shot into the air, then blotted out the jet-black canvas with a shower of sparks.

Ms. Iwato swayed, then lay down, resting her head on my knees.

The nape of her neck, her ear, her slim throat. Those eyelashes that reached up into the darkness. The breeze played with a few escaped strands of her hair. Her head weighed about as much as a melon; I set my hand on it, then gently moved the hand to her shoulder, supporting her back.

"If I disappear or something, don't look for me, all right?"

She sounded as if she was joking. At the same time, though, she seemed to be foretelling our fate.

It scared me.

A frighteningly long time passed before I spoke; my lips were trembling. "Are you planning to disappear?"

"Huh? Don't take things so seriously."

Ms. Iwato sat up and thumped me hard on the shoulder.

Red and green lights raced each other high into the sky, then bloomed in all directions. The two would never meet, and there was something lonely about that, but the contrast between the colors was beautiful.

"Um...," I said, barely managing to squeeze it out. I needed a clear answer already. "Why are you with me? Summer's really short, remember? Is it okay for you to spend time on me like this?"

I'd put a little force behind the words, but Ms. Iwato wasn't looking at me. Maybe she hadn't heard me over the fireworks.

"Why would you ask a thing like that?"

"What am I to you, Ms. Iwa—?"

"I'm glad it was you, Natsuki. I mean that," she said, interrupting me.

"O-okay."

"And so I'd really like you to be happy."

"Huh?"

A star mine burst behind me and cascaded like a waterfall. I cupped my hand to my ear, leaning closer to Ms. Iwato. However, no matter how close I got, I wasn't able to catch what she said. She spoke so softly it was like an afterthought to her breathing.

"I hope you find a cute girlfriend before too long."

"Wh-what?! I can't hear a thing!"

My voice, her voice, and everything else were pulled into the explosion of light.

In the darkness, only the warmth of her shoulder against my hand proved she was there.

4

The long university summer break ended, and all the clubs and executive committees launched into preparations for the school festival. GTR was only providing beer cocktails, and I hadn't shown up since the planning meetings, so they hadn't included me in the sales staff.

On the day of the festival, I was at the station with Tomomi.

The station platform was plastered with a dense row of posters advertising the festival. It was a joint effort between the College of Art and the general ed departments. I kept waking up my smartphone and checking my chat app icon for a red "1" whenever Tomomi wasn't looking.

Atsushi finally showed up, wearing a foolish grin. Tomomi scolded him. "Don't you smirk at me when you're late. Natsuki's been glued to his phone the whole time, and the boredom's killing me."

She shot me a look, and I hastily slipped my phone back into my pocket.

"Yeah, sorry about that," said Atsushi. "There was this girl who looked like she was here for the festival; I started talking to her, and it held me up."

"So how'd that go?"

"I just barely didn't get her e-mail."

Atsushi shrugged clownishly. You couldn't hate that smile.

Come to think of it, the only parts of him that tended to stick in my mind were the shape of his ears and the length of his sideburns.

The crowd around us was almost all teenagers, but I saw some parents with kids here and there. A few high school students were walking around with vocabulary flashcards in one hand, their faces set as if they were going to war.

Right inside the school gate, there was a blood donation booth whose workers enthusiastically pressed us to give. After politely refusing, we headed over to the reception tent. We ran into a few acquaintances there, talked with them for a little while, then accepted our guidebooks. Staged yells from a fight scene and powerful audio with heavy bass notes surged over me from the central plaza.

"Where should we go first?"

The guidebook listed what the clubs were doing and the schedule for the stage performances. The gaps in between were jammed with ads for restaurants near campus.

"What about this?" Atsushi was pointing at the words *Barrier-Free Research Club*. That seemed pretty straitlaced for a guy like Atsushi.

"What, is it that weird? I'm pretty interested in welfare, all right?"

"I hear it doesn't pay, and the work is rough."

"But you get to work with people. It's gotta be better than spending your life in front of a computer staring at numbers, at least."

Oh, I see. That was why I tended to only remember the shape of Atsushi's ears and the length of his sideburns. It was because he was always focused forward, and I was always off to the side watching him.

"…I didn't think you had such a clear dream, Atsushi." I have no idea what my face looked like just then. All I remember is that the expression used the muscles in my cheeks.

"Well, you're gonna be a novelist, right? Get big and write a book about my life."

Atsushi's carefree smile was both dazzling and oppressive.

I hadn't told anyone else, but these two knew I was writing a book. If I hadn't told them, they really would have thought I was an empty shell of a human, and I wouldn't have been able to build a relationship with them as equals.

Even so.

"There's no way. I told you—I'm not planning to be a novelist."

You mean you can't be one, I corrected myself silently.

Atsushi looked openly disappointed, so I gave him a clumsy smile and let the matter slide. Frankly, it was rough having people think it was my dream to be a novelist.

Up on a semicircular stage that reminded me of the Colosseum, the Fight Scene Research Club took their final bow, and then girls in frilly costumes formed ranks and walked on to replace them.

The Music Department's two outdoor speakers immediately started blaring a girlie K-pop song.

"Hey, doesn't this look good?!"

Amid the roar, Tomomi's slim finger, decorated with black nail polish, pointed toward a certain circle's offering. It was the Coffee Research Club, selling a drink labeled MAFFEE.

"What's this mystery liquid supposed to be?!"

"It's got three layers—coffee, matcha, and milk!"

Matcha plus coffee apparently equaled "maffee."

"I'm thirsty. Why don't we go here first?!" Tomomi suggested, and Atsushi agreed.

I grabbed the chance to get out my phone and check for messages.

"Natsuki, come on." Tomomi peeked at my face. "What's up? Is there an event in some phone game?"

I shook my head. Seriously, though, what was going on?

Three days earlier, Ms. Iwato had fallen out of touch.

Up until then, we'd usually talked ten times a day, and once or twice at the very least. On September 22, though, she'd suddenly stopped responding. The last conversation we'd had was about a late-night comedy show. Ms. Iwato had asked me whether I liked comedy sketches or stand-up comic duos better, and while I was trying to pick one, the date had changed.

That was the last I'd heard from her.

On the one hand, I was worried something might have happened; on the other, as I kept telling myself, it had been only three days.

The thing was, the chat app was the one way I had to contact her.

"Sorry I'm so restless."

"That's not it." Tomomi's eyebrows scrunched together, and her tone turned serious. "I'm worried about you, Natsuki. It's…Ms. Iwato, isn't it?"

I clammed up. There hadn't been anything hostile or nosy about the way she said it, though.

"Can I get your take on this later?" I asked.

Tomomi's pierced lip stretched in a grin. "Sure, if you buy me a bubble tea."

The Coffee Research Club's café was on the second floor of the east school building, so the three of us walked down the wide road that cut vertically across campus. The area was crowded with stalls, and a smell that was a chaotic mixture of chocolate, fried chicken, stewed vegetables, and *yakisoba* hung in the air.

Just then, I got the feeling I'd seen something odd, and I widened my eyes.

Two guys were walking toward us, looking as if they were having a great time. One of them was a head shorter than the other. The taller one had a neatly trimmed bowl cut, while the other's hair didn't even reach his eyebrows. What would you call that, a super-short cut?

However, for some reason, the smaller figure's silhouette grabbed my attention.

His back was straight as a rod, and his limbs radiated poise. As he passed me, I doubted my eyes. That wasn't a guy.

It was Yuki Iwato, hair cropped short, wearing jeans and a solid-colored shirt with a band collar.

In that moment, our eyes met, and it felt as if time had frozen. I stared. That two-block haircut looked startlingly good on her, and the clean line of her jaw highlighted the fine features of her face. Ms. Iwato looked as polished as a cut jewel, and the sight made it impossible to put even 1 percent of what I was thinking into words.

A few seconds late, one brief word tumbled out of my mouth.

"Hello."

I nodded to her.

Ms. Iwato's steps slowed slightly. "Hello," she said, then promptly lowered her eyes.

The guy with the mushroom cut glanced over and checked Ms. Iwato's expression. Without telling him anything, she turned on her heel and walked away as if nothing had happened.

Tomomi, who'd been having an enthusiastic conversation with Atsushi, noticed me and ran over. I was gazing after the couple, dazed. Tomomi shot them a look that was pretty close to hostile. She seemed ready to take off after them, and I grabbed her hand, holding her back. "It's fine."

"But that's—"

"I was wrong." Right now, it was all I could do to keep a lid on my feelings. "It was all me. I just had the wrong idea."

Ms. Iwato's back grew smaller and smaller, and once she'd climbed the stone steps to the north school building, it vanished.

5

The vending machines one floor up from the seminar rooms were always out of water. Resigning myself, I hit the button for the next cheapest thing, a sports drink.

"Brr, it's cold. Has November always been this frigid? Man, I wish they'd quit giving us phys ed first thing in the morning," Atsushi grumbled. He was watching me steadily, one finger on the pull tab of his can of hot coffee.

I twisted the cap of my sports drink, but the soft bottle crumpled a little, and the contents splashed over, making my hand sticky. When I tried to take my handkerchief out of my back pocket, I dropped it, and when I bent to pick it up, pain ran through my lower back.

Everything had been going like that lately. No matter what I did, nothing went smoothly. It felt as if I were missing one vital gear.

"I had no idea you were actually dating *the* Ms. Iwato," Atsushi said.

Holding the bottle tightly, I gulped down my sports drink. The scent of lime and artificial sweetener shot up my nose.

Down below, a group of people with a big camera, a tripod, and two cattail-shaped sound collectors was milling around, mingling with the students who were headed for the main gate. Every so often, the College of Art sent people over here from next door to film.

"Maybe I shouldn't be talking, but for now, it's good that it's over. Ms. Iwato's bad news."

The bottle crunched in my hand. If not now, when would have been the right time?

The students with the camera and sound collectors kept moving around, chasing the perfect angle like adventurers following a treasure map. What were they making, a movie? A music video? I'd heard that the College of Art had too many weirdos, so when the Film Club wanted to film "a normal university scene," they came over here.

If they got a chance to enter a competition, would they say it was too soon? If they had an encounter that might change their lives, would they just let it slip away?

"There are lots of rumors about her. I heard some of them from an upperclassman on the school festival executive committee. Apparently, she's kind of a man-eater. She's always got a new one."

I'd always understood that there was something unknowable about Ms. Iwato.

I'd seen it, and I'd made up my mind anyway. And so...

"You'd have to be the president of an IT venture to handle a love monster like that. And I mean, we're first-years, remember?"

"I guess I didn't know anything about her, huh?"

Setting his coffee on the windowsill, Atsushi turned to face me squarely. "You got that right. None of this is your fault. She was the one out of line." He poked my chest.

A yell of "Cut!" drifted in from outside.

"I'll have to learn, then. I need to get to know her a lot better."

Atsushi looked dumbfounded. His mouth flapped soundlessly.

"Natsuki, I'm being real with you here," he said at last.

"Me too." I looked him straight in the eye, saying exactly what I thought. If this wasn't serious, what was? It was the first time I'd ever been this confident. "Did I say something embarrassing?"

Atsushi shut his mouth.

"If not, then tell me the name of that upperclassman."

I made my move the next day.

I walked past the College of Art's campus on my way to school, so I was used to seeing it from the outside, but I'd never been in it before. Just inside the main gate, my attention was snagged by a tall woman with an Afro who was walking toward me; right after that, a guy in coveralls splotched with all the colors of the rainbow ran past. Then I saw a gaggle of about a dozen people with cameras around their necks being spurred on loudly by an elderly man with bushy white whiskers.

I walked along a tree-lined path until a dome-shaped building came into view on the right. Looking around restlessly, I stepped into the fine arts building. In the center of the dim lobby, a sculpture of a decapitated, armless male body and a host of fresco angels seemed intent on forbidding my entry.

I traveled down a gloomy corridor that echoed with every step I took, making me feel jumpy. Before long, I saw sharp light seeping out of a room. A plate by its door read SKETCHING ROOM.

When I poked my head in timidly, the smell of sawdust, paint, and oil socked me in the nose.

I saw several big wooden worktables, drafting boards, a cutting machine, and a power saw. There was a basket of fruit sitting on a platform, and half a dozen men and women were gazing at it, running their pencils over huge sketchbooks they'd placed on wooden easels.

They'd draw several lines, then erase. Draw more lines, then erase more than they'd added. The only thing breaking the silence was the sound of pencils skimming over paper. I crept closer and spoke to a man on my side of the group whose hair was tied back in a ponytail. "Excuse me."

The man looked up. He had a prominent nose and narrow, almond-shaped eyes. His gaze was sharp and focused, but as he shifted his attention from his work to me, it grew milder. "Sure. What do you need?"

"I'm looking for somebody."

The man seemed perplexed; his eyebrows came together, but then his expression turned gentle again. "Are you visiting from another school?"

"I came over from the Literature Department next door."

"Oh, the general ed…" The man nodded as if it all made sense now. He set down his blackened kneaded eraser and turned to face me. "Who are you looking for?"

"His name is Shuji Ishikawa."

The man's mouth dropped open. Then he smiled amicably. "That would be me."

I made a dumb-sounding noise. So this was Shuji Ishikawa. It was true that executive committee members needed solid people skills, so a good-natured person like him was probably tailor-made for the job.

"There's no need to be formal with me, by the way. I'm not a 'respect' kind of guy."

"All right. I mean… O-okay." Feeling an awkward, uncomfortable sensation in my lower jaw, I forced out the word "Understood."

"Why don't we go talk in the smoking booth?" Ishikawa got to his feet, back cracking stiffly.

The smoking booth was just off the lobby. It had a wooden loft across the back, chairs shaped like fruits, and tables shaped like animals. It would have looked right at home in an amusement park. There were more people than I'd expected inside; a few of them were even digging into their lunches amid the swirling smoke.

Ishikawa sat down on an apple chair, while I took a seat across from him on a banana. It was smooth enough that it felt like I'd slip off if I wasn't careful.

"So what did you need?"

Ishikawa took a crushed pack of cigarettes from his breast pocket, slipped one out, then lit it with a Zippo lighter.

I averted my face slightly. "Do you know Yuki Iwato, a second-year oil painting major?"

The moment I said her name, every eye in the room snapped to me. It was like something out of a play.

Time seemed to freeze over. In the stillness, my heart thudded loudly.

"Oh, man. How do you know that name?" With an abrupt, off-putting smile, Ishikawa broke the silence.

"Well, I, um…" I faltered.

He watched me flounder for a while. Then he nodded a few times, as if everything had clicked into place for him. "So that's how it is, hmm?"

Then he said, "She doesn't come to school in the winter."

Was that some kind of riddle? Or did he mean she was going somewhere on exchange over winter term? I couldn't read any information in his narrow, inscrutable eyes.

"Hey, don't give me that look. Frankly, I don't know much about it myself."

"You mean she just doesn't come to class for the whole winter? Not even once?"

"That's not all. Her chat app, Facebook, and Twitter accounts all shut down. She goes completely silent. Not that she has that big an online presence to begin with."

Ishikawa exhaled a big puff of smoke, and I shut my mouth tightly. Stubbing his butt out in the ashtray, he fanned the smoke away from me with his other hand. "Sorry. Not a fan of tobacco, huh?"

"I'm sorry. I'm just not used to it yet."

"No, no. We smokers should be more considerate."

When Ishikawa saw how disconcerted I was, something seemed to dawn on him. "An underclassman from the Literature Department who doesn't like cigarettes... I see. So you're the first-year."

"Did Ms. Iwato say something about me?" I leaned forward.

Ishikawa looked a little uneasy. "Mm, well... She said you were a hassle. Some annoying kid who followed her around."

I was speechless. It felt like I'd been stabbed: Pain ran through my heart, then radiated to the rest of my body, making all my joints stiffen up. My ears were ringing, and everything in front of me seemed to recede.

As I was mulling his words over, dazed, Ishikawa broke into a mischievous smile. "Kidding... She said she felt bad for what she'd done to you. That it had been mean to make you think the two of you could be together when she couldn't stay. She's as arrogant as they come, isn't she? Really selfish."

Ishikawa gazed into the distance, his expression softening slightly.

"She's cute, though, so people end up falling for her."

Then he went quiet for a while.

6

"Excuse me—"

Apparently, I'd sounded a bit too demanding; the guys gathered in the first-floor sketching room swiveled around, startled.

Three of the five frowned and looked down. Of the remaining two, the one with glasses looked like he didn't know what to do, while the one in the baseball hat glared at me. "Why are you asking about that?" he said. His tone was as prickly as his gaze.

"I have some personal business with her."

The guy watched me suspiciously, but then his expression turned to pity.

"Hey, *Yuki Iwato* sounds sort of familiar, doesn't it?" the guy with glasses said to the other four.

"What, you don't know? The whole Fine Arts Department has heard of Yuki." One of the other three guys glanced up, unpleasantness in his voice.

"You another victim?" the one in the hat asked me.

"What do you mean, 'victim'?"

"Just what it sounds like. Some sucker she used and threw away."

"Hey, Ryuutarou. You don't have to put it like that." The guy with glasses shoved the other guy's shoulder. "Sorry about him. He had a bit of a run-in with Ms. Iwato, too," he told me, apologizing humbly.

"Man, shut up. I dumped her." The guy in the baseball cap knocked his heel into the table leg, and a nearly empty bottle of black tea fell over with a light clatter. "Who needs that slut?"

I gritted my teeth, glaring at the bottle.

I'd run around the second and third floors, all the way to the department office on the fourth floor, talking to people. All I'd learned was that Yuki Iwato's relationship history included a whole lot of male students, and that she didn't come to school during the winter. All the students in her department grimaced at the sound of her name, and the staff in the office had insisted there was nothing they could tell me.

What demons was Yuki Iwato fighting?

Or was this all an overreaction on my part? Was she sleeping peacefully in somebody else's arms right now…?

"No!"

I shook my head, spitting out the murkiness that was building up in my heart. I still couldn't stop myself from hoping that I might find a clue to her somewhere.

The setting sun lanced through the corridor, searingly bright, all the way to the doors of the classrooms on the opposite side. Worn out, I reached the top of the stairs that led to the roof and practically fell through the emergency exit.

The only thing there was a vast stretch of concrete reflecting the sun's red light.

It was hard to breathe. My heart ached fiercely, and the sense of futility and loneliness changed something in me.

"Yuki Iwatoooooo!!"

I was desperate. My cracked voice flew right over the urban residential street. Below me, several people looked up. Hastily, I ducked back from the void.

"Yowza."

My exhausted heart gave another startled thump. Timidly, still panting, I turned around.

"That was quite a yell."

"Oh… Uh, no, this isn't…"

"Feel free to keep going."

A tall man was standing in front of the emergency exit, clapping at waist level. He had a bowl cut, and he was wearing a beige Chester coat and black turtleneck. Something seemed off, though. The voice I'd heard had been low, but female.

I remembered seeing this person before. It had been on the day of the school festival, the last time I'd seen Yuki Iwato. At the time, I'd just assumed her friend was a guy, but—

"Um, excuse me… Have we met?"

"Just once." The woman's expression was dignified, and she had the perfect posture of a model as she held a hand above her eyes to shield them from the glare. "We passed each other at the school festival, I believe. At the time, you seemed rather, what's the word…paralyzed."

"Are you a friend of Ms. Iwato's?"

"A friend, yes. Her only friend. She's completely reliant on me."

Because this was coming from a woman, I felt relief well up inside me.

"I'm Ena Shimoki."

"My name is Uzume…"

"I know about you, Natsuki, of course. There's no way I wouldn't." Ena withdrew her hand from her pocket and held it out to me. It was big, but her fingers were long and slender. Her skin was soft, as if she was wearing hand cream.

We relocated to a bench in a corner and sat down.

"If you scream like that, you'll end up violating her privacy."

"I'm sorry you had to see that." I bowed.

"There's no sense in apologizing to me," Ena said, smiling wryly. She was right, but I didn't even know which direction to apologize in.

"Did it hurt so much it made you want to scream, Natsuki?"

Little bubbles of moss were growing in a gap in the concrete, and two blades of grass sprouted from the moss, drooping limply onto the ground.

"Then no doubt she's been screaming for a while now, too," she continued.

"Ms. Shimoki, do you know anything about Ms. Iwato?"

"She's told me everything. Literally everything."

"Then tell me, please! Where is she now, and what is she doing?"

"She's at her parents' house."

"Where's…?"

Ena held her index finger to her full, slightly flushed lips. "I can't say more than that."

"Why not?!"

"Because Yuki doesn't want me to."

"She doesn't want…?"

Ena nodded once, firmly. Ms. Iwato didn't want that. I chewed those words over, trying to process them, but it was hopeless.

"Winter is that great an Achilles' heel for her, you see."

The kind of intense gust peculiar to roofs blew through, and cold seeped into me. Ena hunched her shoulders up, shoved her hands into the pockets of her coat, and pulled it tighter around her.

"Have I been dumped?" I asked.

Now, when it was about to get much colder? Now, when there were so many fun things waiting for us? At a time like this…

"What do you think?" She tilted her head, giving me a clammy look. "Say you wouldn't be able to see her all winter long. No matter how you begged, no matter how you plotted or schemed, say you'd always be alone in winter. Could you call that 'being dumped'?"

"If I can see her again, I'll wait as long as I have to," I said firmly.

Her lips stretched into a grin, a flat smile that suffused her entire face. "You've got it bad," she said with a little laugh. "Either way, if you want to know the truth, you'll have to ask her in person."

Ena wasn't like any of the others. She didn't try to make me feel better, and she didn't sneer at me. She was just there, in a perfectly neutral position, as transparent as air.

"Although by that time, you're bound to be in love with somebody else," she mused.

"Why would you say that?"

"Well, that's how student relationships go, isn't it?"

I couldn't nod. I just gazed stiffly at the ground.

"Isn't there anyone else you like?"

"I like Ms. Iwato."

"You mean you like her, *too*. Biologically, that's nonsense. You're fully capable of falling for somebody else. A female friend you're close to, say."

For a moment, Tomomi popped into my mind, and I hastily banished the image.

"Why Yuki?"

Ena didn't ask me any more than that. Maybe she didn't need to. After all, my throat had closed up, and I couldn't talk. I just hung my head, glaring at the ground.

7

The train arrived, and a crowd of people flowed in. Most of them seemed to be students. Over half of them were wearing earbuds or headphones. Several were probably in love at the moment.

In this day and age, there was no standard way to date.

There wasn't any point in putting a label on human relationships, and it was even more pointless to limit your relationship with a name. If relationships were simply two unembellished humans being together, then the word *love* might be nothing more than an indulgence that allowed you to stay with somebody else.

Five or six trains had passed through. I could tell by the noise.

"Hey, it's Natsuki."

A voice abruptly called out to me from behind, and I twisted around. It was Tomomi.

"What're you doing here?" she asked.

She'd spoken to me twice now, so I felt like I had to look up. At some point, the sky had dimmed to navy blue. My coat hung down over the edge of the bench, and I realized my legs were trembling slightly beneath it.

The cold was circulating through my body like a poison.

"Isn't it obvious? I'm waiting for a train."

"Where exactly are you planning to go at this hour? You live around here," Tomomi said. She was teasing, but her expression seemed a little subdued.

"Being here sort of calms me down."

"But you went through the ticket barrier."

"I'll tell them I made a mistake and get the money back at the adjustment counter later."

"Cheating much?" Tomomi said, her gaze flat.

At that point, I realized there was something different about her. She'd taken the piercing out of her lower lip and dyed her brown hair black. "Tomomi, where's your piercing?"

"My new part-time job wouldn't let me wear it."

"You're working a proper job. That's impressive."

"Well, you're writing a novel, Natsuki. You think that's not impressive?" Tomomi looked down a little, then murmured, "The thing is, I've only got one parent, and my brother dropped out of university. He's at home all the time. That means I have to work."

At times like this, I wished I could respond immediately. I always spent so long choosing the right words that I lost the chance to say them.

Actually…had I ever managed to say anything straight from the heart to anybody?

"Listen, remember the Baggages show I was telling you about?"

"Yeah."

"Their bass player screwed up and caused a scandal, so their show got canceled. They say all bass players are pervs, and I guess it's true. They refunded my ticket, but that other one…"

"You're always really earnest about stuff, aren't you, Tomomi? That's, um, how do I put this…? I think it's incredible. It's very cool."

"Whoa. Where's this coming from?"

"Why do you like them so much? That specific band."

"Why...? Geez, way to ask a really hard question. I've been following the Baggages since nobody knew who they were; I'm an original fan. The drummer, Naa, is a particular favorite of mine. Maybe it's because he's got a big brother, too, and the homes we come from are similar..."

Tomomi thought hard for a bit, then spoke as if she were dredging the answer up from the gloomy depths of her mind. "But listen, love isn't an on-off sort of thing. It's a process, isn't it?"

Oh, I see.

Yeah, you're right.

Who said we had to like each other right from the start? Was there some law that I couldn't be intrigued by her if I didn't love her?

Why Yuki? Heck, even I didn't know.

But that was exactly why I wanted to find out. There was nothing wrong with that.

Tomomi was staring at me as if I made no sense. I felt kind of bad about it, but I thought I'd finally grasped the words on the tip of my tongue. "I have to find her."

"You mean Ms. Iwato, don't you? I...know those rumors, too, you know." Her expression had turned grim, and she peered into my face. "I wouldn't mess with that. She'll just play you. You're the one who'll end up getting hurt, Natsuki."

Not even her birthday had been on Facebook, let alone her address. I couldn't give up yet, though. I jumped to my feet and took off running. "I'm sorry. I have to go."

"Huh? Hold it, where—?"

As I ran up the right-hand side of the escalator, I glanced back, just once. "I think that's a good look on you!"

She called after me, trying to stop me, but I shook her voice off and clattered my way up the escalator.

I dashed back to the College of Art campus, traveling against the flow of people heading home. When I reached the fourth floor of the fine arts building, they were just getting ready to turn off the lights in the faculty room. I flattened myself against a pillar, peeked out from behind it, and saw a moving shape on the other side of the frosted glass. The shadow shifted into a physical body: A woman dressed like a clerical worker left the dark room and trotted quickly toward the toilets.

Her footsteps echoed in the darkness. After they'd faded into silence, I turned on my smartphone's light and dashed through the door.

The school register would have Ms. Iwato's parents' address listed as a secondary emergency contact. I visualized the Literature Department's faculty room in my head. The layout was pretty similar, but naturally, the desks and the printer were in different places. Most noticeably, a plaster bust and unused easels and canvases took up part of the space, and I didn't see the cabinet that held important documents.

Would that cabinet even be unlocked?

My eyes had adjusted to the darkness, and I began going through every cabinet I could find by the light of my smartphone. Midterm tests, seminars, club materials: The folders with labels weren't so bad. When they had nothing written on them, I had to read three or four pages of the contents before I even had a clue what the folder was for.

The woman had been gone for quite a while. I'd left the door open a crack, and the light from the emergency lamp crept in eerily.

What was I doing? I didn't have any idea where to look, and if I got caught, I was definitely going to get suspended. What had possessed me to do something this crazy?

Dammit!

Compressing my scream into a whisper, I spat it out through pursed lips.

Where is it, where?!

A plastic drawer stuck, and I tugged a little harder. Too hard: The tray popped out, sending a clatter echoing through the darkness.

Just then, the sound of quiet footsteps joined it, and I think my heart actually stopped for a few seconds.

"Is somebody there?"

I shrank back, holding my breath. Moving so I couldn't be seen from the doorway, I took cover under a desk. Tucking my head into the space between my knees, I covered my mouth with both hands.

Only the woman's footsteps told me she was there. However, slowly but steadily, they were getting louder.

"You are there, aren't you?"

The footsteps stopped, and I heard a click. The light streaming through the door cast the woman's shadow onto the floor.

"Ah, you've caught me," came a man's voice.

The new set of footsteps was heavier and more deliberate.

"Oh, goodness, it's you, Professor. Is something the matter?"

"I just came to leave a few things. My makeup classes are finally over. Am I too late?"

"It is quite late, yes." The woman's tone was mild, but she seemed to be trying to cover up her irritation. "Was this another private lesson?"

"It was. Today's young lady has marvelous design skills, and there's something dazzling about her compositions. But she seems to be, what's the word…stuck. What she really thinks doesn't come through."

The footsteps came closer, circling the desk, and pointed purple patent-leather shoes and the legs of a suit in the same color passed right in front of me.

"Peeling that away layer by layer is a teacher's duty, don't you—…?" The feet stopped in front of me. "There's a tray on the floor here."

"Huh? Is there really?"

"Yes. You really need to take proper care of these things." Abruptly, the man's tone grew firm and authoritative. "I swear, young people these days…"

"You're quite young yourself, Professor Kanzaki."

I latched on to that name. Professor Kanzaki… I was pretty sure he was in charge of a class Ms. Iwato attended.

"Oh, I'm always young at heart."

Kanzaki bent down, and his shadow bent with him. The tray returned to its former position, and something was set down on top of the desk. I felt the vibrations from both in my back.

"Would you like to come out for a drink with me?" the professor asked. "Just the two of us."

"Another time, maybe…"

Their footsteps receded. The door clicked shut. Then, for a little while, I could hear their muffled voices as they waited for the elevator. The woman continued gently refusing him, but Kanzaki stubbornly kept after her.

When the voices vanished, true night enveloped my stiff, cringing body.

A sense that I was safe mingled with the loneliness of being on my own.

Relieved, I tried to stand up. My skull crashed into the underside of the desk with a pretty loud thud, and pain ran through me.

Rubbing my head, I straightened up.

When I shone my light on the desk, I found a leather bag from a designer brand, tossed carelessly on top of a pile of papers. I unbuttoned the flap and looked inside. There were a couple of books, a half-empty bottle of green tea, and a plastic file full of documents. Inside the file… There it was: the student register.

A two-column frame held a long list of names, student ID numbers, and addresses. *Iwato, Iwato, Iwato…* My eyes ran down the list, searching for the first character in her name, and finally stopping on *Iwato, Yuki.*

I'd found her. I saw the words *Nagoya City.*

I promptly activated my phone's camera, took a few photos with the flash, then put the papers back in the order I'd found them and returned them to the bag.

I hadn't noticed until just now, but my entire body was covered in goose bumps. The heat to the faculty room had been shut off, and it seemed to be getting colder and colder.

Looking around cautiously, I left the room, then dove into the elevator.

On my way down, I opened the photo folder on my phone.

P02-50221   Iwato, Yuki   2-2 Taikou District, Taikou Ward, Nagoya City, Aichi Prefecture

In the elevator, all alone, I called Tomomi. She picked up on the second ring, and I heard her cheerful voice ask, *"What's up?"*

"Do you still have that ticket?"

"I told you—they refunded it."

"Not that one. The night-bus ticket."

After I left the elevator, I discovered that the front gate was closed off by a big mobile barricade. I started walking through campus, following the map in my memory.

"Yeah, I have it. They said even if I got it refunded now, I'd lose seventy percent in fees…"

"I'll buy it from you," I said, stopping at a red light.

"Still, having blown three thousand yen bites… Wait, huh? What?"

Tomomi sounded genuinely bewildered. It was probably because this was coming from me: Even the most diplomatic person wouldn't have said I was a big spender.

"That would be a huge help, but what gives? I mean, it's a ticket for Nagoya—"

At that point, she broke off.

In the silence, the traffic signal changed, and the students who'd lined up beside me started across the street. My feet stayed firmly planted on the yellow tactile paving square at the sidewalk's edge.

"I see. So that's it. This is about Ms. Iwato again." Abruptly, Tomomi's voice grew heavier. Then it became a sharp point that she thrust at my ears. *"Natsuki. Just don't."*

"How do you know this is about her?"

"My brother knows her, that's all. It sounds like you're trying to go to her house."

"Yeah," I said, without hesitating.

Tomomi's voice turned shrill and cracked. *"You know that's not right! Natsuki, you've been weird since July. I didn't think you were the type to fall for someone so hard."*

She might have been right about that. I was well aware of how tough it was to like someone or something. This time was different, though. I couldn't pinpoint what that difference was, but it was there.

"Listen, I get it. You're lonely, right? If you need to talk, I'll listen! So seriously, enough of this."

I knew Tomomi was sincerely worried about me. Maybe she'd picked up on how scary Yuki Iwato was using some instinct guys didn't have.

This had passed the point of asking for advice, though.

"I'm sorry. I've already decided what I'm going to do."

"……"

Tomomi was silent. Was she pitying me for being an idiot? Even if she was, it was too late for me to change what I was going to say next.

"I'll buy the ticket on my own. Thanks."

As I hung up, I saw that the back gate was open, and I hurried off campus before a security guard could spot me.

8

The night bus with "extra room" seats was surprisingly spacious. The warm air from the heater at my feet was hot, though, and the happy-sounding breathing of the guy passed out in the seat next to mine pushed me even further from sleep.

We reached the terminal at dawn, and I took refuge in a McDonald's. Even in unfamiliar places, chain restaurants were always the same, and it was vaguely soothing. I ordered from the breakfast menu, then lowered myself into a corner seat I was lucky enough to find. As I was drinking a Fanta melon soda, resting my chin on my hand, the sandman jumped me.

When I raised my head, I had a faint headache, and there was something stuck to my cheek. It crackled as I peeled it off; it was a paper napkin. My lips were stiff with drool.

Something in my pocket was hot. When I hastily took it out, I realized my phone had been in camera mode for a good long time, and the battery was down to 10 percent.

It was about half past ten. I crammed a cold Egg McMuffin and hash browns into my mouth, washed them down with watery Fanta, then left the restaurant.

Forcing my sleep-dazed eyes to get back to work, I followed the yellow overhead marks for the Higashiyama Line. The underground shopping mall had a whole lot of beauty supply stores and apparel shops for older people. Overall, it seemed to be geared toward a slightly higher age demographic than the malls in Tokyo.

When I asked the station employee near the ticket barrier how to get to the Taikou District, I was told to take the Higashiyama Line bound for Takabata, then get off at Honjin Station.

The dingy bench on the platform had plastic bottles and bags lying under it. A nostalgic-sounding alert played, and then the train arrived, pushing musty, lukewarm wind ahead of it.

The train was pretty empty, and the only people sitting down were old. As I lowered myself into a burgundy seat, I felt my stomach start to squirm uneasily.

"The next stop is Kamejima, Kamejima. For My Dome, the batting center that entertains you with virtual imagery, get off at the next stop."

An announcement played. We stopped at Kamejima Station, but almost nobody got on or off.

"The next stop is Honjin, Honjin. For Honjin, your destination for medicinal herb specialty stores and Chinese medicine, get off at the next stop."

That was me. I stood up, grabbing the pole near the door for support. The train car rocked violently, and there was a low *vvvumm* that made me want to cover my ears.

In the truest sense of the word, I was all alone here.

Ms. Iwato.

With that name as my only guidepost, I stepped off the train and followed the directions on my map app.

Out here, the streets were a whole lot wider than they were in the city center. For what was probably the first time in my life, I passed several old people in a row all pushing those combination chair-walkers.

After I turned off the main street, the roads grew narrower, until finally I reached the cul-de-sac marked with a red pin on my map. The app had said it was a five-minute walk from the station, but it had definitely taken more than twenty minutes.

My destination was a brown two-story house. The front walk was covered with smooth, tumbled gravel, and there was a Toyota sedan in the small covered carport.

The name Iwato was chiseled into the marble nameplate. I saw it with my own two eyes.

I hadn't been wrong.

Feeling as if my efforts had been rewarded, I stood there in a daze.

I hadn't resolved anything yet, though. Just as I came to that realization, a gust of November wind blew through, cooling my feverish head. I felt like I had back when I was a kid and my cram school teacher had told me the method I'd been using to solve a math problem was actually wrong. I'd spent several days doubting what he'd said, twisting my own method in several different ways and reaching the answer through brute force.

If I was going to take action, I had to start by believing in myself. If I didn't, I'd lose my chance before I could do anything. I'd end up being "that guy who failed to act."

What exactly was I doing now, though? I'd spent 4,500 yen plus train fare and traveled three hundred kilometers, staking all that money and distance on only a vague possibility. All because I'd listened to the "genuine feelings" I might (or might not) have found inside myself.

But nobody was going to acknowledge my feelings now that I'd gone this far. This was… Yeah, what I was doing was basically—

"Agh! Stalker!"

A girl was standing in front of me, holding a plastic shopping bag. She had light-brown hair tied up in two pigtails, and big eyes that slanted up at the outer corners. She was glaring at me suspiciously.

I took a step forward. The girl stepped back. Slowly, she drew her hand out of the pocket of her hoodie. "Stay right where you are, or I'll report you!"

She was holding her smartphone, and the screen already showed "110," the emergency number.

"No, I'm not—"

"Don't move."

I put both hands up and froze.

"I'll call the police. I'll yell," she said.

"No, like I said—"

"Just get out of here! There's somebody I need to protect!"

Her tense voice echoed in the cul-de-sac. At that point, I noticed something.

Those upturned eyes. Their almond shape. She'd dyed her hair brown, but there was a little lustrous black near the roots. All these features reminded me vaguely of Yuki Iwato.

Her makeup, her clothes, and the aura she projected were all polar opposites of trim Ms. Iwato, but that made the similarities stand out even more sharply.

"Are you maybe Ms. Iwato's…?"

The wariness in the girl's face faded, and she lowered her smartphone to waist level. "You know my sister?"

"I'm a year below her at school. We're in the same club."

The girl sighed. She wasn't wary anymore, although she wasn't acting friendly, either. "You're in college? You look like a high school student, so I just assumed."

As a matter of fact, I had been one until last year. Was she saying I looked like a kid? She didn't have to be so blunt about it...

"We get a few of those sometimes. Morons who hear the rumors about my sister and come to gawk."

"Rumors...?"

"Yeah. Cruddy, insulting rumors." The girl frowned, staring at me. "Hang on. Her club? Do you mean the one with the three-letter acronym?"

"GTR," I told her.

The girl's mouth fell open in astonishment. "Then you're the one she was talking about."

Her eyes abruptly grew sharp, and she shot me a look that pierced me like an arrow. "Follow me, then. She said to let you in if you came... It ticks me off," she added resentfully. "But those were my sister's orders. So."

She walked right past me, opened the garden gate, tromped noisily up the pebble-covered path, and stuck her key in the door.

9

The girl turned our shoes around so that they pointed toward the exit, then pinched the heels together, lining them up properly.

A paper-clay figurine of two snowmen holding hands sat on the cupboard in the entryway. Next to it was something I suspected might be a miniature humidifier: a teardrop-shaped vase that puffed out rings of vapor.

The place had that fresh, slightly sweet scent unique to other people's houses.

There was no wall between the kitchen and what I assumed was the living room; the space held an imposing wooden table that could have seated six people, and the walls were covered with metal shelves. There were four wooden chairs whose design matched the table, and one plastic chair with armrests that stuck out like a sore thumb.

A frame on the wall held a sketch of what appeared to be a convenience store on a dark night, done in delicate colored pencil. Down in the right-hand corner of the paper, I could make out Yuki Iwato's tiny signature.

The girl set her shopping bag down on the table, then pulled out one of the wooden chairs. She promptly pointed, indicating the spot where I was supposed to sit.

"The name's Fuyumi. *Fu* as in *fukanou*, 'impossible.' *Yu* as in *yurai*, 'origin.' *Bi* as in *bijin*, 'beauty,' but read *mi*," the girl—Fuyumi—told me in a flat voice as soon as I sat down.

"I'm—"

"Don't bother; I know your name. Natsuki Uzume."

"If you're her little sister, what year of college are you in?"

"Huh?" Fuyumi's eyes narrowed to slits, and she gave me a look saturated with contempt. "I guess I look pretty old for my age. I'm in high school. Second year."

"In high school…"

For a high schooler, her attitude was extremely direct. When I took another look, I could tell she was young, but I picked up on a kind of resolution in her, too. That was what gave her the sharp eyes and forceful words that made her seem so much older.

"But then, what about your uniform? Actually, what about school?"

"Mom had some business she couldn't reschedule today."

Fuyumi took a plastic container out of her bag, stripped off the thin wrapper, and opened the lid. Faint steam rose from the cream-and-spicy-fish-egg pasta.

"Somebody has to watch her, you know. That 'somebody' was me today, that's all."

She sank a plastic fork into the convenience store pasta, then twirled it. Opening her mouth wide, she began quietly eating her way through the dish, without slurping it.

"You'll have to excuse me. It's my first meal of the day."

"No, please, take your time."

"I'll do that with or without your permission, thanks," Fuyumi said curtly. Both her hand and her jaws kept moving. The mass of pasta began to shrink, and in no time at all, she'd finished it. She shoved the fork and the plastic wrapper into the container, jammed the lid back on, and tossed it into the kitchen trash.

Returning to the table with a bottle of green tea, Fuyumi glanced at her watch. Then she looked at me as if she thought I was a pain. "Is my sister's university a good place?"

Ms. Iwato and I went to the same university. Our campuses were right next to each other; only our departments were different, and yet—I couldn't answer her sister's question.

"...I'm sorry. She's in another department, so I don't—"

"Yeah, that figures." Fuyumi checked her watch again. She started chugging her tea, squeezing the plastic bottle, then wiped her mouth forcefully on the sleeve of her hoodie. "My sister said you might come. She said to let you into the house and treat you politely if you did."

Ms. Iwato had told her sister about me. Not only that, she'd thought I might come! That alone was enough to keep me breathing.

"I'm not happy about it, though. In the first place, why come all the way from Tokyo? And then you just stood in front of our house. What would you have done if I hadn't come along?"

"Well..."

I'd been trying not to think about it. I'd had the idea that thinking would paralyze me, just like it always had before.

I'd been intentionally spontaneous, acting even though I felt shaky about it.

But as a result, I—

"Right now, I'll turn a blind eye to everything. I'm busy, after all. However, before you meet my sister, I have to ask you this: Why did you come here?"

Was she asking for herself, or on Ms. Iwato's behalf? Fuyumi glared at me again.

"I was worried," I said, keeping a careful eye on her expression. "Ms. Iwato, I mean Yuki, fell out of touch with me abruptly. Other people in her department said she didn't come to school in the winter, and it looks like she hasn't been updating her Facebook. I felt…really uneasy."

"I see. That's a relief." Fuyumi's face softened a bit, and she put on a mild expression. "If that's all, then taking you upstairs shouldn't be a problem."

She smiled brightly, clasping both hands in front of her chest.

Just then, an alarm rang out from somewhere above us. Looking up, Fuyumi murmured, "Great timing."

"Can I see Yuki?"

"Sure, you can see her." Fuyumi quirked one eyebrow sarcastically. "She won't see you, though. If that's good enough, then…"

What was that supposed to mean?

Either way, I had no choice but to nod.

There were framed pictures on the stairway wall and landing. On the lower steps, the pictures were mostly bright watercolors, but as we went up, the number of oil paintings grew. At the same time, the backgrounds got darker, and more of the paintings had clearly delineated areas of light and shadow.

"My sister painted these." Fuyumi was climbing ahead of me, one hand holding her skirt against her legs. "She started drawing around the time I was born, and the house is covered in pictures she painted between then and five years ago. Mom suggested hanging up the ones we'd stored in the closet."

"They're pretty. The mostly dark-colored backgrounds and vaguely shadowed feeling remind me of Yuki."

"Do they? I can't see it. If you can, Mr. Uzume, you might get along with my mother." Fuyumi sounded a bit sarcastic.

The stairs creaked beneath our feet. When we reached the second floor, there was a single corridor with multiple rooms opening off it. The one at the very back seemed to be Ms. Iwato's: A plate that looked like a slice from a small log hung on the closed door, with YUKI written on it in flowing script. I could still hear the alarm sporadically. It seemed to be filtering out through her door.

"Wait." Fuyumi's hand was on the doorknob, but I stopped her. "Is it really okay for me to go in there?"

She shot me a glance, then turned the doorknob without answering. With no regard for my hesitation, the door swung open easily.

Immediately, I was enveloped by the faint smell of oil and by warm air just this side of hot.

Lots of pictures hung on the walls. I saw everything from a girl in a blue turban and Dalí's melted clocks to a retouched photo of the city center at night...and in among those were glossy photos of Yoshimoto comedians. In a corner of the room was a big medical bed, and on that bed lay Ms. Iwato, asleep and breathing peacefully.

Her face was so terribly calm and elegant that for a moment I was afraid she might be dead. In fact, that might have been the first time I'd ever heard her breathe while she slept. Who would have thought it would sound so tranquil?

"Ms. Iwato," I called loudly, gripped by relief that I'd managed to see her again and an equal quantity of unease.

Fuyumi scowled and shushed me, index finger to her lips. "Quiet in the bedroom."

The source of that intermittent noise turned out to be the transfusion pump attached to the IV stand. One of the tubes running out from below the coverlet was connected to a transparent pouch, and that pouch had gone flat.

When Fuyumi hit a blue button on the pump, the alarm stopped. She folded the coverlet down to Ms. Iwato's stomach, removed the tube from the needle that was stuck into her right arm, squirted a clear fluid into the needle from a syringe, then connected the needle to a new tube and pouch. Restarting the pump, she twisted something that looked like a clip, adjusting the flow of the replenished fluid. Through all of this, she never showed an ounce of hesitation.

"She's just sleeping," Fuyumi said.

My attention had been drifting in a daze until her voice pulled me back. "Sleeping...?" I asked.

"Yes. Literally. My sister's only asleep." She crouched down with her back against the side of the bed, then bent her knees, pulling her legs in close. "She sleeps all winter long."

"All winter...?"

Fuyumi's face was hidden by her knees, but her voice was cold. I was leaning forward, ready to run to the bed at any minute, but that voice held me back.

Even if it hadn't, I wouldn't have been able to move. An invisible rift ran between me and that bed, wordlessly rebuffing me.

"Yes, the whole time. If she's early, she sleeps from the end of October until about February twentieth."

"But that…that sounds like…"

Fuyumi didn't seem to be teasing me. She also didn't have a single reason to lie.

"It sounds almost like she's hibernating," I said at last.

A long road unfolds before me.
It doesn't look daunting when I see it from a distance, but when
I strain my eyes and stare, it glares back with the dignity of a dragon.
Every time I remember how long that road is, I freeze as if I've been
sewn to the ground. I've seen it before, over and over. It's part of the world,
and I need to accept it, but the fear and the despair never lose their edge.
I'm waiting to wake up.
In order to wake up, I walk across that long, silent wilderness.

CHAPTER 2
THE CONVENIENCE STORE AT NIGHT

1

"Good evening, Ms. Iwato."

For the first time in my life, I was in a girl's bedroom. It was a perfectly ordinary single-occupant room, though the medical bed and IV stand made it seem a little cramped.

Without the mechanical beep of the pump, the room was very quiet, and the ticking of the desk clock seemed exceptionally loud. It read 3:23 PM.

I leaned against the wall and slid down it into a crouch. From there, I looked up at the thick mattress, which was supported by those white metal pillars.

"Sorry for barging into your room like this."

Drops were falling into a capsule about the size of an index finger, one by one, sending ripples across the tiny pool within. Speed safely regulated, the fluid traveled through the tube, acquiring a few miniature air bubbles on its way into Yuki's arm.

"I came all this way to visit you, and it seems you won't talk to me."

There was no response.

"If you sleep too long, I'll watch the last episode of *Stranger Things*. I've been waiting this whole time."

I couldn't even hear her breathe.

I got to my feet and went over to the bed. The sight of her pale lips and shockingly white face made me take a step back. Sweat broke out on my palms. Being told she was only sleeping started to sound like a euphemism, and the idea that she might actually be dead flitted through my mind. I chafed her shoulders, held my hand in front of her face, and clapped sharply next to her ears, but Ms. Iwato didn't budge.

"Playing possum isn't funny. Would you stop?"

I glanced at the door, then caught Ms. Iwato's shoulders and shook her hard. I pinched her cheek and called her name right in her ear.

"She really won't wake up...," I murmured, astonished.

The preposterous situation was gradually eroding my sense of reality.

Once I fixed the rumpled coverlet, I could tell that its surface was rising and falling slightly. The pace of her breathing, however, was extremely slow. Each inhale and exhale took more than five times longer than one of mine.

When I set a hand on her chest, I felt her heart beat once. It was almost enough to make me leap up and break into song. And yet, though I waited and waited, the next beat didn't come. My elation receded like a wave. Then, just as I was about to pull her into my arms and beg her not to go, there was another beat.

I touched her cheeks. They looked lifeless. Slowly, I bent down and gazed into her face. Her breath brushed the tip of my nose like a breeze.

"Just tell me one thing," I asked her. "Did you abandon me, or...?"

Just then, I heard hasty footsteps. The door burst open, and Fuyumi poked her head in. She had a pair of headphones around her neck and a set of vocabulary flashcards in one hand. "Trouble, Uzu— Eek!"

Her shrill shriek echoed in the room, and my head snapped up. Fuyumi had covered her face with both hands, but she was glaring at me through the gaps between her fingers.

"You've got the wrong idea!" I yelped.

"It seems pretty clear to me what you were up to!"

"I was just talking to her—"

"'Just talking,' from that position?"

When I thought about it, I really had no excuse.

"One instance of sexual harassment while she's asleep. I'm so completely reporting that."

The awkward way she put it made the situation even more embarrassing.

"Never mind, you've got to hide!" Fuyumi said in a stifled shriek. "Hurry!" She pushed her way into the room, her face tense.

"Hide? Why?"

"My mom's back earlier than she said!"

"But didn't you promise your sister to—?"

"Letting you in was a promise between my sister and me. My parents don't know."

Stunned, I thought about what that meant. Little by little, anxiety crept from my toes up through my body.

This was an emergency. Any sane person would have known that hiding wasn't a practical option.

In other words, neither of us was sane.

"I'd better hide…!" Making up my mind, I started searching for a good spot. The first one I thought of was under the bed. I bent down to check but discovered there wasn't much room under medical beds; even just my arm barely fit. The only other possibility was behind the art supplies leaning against the wall.

"Oh, the entryway. My shoes…," I murmured.

Fuyumi went white. In the meantime, the sound of footsteps on the stairs was getting louder.

Fuyumi opened the closet and grabbed my arm with a grip that left no room for argument. "It's fine; just get out of sight."

The closet was the built-in sort, part of the wall. Inside, I saw a clothes chest made of translucent plastic, filled with camisoles and underwear—and next to it, a narrow space that a child might have been able to fit into. Fuyumi started trying to shove me in.

Even to me, that seemed a bridge too far.

As we struggled, I caught a faint whiff of Ms. Iwato's scent, and it reminded me why I was here.

"No," I said, planting my hands on the closet's doorframe. "I came to see Ms. Iwato."

"This isn't the time!"

"It's nothing to feel guilty about!"

And then the door opened to reveal a slender woman holding a shopping bag.

The pressure on my back gradually weakened. Fuyumi's mouth was wide open, her expression halfway between laughing and crying.

It was a three-way standoff. None of us so much as twitched.

Finally, without a word, I bowed to the woman. She bowed back. When she spoke, her voice was as faint as a butterfly's wingbeat. "Who are you?"

"Um, my name is Natsuki Uzume."

"I see. Were the sneakers downstairs yours?"

"Yes, ma'am."

"I see…" The woman nodded slowly two or three times, then glanced at the bed. "There are better places for this. Let's go downstairs." She smiled.

Fuyumi and I both nodded and followed the woman.

This was apparently the Iwato girls' mother, Touko.

Once we arrived in the living room, Touko motioned for Fuyumi and me to sit on the sofa. She didn't seem angry, but neither of us dared disobey. Although the sofa could seat three comfortably, we sat down on opposite ends of it, as if clinging to the edges.

Fuyumi looked at me as if I were filthy. "Mom, listen. You've got the wrong idea."

Touko was putting the groceries she'd just brought home into the refrigerator. She didn't turn around. "Do I?"

"I didn't let him in."

I looked at Fuyumi, shocked. She was leaning against the armrest, and she turned her face away uncomfortably. "I told him it wasn't okay, but he just forced his way—"

"Fuyumi," said her mother, "don't tell silly lies." I hadn't even had to correct her. Touko's tense voice echoed across the living room. "How did he get into the house if you didn't let him in?"

"But, um…"

"Lie one more time, and I'll have Dad reduce your allowance."

Fuyumi looked down, dejected.

"Natsuki, wasn't it?" said her mother, looking at me.

"Yes'm." I sat up straighter.

"What are you to Yuki?"

"I'm her friend." That was the first answer I thought of? I was disgusted with myself. "Just a regular friend." I tried to fix it, but it was no good. My mouth just kept moving on its own. "From university. We're both in this film club, GTR…"

Touko had finished what she was doing. Now she came over to me, bent down, and gazed steadily into my face. Her fiery red lipstick contrasted with the frigid calm in her eyes.

I swallowed hard.

"Thank you for looking out for Yuki." Touko's expression turned cheerful, as if a soft light had come on inside it. I felt the tension drain out of my shoulders. "Really, thank you so much for coming all this way. You came because you were worried about her, didn't you?"

"Yes, well…"

"I'm sure it was a long trip. It must have cost you close to twenty thousand yen, including the way back. We'll reimburse you for it later."

"Oh, no, I just came because I wanted to. I couldn't possibly…"

"Don't worry about it. Also, I hope you'll stay with us tonight."

"Mom?!" Fuyumi spoke up, as if she couldn't just stand by and watch this. "Are you serious?"

"Yes. Did I say anything strange?"

"No, but… You just met him."

"But he's your sister's friend, isn't he?"

"No. He's probably her—"

"He's her friend. Isn't he?" Touko said, shutting her down. Fuyumi looked at the floor, at a loss for words. "And after he came all this way." Touko turned to me again. "I'm sorry. With Yuki in that state…"

"Hibernating…" The word slipped out.

Touko's eyebrows twitched. "Oh. I suppose you could call it that, couldn't you?" Her gaze traveled restlessly around the room. "It began when she was five, and she's been this way ever since. When winter comes, she… You know. She sleeps a bit more than most people. That's all it is. You didn't know anything about it, though, did you?"

"No… It really startled me."

"Startled" wasn't even the half of it. That had been… I mean, she'd looked like she was dead. The last time I'd touched human skin that cold had been at my grandfather's funeral.

That hadn't been the temperature of a living human being.

"Um, she—! She really is…alive, right…?"

Touko went still, gazing into empty space. Then she nodded. She put a hand to her throat. "…She may be like that now, but the fact that she has someone who'd come all this way to see her makes me truly happy. You really must have tea with us. I think I have some from Shizuoka; it was a gift from another member of my mothers' group. Wait just a moment."

Touko headed back into the kitchen.

Grabbing her chance, Fuyumi closed the distance between us in one move. Her tights-clad heel came down hard on my toes. "My sister's 'regular friend'?" Her eyes blazed belligerently. "That's an impressive load of bull."

"Well, what was I supposed to say?"

"Come on. There's no way someone like her could make 'a regular friend.'"

I couldn't believe my ears. No matter what their relationship was like, how could she talk about her own sister like that?

"The odds are extremely good that you're just here to sexually harass her."

"Not true. And kids should keep their noses out of adult relationships."

"I'm only two years younger than you!"

Somewhere along the line, Fuyumi and I had started shouting at each other. Our criticism of things the other had done turned into criticism of our personalities, then insults about our characters.

At a certain point, Fuyumi heaved a deep sigh. "I swear… I only agreed to let you in because I had to, because Yuki said to," she whispered. "I would have liked to never meet you. You're just going to hurt her in the end."

In the end? Hurt her?

At the time, I had no idea what Fuyumi was talking about.

"Seriously, just go home already. I mean it," she said through gritted teeth.

A little while later, Touko came back with a tray holding a teapot, three teacups, and refreshments, and she transferred all of it to the coffee table. The tea sweets were a type I'd never seen before: a dollop of sweet red bean jam molded into a ridged leaflike shape.

"These are called *akafuku*. They're a famous traditional sweet in this part of the country. They're the reverse of an ordinary bean jam bun; with these, the jam is on the outside of the mochi," Touko explained, picking up on my curiosity. "Go ahead, help yourself."

After sitting down in a side chair, she began to pour for us. Steam rose from the stream of clear, light-green liquid, and I caught the fresh fragrance of Japanese tea.

"And how is Yuki at school?" Touko asked, glancing at me. "She doesn't tell me much about it. Is she getting along all right? How does it seem to you?"

I tried to dig up some memories from school, but all that came to mind was how Ms. Iwato looked when she was at my place at three in the morning. I knew all sorts of things she wouldn't want others to know, and yet I knew frighteningly little about the version of herself she showed other people.

"We're in different departments, so I don't know what she's usually like. She's a very serious upperclassman, though, and I respect her. I'm studying literature, so watching her paint always fascinates me."

As I spoke, I began to feel uneasy. Every time I said I knew Ms. Iwato, the fact that I didn't became clearer and clearer.

This won't work, I thought vaguely.

"I'm sorry. I don't actually know anything."

Touko didn't seem startled. She just waited for me to go on.

"We hung out together from time to time, and we only met off campus, so… We really didn't know anything about each other, and then we…"

What sort of colors did she use? What topics did she paint? What art styles did she like?

I knew none of that. I didn't even know what Ms. Iwato had thought we were.

All I'd seen was the version of her I'd wanted to see.

"She said it was just a summer relationship. I thought she was kidding or something. From late September on, though, she wouldn't even look at me. It made me wonder what was wrong, or if something had happened. I looked up her address in the faculty room and came here—"

By the time I'd finished saying it, I felt five kilograms lighter.

At the same time, I braced myself for her family's disillusionment.

"She's like that sometimes. I'm sorry she manipulated you." Touko looked up at the ceiling, then bowed to me, like a parent apologizing for her child's mischief. "I'm sure she had her reasons, though. Unfortunately, there's no way to know what they were right now, but…" She smiled, pointing at the ceiling. "Why not come back next February and ask her in person?"

"Mom!" Fuyumi yelled.

I couldn't blame her, but Touko glared at her sternly and told her to go study.

Fuyumi was left speechless again, and I felt a little bad for her.

"You really wouldn't mind?" I asked, after I'd taken a sip of tea.

Touko smiled and nodded.

"Do you really think she'll wake up?"

Partly because Touko had ordered her to, Fuyumi was reluctantly walking me to the station. She'd broken a long silence with that question.

"I'm just asking. Taking a survey. When you first saw my sister, what did you think? I'll use the survey's results to improve the Iwato family's hospitality service."

Her sarcasm was even more biting than usual.

There was no way I could know. After all, I hadn't even heard why Ms. Iwato hibernated. Fuyumi was well aware of that, though.

"I trust that she will."

"Hmm. So you're an optimist."

There was aloof mockery in Fuyumi's tone.

She couldn't have been more right, and I had no comeback. I'd only been a guest today. A guest who'd learned about Ms. Iwato's background for the first time, hadn't been able to process it completely, and was still confused.

But this girl was different. For at least ten years, since early childhood, she'd been facing her sister's hibernations as a member of her family.

"I'd like to believe that myself," she said. "I want to think that what happened eight years ago couldn't happen again."

"Eight years ago?"

"My mom didn't mention it, but…" Fuyumi broke off for a moment, then went on. "It was incredibly cold that year; they said it was the biggest cold wave ever or something. My sister's switch had flipped by the end of September, and she fell asleep in mid-October. Then she didn't wake up in February, or March, or when the cherry trees bloomed—"

Or when they changed from spring to summer uniforms. Or when they started thinking about what presents to ask Santa for. Or when they reached the season where you felt even more grateful for every warm bath and meal...

What kind of anxiety had this girl lived through, eight years ago?

"That time, it took her a year and five months to wake up."

"Huh?!"

A yelp even I thought was pathetic escaped me with a puff of white breath.

I whirled around, looking back down the road we'd just walked. The corner room on the second floor of the Iwatos' house was already lost, buried in the townscape.

My heart wanted to take off running right that second, but the girl gatekeeper shut it down. "You're no prince. Kissing her won't wake her up."

Her gaze was fixed on Honjin Station, which also housed the bus terminal.

"All right. Let's meet at 'the ritual' next year. Assuming there is a next year."

2

The lights in the classroom flipped on, and I squinted against the glare. I could barely make out the back of Professor Takeda, the modern film history teacher, as he left the classroom.

His assistant retracted the screen, then started collecting attendance cards. Hastily wiping my drool away, I hunted for my card but couldn't find it. *Where is it, where?!* As I was looking around, a voice jabbed into my back.

"Here, right here!"

My unfocused eyes had gone farsighted on me, and I couldn't tell who the figures directly behind me were.

"Hang on, this is hilarious. I'm getting a photo."

"Huh? What?"

"Like I said, it's right here."

When I rubbed my eyes and got my sight back to normal, I saw Tomomi and Atsushi. Atsushi was looking at me with pity in his eyes, while Tomomi was holding her smartphone at the ready and pointing repeatedly at her cheek with her free hand.

"On your face."

Feeling across my cheek with my fingertips, I found the card, stiff with drool and glued to my skin.

I gathered the scattered printouts from my desk, then folded up my Bluetooth keyboard. My smartphone still sat horizontally on its stand, displaying the notebook app I'd been using to supplement my written notes.

"How long have you two been there?" I asked.

"We got in kind of late. I bet you were conked out the whole time, huh?" Atsushi sounded a little disgusted.

Even though she acted like it was a pain, Tomomi dug a spare attendance card out of her bag and handed it to me. She really looked out for other people, and I was deeply indebted to her for it.

"I haven't seen you much lately. Are you coming to school like you're supposed to?" Tomomi asked, after I'd handed over the card and we'd left the classroom.

"Yeah, mostly."

"How did things go with Ms. Iwato?"

I tilted my head, scratching at the back of my neck, trying to escape Tomomi's searching gaze. "Why would you ask about that?"

"Well…because I'm worried, obviously. About you."

"It sounds like you've been writing a ton lately. I can't wait to read it," Atsushi said quietly, as if he was trying cancel out Tomomi's remark.

"Y-yeah…"

Even that vague answer earned a smile from him.

I'd liked arts and crafts ever since kindergarten. I enjoyed using the tools available to make a work of art and then getting praised for it. Creative work was an extension of that. I'd started writing my first novel in middle school, and I'd had several of my friends read it. Even now, I could remember how tense I'd felt as I watched them try to figure out what they thought of it. It was easy to turn ordinary days into an adventure.

However, when high school entrance exams came around, the number of friends who'd read for me dwindled. I'd joined this university's Literature Department without talking it over with my teachers or my parents. I hadn't told my parents that I'd chosen it because it had a College of Art next door, which meant I'd have the chance to switch departments.

My future had stalled right there, when I hadn't been able to boldly put down *Writer* as my desired career.

I wished I hadn't told these two about it. It was a problem I should have kept to myself.

As I thought about all this, I continued responding absentmindedly to the conversation. On our way to the cafeteria, we passed the semicircular stage like the one at the Colosseum. It was typically used for events and dance club practices, but now, oddly, a large figure in a military coat was up there, bending over something that seemed to be on fire.

Thinking this was weird, I slowed down. Atsushi looked over at me and asked what was up, so I pointed the figure out to him.

The flames were escaping from a small metal stand, and the figure set something that appeared to be a skillet down on top of them.

"They're camping," I said.

Tomomi's attention was on the stage now, too. "You're right." She sounded shocked.

Cutting in front of her, Atsushi headed over, as if the stage were beckoning him. Tomomi and I followed. Then, without thinking, I called out to the figure. "Ms.…Shimoki."

She was wearing a military coat and had broad shoulders, and I'd only been able to see her back, so I'd just assumed she was a guy. That was the second time I'd made that mistake.

"Friend of yours?" Tomomi glanced at me dubiously.

"Well, um…"

"You hesitating means it's related to Ms. Iwato, doesn't it?"

I clammed up.

"Huh. Guess I called it," Tomomi said, arbitrarily deciding she was right.

Just then, Ena looked our way and beckoned us over with a leisurely gesture. I climbed the stone steps she was sitting on and stopped one step below her.

"Hi there," she said.

"Hello." I ducked my head in a casual bow, a little late.

A hinged pair of iron plates sat on top of a simple camp stove. Ena opened them, checking the contents, then flipped the plates.

"What are you doing, Ms. Shimoki?"

"Exactly what it looks like. I'm making a grilled sandwich."

"A grilled sandwich…"

"I bought sandwich bread, cheese, and ham over there." Ena pointed to the convenience store annexed to the cafeteria. "Now I'm grilling them." She adjusted the valve on the gas stove, and the red flames dwindled to a feeble blue.

"But why here? Are you auditing a Literature Department class?"

"Auditing? This is my department. I'm in my third year of studying German literature."

"Huh?! …So you're not from the College of Art?"

No way.

"I never claimed to be, you know." Ena smiled faintly, then shifted her focus to a point behind me and gave a deep nod in greeting. Tomomi and Atsushi hastily nodded back.

After taking the plates from the flames, she turned off the gas, then opened them. Steam billowed from a flattened, crustless, toasty brown sandwich.

"Want some?"

Ena broke the grilled sandwich in two. Cheese oozed out, spinning into threads as she offered half to me.

"N-no thank you."

"If you're sure." Casually, Ena set that half on a plate and started in on the half she was holding. "Do you ever get the overwhelming urge to camp?"

"Well, uh…"

"Quietly, by yourself, at night when no one's around."

"Wouldn't you get lonely?"

"Would you prefer to camp with a large group, then?"

"Well, camping isn't something I generally…"

"This guy's a hard-core indoor type," said Atsushi, breaking in suddenly. "He says he's got no plans for either December or January. He's working part-time and everything, so he really should take at least one trip, right?!"

Tomomi looked startled at the interruption. However, Ena listened to Atsushi calmly while she devoured her grilled sandwich. "I'd imagine that's true. You can tell just by looking at him." Atsushi was taken aback by her unexpected total agreement. "Even if he were the outdoorsy type, though, this winter, he's—"

Ena broke off midsentence. Then, with an unsettling smile, she tilted her head, letting her gaze wander through space.

"You saw her, didn't you?" The question could have been directed at anybody. She'd definitely meant it for me, though. "It's clear from the way you're acting. You saw her, and you came back shattered. I imagine you're privately nursing a broken heart right about now."

"Um…" At that point, Tomomi broke in. Projecting a wariness just shy of hostility, she spoke from a step behind Atsushi and me. "Excuse me. May I ask what your relationship is to Natsuki?"

"When one feels a question needs excusing, it's best not to ask it," Ena said spitefully, but Tomomi didn't back down.

After a deliberate pause, Ena answered. "He's had a little trouble with a friend of mine. I suppose you could call me his supporter."

She wanted me to succeed here? That was the first I'd heard of it.

Atsushi looked Ena up and down, repeatedly almost saying something and then deciding not to. Tomomi remained as wary as ever.

Ena cast the two of them a sidelong glance. "Say, underclassmen. May I borrow your friend for a few minutes?"

When we opened the emergency door, cold wind blew in, sending a shiver through me. In front of me, the tail of Ena's coat flapped as if the wind were trying to tear it away.

Someone had gotten to the roof ahead of us: A petite girl and a tall, gangly guy were there, sharing a single caffe latte.

We hadn't spoken much while we were on the move: Ena was an

abnormally fast walker. Getting my breathing under control quietly so she wouldn't notice, I lowered myself onto a bench.

"This place really is calming," Ena said, raising to her lips the hot matcha au lait she'd picked up on our way here. I opened the coffee she'd bought for me. "Did I walk a bit too fast?"

She'd seen through me, and I flinched internally. "Just…a little."

"Sorry. Yuki usually keeps up with me."

For some reason, it was a relief to hear that name from Ena. She glanced at me, then set her elbows on her knees, laced her fingers together, and rested her forehead on her clasped hands as if she were praying. "Ever since high school, I've walked as if I were running away. I was too big for a girl, and I was afraid everyone would make fun of me."

Ena was over 170 centimeters tall. Compared with the average, that really was pretty big.

"I believed I'd be able to change once I got to university, but I was wrong. It's only natural, when you think about it. High schoolers become college students just as they are. They don't shed their skins or emerge from chrysalides. The fact that I thought changing my environment would change anything else is embarrassing to me now."

A self-mocking smile spread over Ena's face. The words "It's chilly out here" passed in front of us, and the couple went back into the building, their shoulders rubbing together. For a moment, Ena's eyes followed the girl's back as she disappeared through the door.

"Did you attend a new student event?"

"Yes, technically."

"So did I. And that's where I met Yuki."

Something about that statement tugged at me.

Ena was gazing at the sky, beyond the fence around the building's edge. "At the time, I didn't know drinking parties were like that. Nor did I know how terrifying alcohol was, or how deep the night could be. On the other hand, she was really used to it. For a college first-year, everything about her was incredibly polished."

It was as if she were reliving her first encounter with Ms. Iwato.

I never suspected Ena might have had an experience like mine. A sudden sense of kinship welled up inside me.

"People urged me to drink, so I did. Then my vision grew unsteady, and their voices began to echo. It felt like sinking underwater. Even so, I toughed it out until the party ended. As I left the pub, I remember leaning on Yuki's shoulder for support. When I woke up, I was lying in the bicycle parking lot of a pachinko parlor. When she saw I was awake, Yuki handed me a bottle of water."

As I listened, I remembered Ms. Iwato's back as she walked through the night.

"I asked, and she'd apparently stayed with me the whole time I was asleep. We'd only just met, but she stayed with me for hours."

"Wait a second." Realizing that what had felt odd about her story was something very simple, I hastily stopped her. "Aren't you in your third year here, Ms. Shimoki?"

"Yes...?"

"Why were you and Ms. Iwato at the same new student event?"

Ena nodded. "So you haven't heard yet," she said, taking a sip of her matcha au lait. "She and I started university at the same time. I was twenty-one, though, while she was twenty-two, born in the first quarter of the year."

The words didn't feel real to me, but when I thought about my own eighteen years, their meaning sank in. When I was still in middle school, Ms. Iwato had already been old enough to start college.

I didn't know what to say, and my head grew heavy, tilting down on its own. I didn't care about Ms. Iwato's age. It was not having been able to hear it from her in person that got to me.

"From the looks of it..." Ena scrutinized my face. I knew right away what she was asking. "You really did meet her, didn't you?"

I nodded wordlessly.

"I see," she said in a low voice; she didn't seem surprised. I drained my coffee, which had cooled some time ago, then set the can behind my heel.

"Congratulations. Welcome to the fellowship of stalkers."

I wasn't the least bit happy about that.

"That's what her little sister called me, too..."

"Well, it's a fact, isn't it? Going to her house is lunacy."

Ena was completely right. I'd crossed a line.

She put an arm around my shoulders and pulled me into a side hug, the way a male friend might do. "Well, don't let it discourage you. You're not the only one who's been enthralled by the abyss."

"Huh…?"

"She has something that drives people mad."

Ena's sympathetic voice whispered in my ear. She hugged my shoulder tighter, to the point where it hurt a little.

Something that drove people mad. In that case, I was already long—

"And I'm sorry for you. Now you've got one foot stuck in this, too. It's on its way. Your first winter."

Ena pointed up at the cloud-covered sky.

A gust of wind blew through. The can I'd set by my foot tipped over with a clatter and bounced and tumbled at random over the roof. I ran after it, watching for the moment when it slowed down, then stomped it flat.

"It only takes a slight difference for people to pass each other by. On top of that, we're students; we haven't even found our feet yet. I wonder how long you'll last."

When I turned back, Ena had stood up, too. The hem of her military coat rippled in an unsettling way, like the twin tails of a monster cat.

"I'm fine! It doesn't hurt!" I shot back, trying to be intimidating. I wasn't cold or anything.

"I'm not so sure about that." Ena gave a low laugh. "Are you lonely?"

"No," I said immediately. This wasn't good-bye forever. I'd see her again in March. Of course I could wait that long.

"But soon real winter will arrive."

I was sure I'd be fine.

The wind was as strong as ever, and my fingertips were going numb.

"You'll be in love with someone else by then."

From a classroom somewhere, I heard a clear soprano voice.

I remembered the weather forecaster on the news that morning saying this year was going to be colder than usual.

3

One step outside Choufu Station, I found myself in a mazelike residential district. I checked my smartphone one-handed; the other hand was holding a plastic bag with two bottles of sake. The GPS seemed to be having a bad day: The map kept turning this way and that like a weathervane.

As the compass finally pointed out the direction I should go, out of the corner of my eye, I saw a woman running.

"...Tomomi?"

Had she lost a game of Tycoon and been sent on an errand or something?

When the map app told me I'd reached my destination, it turned out to be a big building surrounded by a fence. I pushed the gate open, then punched in the apartment number at the building's entrance.

Atsushi came down in the elevator, then passed me rather hastily and ducked outside to take a look around.

"I saw Tomomi go running by."

"Oh... For real?" Atsushi glanced at me, then crossed his arms and leaned back against the corner of the elevator.

"How many people ended up coming?" I asked.

"Six. Or no, seven counting you."

"So there's eight?"

"No, seven. I counted me, too."

I'd asked him how many people *came*, though... The sound of the elevator doors opening interrupted my train of thought.

We got out on the sixth floor, then walked to number 9. The door opened, and Keiya from the same seminar poked his head out. He was a slim, pale guy with clear-cut features and blond hair the color of tempura. I didn't know him well, but Tomomi had told me he played guitar in the Pop Music Club.

"Hey," Keiya said casually as soon as he saw me.

"...It's been a while."

Keiya gave me an odd look, then went back into the apartment. He'd just barely managed to find room for his feet in the messy entryway, and he staggered a bit as he went.

"Keiya looks"—I straightened up the shoes in the entryway—"like he'd be popular with girls."

"Him?" Atsushi held the door for me as I worked. "He's pretty dumb, though. I bet they'd give up on him after one or two dates."

"I can kind of see that."

"He has a girlfriend now, though," Atsushi said, teasing me, and I flipped him off, joking right back.

There were a lot of cardboard boxes piled against the wall in front of the bathroom. I hesitated, gazing at them, and Atsushi hurried me along from just outside the door. "Come on, they're going to start on the food. Sorry the hall's such a tight fit."

"Nah, it's fine."

Atsushi wouldn't step through the door until I started walking.

His place was a studio apartment, but he'd managed to separate the bedroom and living areas. His desk was in the bedroom, so the living room had a lot of space, and there was a low, heated *kotatsu* table.

When I stepped inside, everyone's eyes snapped to me, and greetings flew back and forth. The eyes that had been on my face soon shifted to the bag I was holding.

"Sake?! Why did everyone bring sake?!" Keiya thunked his head on the floor, yelling like it was the end of the world. Saori and Aina backed him up, sending me disappointed looks across the bubbling hot pot.

"Hey, it's fine. We'll drink it later." Jun, who was sitting next to Aina, got up and headed over to the cupboard, then tossed me a cushion like a Frisbee. "There you go. There's space next to me; c'mon over," he said easily, returning to his spot in front of the hot pot.

The *kotatsu* table, built for four, had been set out in the living room. On it, pale-blue flames flickered above a portable gas stove. When the lid of the clay pot was lifted, steam billowed out, and water dripped from the lid onto the quilt that covered the *kotatsu*. It was a Korean seafood hot pot. The dishes were miso soup bowls, rice bowls, and even mugs; there was no rhyme or reason here. Keiya took his turn first and stuck his own chopsticks into the hot pot, saying he hadn't used them yet, so it was fine. He scooped red octopus and bok choy and glass noodles into a miso soup bowl.

"Hot!"

Something in the pot burst, sending droplets of broth flying. Keiya scrambled out from the *kotatsu*, rubbing at his cheek. Saori ran over to him, looking worried, and knocked over a big empty sake bottle that rolled across the floor.

"What is this stuff?!" Keiya yelled. "It's spicy, and the flavor's way too strong!" Laughing, Atsushi handed him a two-liter bottle of mineral water straight from the fridge.

Somehow, everything felt unreal, and I didn't notice that the guy next to me was trying to hand me a rice bowl.

"You're spacing out."

At the sound of Jun's voice, I turned. After hastily accepting the bowl, I started to help myself to the hot pot. "I was just thinking, 'When college kids live on their own, it's the same everywhere,'" I said.

"Speaking of, I guess I've never been to your place."

I imagined Jun and several other friends coming over to my apartment. I couldn't have six people sleep on my guest futon. I could put two or three in my twin bed... But we'd slept in that bed, Ms. Iwato and I. She'd held my hand when morning began, and at the end of the night. That had really happened, at least until summer ended.

"What's wrong? Not feeling so good?" Jun's voice was soft and kind.

I shook my head. When I looked over, I could see the sincerity in his eyes.

Jun never said much. We'd had several classes together, though—Theory of Ideas and Thought Experiment Theory, among others. Maybe we were on a similar wavelength.

"The thing is, up until a little while ago, there was a girl I thought things were going pretty well with."

"Going pretty well... Oh, I get it. And?"

"She went away."

I could see genuine interest and worry in his face. I was grateful to him for not giving me a superficial reaction, like *What, she dumped you?* or *Shake it off.*

"Do you know why she left, Natsuki?"

Of course I knew. How could I not?

There was nothing anyone could have done. It was just how her body worked. It wasn't as if she'd betrayed me.

Come to think of it, this might have been the first time I'd actually told somebody that Ms. Iwato had gone away. Jun's straightforward eyes gave me courage.

"See, when winter comes, she always—"

With a jolt, I broke off. Jun looked mystified.

In winter, she always what? Hibernated? Slept for four months straight?

What was I, an idiot?

"I mean, um, she…"

I couldn't say it. There was no way I could say she hibernated. That she fell into a deep sleep and didn't wake up once all winter, that she went into a vegetative state, that she got all her nutrition through tubes one centimeter in diameter.

Jun gave me a searching look. The fact that he wasn't pushing me to answer was really rough on my conscience.

I swallowed my words. Not just with Jun, but with Atsushi, with my parents, with counselors. Except for Ms. Iwato and her family, there wasn't a single person in the world I could talk to about this.

"In winter, she has to go back to her parents' place. She's not here now."

"Did she get called back to help with the family business or something?" As Jun spoke, he turned down the flame on the stove slightly. The bubbling surface of the pot settled down.

I nodded a little, letting my eyes fall to the bright-red broth of my untouched Korean hot pot.

What was I saying? Ms. Iwato didn't see me as her boyfriend. She didn't see me as anything.

The hairiest part was that I still thought I might have a chance. If it weren't for that hope, I wouldn't be hurting, and yet…

"I'm gonna make a convenience store run." Atsushi got up abruptly and disappeared into the entryway. The hot pot was mostly broth at this point, and as Keiya and Saori headed to the kitchen to get more ingredients, I was struck by the feeling that something was missing. Atsushi had said there were seven of us, but the group in here was…

"Huh? Where's Tomomi?"

At the sound of that name, everyone glanced at me, then went quiet. Even Jun gave me an awkward look.

"What's up?" I asked.

"Oh, well, it's fine. Don't worry about it," Saori said. The four of them turned reproachful eyes on me, pressuring me, as if I'd brought up something taboo.

"It sounds like those two are dating. Didn't you know, Natsuki?" Jun asked quietly.

When I looked blank, the reproach turned to sympathy.

That can't be right, I murmured to myself. Neither of them had ever said a word about it. They'd never shown me any signs.

"Since when…?"

"For quite a while now. I think it was just after the spring orientation."

So back when I'd first told them about Ms. Iwato, those two had been a couple already?

"I see. I didn't know. It, um, looks like everybody else did, huh?"

The other four looked at each other and nodded.

"I mean, it's not that hard to notice, right?" Keiya broke in tactlessly. "Like those cardboard boxes. That's obviously Tomomi's stuff, yeah? They must've been living together. When I first got here, you could see what was in those. Women's underwear and camis, things like that. He must've realized he'd messed up. They've been taped shut ever since."

"Cut it out." Aina, who'd been picking up our trash, stretched her lower back.

"Well, it's weird." Keiya smirked, thumping his stomach. "Right, Saori?"

"Yeah…," Saori said quietly, then looked back down at the cutting board.

There was a click, then the sound of shoes being removed. The door opened, and Atsushi walked back in. He tromped heavily over to the bed, leaving no room for argument. A little later, Tomomi poked her head in. Her eyes were slightly red. They seemed moister than usual, and they shone in the light from the ceiling lamp.

"Sorry. The grocery store I went to was pretty far," she said quietly, sitting down on a free cushion. She glanced at me with those red, puffy eyes, then promptly looked down guiltily.

Lying on the bed with his legs kicked out in a big V, Atsushi started reading the second volume of *One Piece*.

I didn't know exactly what had happened between these two. The only thing I could say for sure was that, in this moment, they'd chosen not to acknowledge each other.

And if they'd managed to do that, I was sure they could still talk it out, too. I was probably the only one in this lukewarm room who was feeling the cold right down to his core.

But soon real winter will arrive.

Ms. Shimoki had been right.

The windows were heavily beaded with condensation.

4

Just outside the north exit of Ikebukuro Station was a V-shaped road, and across the street at its base stood an old building. On its first floor, between a karaoke place and a cell phone outlet, there was a timeworn pastry shop.

As a rule, it sold tarts and cream puffs, but as the season drew closer, it offered special cakes decorated for Christmas. A stack of fancy pink boxes sat on a table that had been pulled outside the shop. I stood next to it, wearing an apron, working as a vendor.

I was a robot repeating a preset speech.

I didn't hate being a robot. I was actually pretty grateful for the opportunity.

I put the product into plastic bags and handed it to customers, then either accepted cash or took electronic payment through the handheld terminal. By now, the whole sequence was an ingrained reflex. My heart wasn't in it. People who weren't planning to buy cakes didn't even glance at me. Just as I didn't exist for them, they didn't exist for me.

My mind floated in midair, as if I were having an out-of-body experience.

After making eye contact, a young couple approached me. I tore off a plastic bag, put a box into it, and pushed it forward a little, and they hastily got out their wallet.

The tall, pointy-chinned man grabbed the bag with a muscular arm. Then he put his other arm around the waist of the woman, who was wearing pancake makeup, and they walked off toward the station together. A group went into the karaoke place next door. When the glass doors opened, an incredible din escaped, so I raised my voice to compete with it.

The DVD-viewing place right in front of me was loudly advertising a Christmas discount. The tempura rice bowl shop next to it was offering a "Christmas rice bowl."

What the heck was that? I definitely didn't want one.

A suit-clad businessman with stiffly set hair was walking arm in arm with a woman in a wool coat. They looked restless, and their eyes were gleaming brightly.

They headed up the road on the right branch of the V, walking parallel with the tracks. For a brief moment, I imagined where they'd be twenty minutes later. Then a family passed by, and I looked into the eyes of the timid-looking mother before trying to call her over.

The flow of customers broke off for a moment, and I rested my throat. I'd been yelling for the past two hours. Since I was a robot, though, I felt no pain. Nothing hurt.

The shop gave me one of the unsold cakes, and I went home. Even if these were discounted tomorrow, they wouldn't sell, so they were giving them away to their staff instead.

I carried the fancy box home carefully.

The entrance of the apartment next to mine was decorated with ornaments. I opened the door to my place.

"Welcome home."

For the past two weeks, I'd been imagining that impossible voice constantly.

I set the box on the low table, got out two random plates, then grabbed two forks, and set them all out. I turned on the TV and brought up my usual video streaming service out of habit.

"Oops!"

The cursor had been on the last episode of season 2 of *Stranger Things*, and it started to play on its own. Hastily, I grabbed the remote and stopped it.

If this was how it was going to be, we should have just watched the last episode on September 22.

I opened the cake box and forced the side of my fork through the white mass I'd been selling up until just a little while ago. Then I transferred a slice of the crushed cake onto my plate and another slice onto the other plate.

"Let's dig in."

The sound of the second hand on the clock filled the room.

The slow, spiteful crawl of time was right in my face.

"Thanks for the food."

I threw the cake away.

It was all I could do.

Even so, my stomach felt disgustingly empty. I pulled on my down jacket again and left the house.

Something fell onto my forehead. *Cold.* When I touched my hair, it was a little wet.

I looked up at the sky. The stuff sifting down onto my eyelids wasn't water droplets. It was soft white powder. By the time I realized what it was, it was falling all over town.

Most people didn't stop walking. There was nothing special about it. To me, though, this was snow I'd wanted to see together with somebody.

But that was a wish that would never come true.

Because Yuki Iwato couldn't see snow.

5

The Fine Arts Department studio was a quiet battlefield: Students in coveralls had brought in sleeping bags and cushions and were spending their nights there, finishing up their paintings in preparation for the February submission deadline.

Unexpectedly, Ms. Iwato's painting was in with the others. It was an oil painting on a huge canvas, about 190 by 130 cm, and it showed a drowsy woman slumped over her desk. Its expansive composition and bright colors were striking.

"The style doesn't really match her vibe, does it? It's sort of laid-back," Shuji Ishikawa called to me as he passed by. I'd gotten acquainted with him during my multiple trips to the Fine Arts Department, and we talked sometimes.

Since making that trip to Ms. Iwato's house, I'd checked through school festival pamphlets and the Fine Arts Department homepage and had seen several of her works, so I knew. She liked dark backgrounds, and she almost never drew bright ones where light seemed to engulf the subject like this.

It was pretty.

I genuinely thought so, but after gazing at it for a while, I started to feel as if the painting were pulling me in, and I had to look away.

I couldn't understand why it had that effect.

"If she'd only finished it, she probably would have had a shot at the contest," Ishikawa grumbled. He was putting his own work away in a canvas case.

"Come to think of it, everyone's drawing faces, huh?"

There were a few that had given expressions to inanimate objects and others that seemed to do the reverse, likening people to objects, but from what I could see, most of the paintings showed human faces.

"Well, yeah. The end-of-term topic is self-portraits," Ishikawa answered absently.

I nodded.

Oh, of course. A second later, a sense of understanding seeped through me, and I stared at Ms. Iwato's picture again in astonishment. Even when I wanted to avert my eyes, I forced myself to look right at it.

This painting wasn't laid-back.

After all, it was a self-portrait. In other words—it must represent the ominous journey into hibernation, one from which she might never wake. It had to show Ms. Iwato's fear as she fell into bottomless darkness.

I turned my eyes away, wasn't able to look at it, because this was exactly what I'd been feeling all winter long.

I'd walked through the long, cold season alone, and I'd finally made it to February. I'd kept my focus on that feeling of loneliness, carefully coaxing myself closer and closer to the finish line. But what if Ms. Iwato didn't wake up? What if, as Fuyumi had warned, next year didn't come? What if it was like this unfinished painting? What if she became nothing but matter and slept for a year and five months, or even longer?

"Hey, what's up? You don't look so good," Ishikawa said.

Forcing a smile, I shook my head.

Compared with this fear, loneliness was a joke. It was mere optimism, rooted in the premise that I'd see her again. This love of mine might not even get the chance to end in heartbreak—

No, I couldn't afford to think about it. Imagination was not my friend.

A convenience store I passed on the way home had a Meiji Chocolate streamer dancing outside it, gearing up for Valentine's Day. I kept my eyes down and walked right by, pretending I saw nothing.

6

Beyond the bullet train's round-cornered, double-paned window, transparent-blue scenery rolled away.

I tried to brace my elbow on the window frame, but it was too smooth and narrow, and my elbow couldn't find any purchase. That said, fitting my head into the gap between the seat and the wall wasn't comfortable; the back of my skull felt compressed. I considered lowering the seat table and resting my head on that, but I realized I might break the supports and thought better of it.

Giving up, I sat up straight and folded my arms.

A week earlier, on the evening of February 21, I'd gotten a phone call from Touko Iwato.

I'd been typing a homework essay on my computer. I'd looked down at my vibrating smartphone and let it ring ten times. I hadn't been able to answer it.

I'd just lived through the longest winter of my life. Even though the thought of that one phone call was what had gotten me through it, when it actually came, my hands shook so badly I couldn't pick up.

You're no prince. Kissing her won't wake her up.

Fuyumi's words had been both a light and a curse. Over the past three months, hardly a day had gone by when I hadn't thought about them. I was no prince. Even if the sky fell, there was no way my involvement would improve Ms. Iwato's condition.

That meant Yuki might not wake up.

This phone call might be to let me know that the ritual had been canceled.

The cold had seeped into my desk. I slumped over it and cooled my head against its surface. Then, when I checked my smartphone, there was a voice-mail. I knew it was rude, but I had to wait until after sunset to listen to it.

As the town was settling down for the night, I played back the message. Once I made up my mind to listen, it was over in a moment: Yuki was awake.

She'd awakened.

The next day, I called. I confirmed the statement I'd heard the previous night, then checked again to be sure. The idea that this might annoy her didn't occur to me. Every time I asked, Touko gave me the same answer.

Then she invited me to the Wake-Up Party they were going to hold a week later.

We entered a tunnel, and my ears rang. When I popped them, my head hurt. I braced my elbow on the window frame again. It stayed in place nicely this time, and I managed to rest my chin on my hand.

We got through the tunnel, and a light vibration ran through the train. My elbow slipped off the window frame.

This wasn't like my first visit to Nagoya. This time, at the very least, the whole family knew I was coming.

I had to calm down.

When I got through the ticket gate, my eyes found a clock shaped like a big die. This was the "Silver Clock" Touko had told me about. It was a popular meeting spot, and naturally, there were quite a few people leaning against its base or crouched beside it.

One girl with a sharper look in her eyes than the others was glancing around restlessly. Her hair hung straight, falling a bit below her shoulders, and she seemed a little more grown-up, but it was definitely Fuyumi.

Before I could call out to her, her eyes flicked my way. Her glare was as sharp as the tip of a blade. Then, before anything else, she sighed.

"H-hello…" I greeted her timidly.

"……"

"Thank you for…coming to meet me…"

"……"

"It's, um, been a long time."

"You can't possibly expect me to care," she said, turning away in a huff. She was as unfriendly as ever, and it was actually kind of a relief, but I wasn't about to say so.

As we left the building, I saw a huge sculpture like a swirling tower sitting in the middle of a traffic circle. Walking briskly, Fuyumi headed down into the underground entrance facing the road. I'd been through this place once before and had a faint memory of it, but since my eyes had been glued to my phone's transfer app at the time, the sights of Nagoya Station seemed new to me.

"Who'd have believed he'd actually come...?" Fuyumi muttered as we walked through the shopping street under the station.

I can hear you.

Why did she hate me so much?

After two stations' worth of swaying in the subway, we reached the Taikou District. After that, we walked for a ways. We barely spoke.

I hadn't seen the Iwato residence in three months, but it looked exactly as I remembered. I was shaking, and I quickly realized I couldn't blame the cold or the wind. My legs were trembling, and the vibrations were traveling up through the rest of my body.

Fuyumi had already opened the gate, and she turned back suspiciously. "What are you doing?"

"Well, um..."

I looked down, trying to get my breathing under control. The fear that had abruptly welled up in me was threatening to swallow me whole.

"Hurry up and get in here."

"Is it really okay for me to see her?"

"Huh?" There was irritation and disappointment in her voice. "You're saying that now...? Why, exactly? You came here three months ago, voluntarily. Remember? My sister approved you."

"She might have changed her mind."

Fuyumi took her hand off the gate, tromped back to me, and leaned in so that her face was right in front of mine. "There's a very special ritual today. Frankly, if you keep acting like this, we're going to have a problem."

"But—"

"And you call yourself a man?"

That left me speechless. My embarrassment blew my fear away, and my legs stopped trembling.

Fuyumi reached for the front door. I could hardly wait, and at the same time, I was so scared I couldn't take it. With one hand on the doorknob, she turned back to me. The hostility that had flooded her eyes a moment ago was gone. Instead, I saw something urgent and pleading in them.

Just then, the door swung open.

A woman in a dressing gown stood there, leaning on crutches. Her glossy black hair had grown quite a bit since the last time I saw her; it almost brushed her chin now. Still, her bewitching aura was the same as ever, and she was several times lovelier than she had appeared in my constant daydreams over the past three months, and...

I'd had tens of thousands of words ready and waiting for this moment, and now I realized they were all completely useless.

"Natsuki?"

Ms. Iwato tilted her head, looking mystified. Her voice was clear and musical. I wanted to talk, to tell her things, but I couldn't speak. Even I didn't understand what was wrong with me.

"Yes... That's right—it's me! Natsuki!"

When the words finally came, they were as shrill as a train whistle. Beside me, Fuyumi cracked up.

"How strange. It's really you? The Natsuki I know?"

I nodded firmly several times.

She was awake. Awake and talking. Yuki Iwato was standing right there in front of me.

How long had I been waiting for this?

"I'm glad, though," Ms. Iwato whispered. Her face was transparent, unlit by any emotion. "Go ahead and come in. I'll get dressed."

For the second time, I stepped into the Iwato family home.

7

The curtain rods were decorated with paper chains, and party crackers were laid out on the table. A glance at the living room made it obvious that something was happening that day. I waited there by myself until Ms. Iwato came downstairs. She was wearing jeans and a hooded fleece jacket, and the crutches had been replaced by an aluminum cane she held in her left hand.

"Would you come for a walk with me?" she asked.

There was a big hospital just down the street from the house, and our walk took us along its stone wall. The surrounding buildings were all relatively short, so the cluster of skyscrapers near Nagoya Station seemed to tower at the far edge of the sky.

Ms. Iwato walked slowly down the edge of the street, testing her footing as she went. Bicycles passed us again and again, but they were careful to avoid us when they saw her cane. It still didn't feel safe, so I stuck close, staying one step behind her.

"It's been a while, hasn't it?" she said.

"It really has."

"About how many months, do you think?"

"The last time I saw you was at the end of November, so maybe three."

"It might have been three months for you, but it's been longer for me," Ms. Iwato said, sounding slightly cross. "You saw me asleep, didn't you?"

My heart skipped a beat, and I stopped in my tracks for a moment. Ms. Iwato turned to face me, keeping one hand on the stone wall. "That's what it means that you're here, right?"

"I-I'm sorry!" I shouted impulsively. Her sister or mom had to have told me I'd visited in November. "I'd seen you sleep before that, though."

During the summer—, I almost said, but I stopped myself.

Ms. Iwato seemed to have picked up on the words anyway. She gave me a searching look. "I never let you see me asleep, you know."

The history of that summer was branded onto my brain. I had vividly detailed memories of Ms. Iwato's profile and the scent of her sweat as she lay in that hot, humid bed, asleep and breathing peacefully.

"Is that...right...?" My cheeks flamed up, and I averted my eyes. "So you don't want people seeing you sleep?"

Ms. Iwato shot me an incredulous look, as if surprised I didn't already know. "Well, I mean. I'm not wearing makeup, I'm all sweaty, and my hair's short. I'm not cute at all."

She giggled, then started walking again. Our route took us all around the hospital. As usual, we passed a lot of old people.

"My mom's cooking a lot of food for tonight. I'm really looking forward to this."

"Is it going to be spicy?"

"Just mine. Just a little bit."

There was no way it was going to be "just a little bit" spicy.

"All I've had so far is Ensure, and I'm sick of it. The only yummy flavor is brown sugar, and we always run out of it fast."

Was she talking about the nutritional drinks in those cardboard boxes in the entryway? If she'd been hibernating, it made sense she wouldn't have eaten any solid food in over four months. Her stomach had probably shrunk, and her digestion must have weakened.

"Listen, Natsuki?"

"Yes?"

"Thank you. Both for coming all the way out here and for worrying about me."

I was happy. Having Ms. Iwato tell me she was grateful should have made me delirious with joy.

Something was off, though. I couldn't explain it, but I felt an uneasy, creepy sensation on my back.

"Come up here by me."

"Okay."

"Also, would you stop being so polite?"

"But, Ms. Iwato, you're five years older than—"

"Do you have to say that now?" She smiled, then pressed her lips into a straight line and leaned in close.

Right. I had to do what she said, or else.

"Call me Yuki."

"Okay…"

Maybe it was still hard for her to move, since she'd just woken up. Her speech was a little halting, and her voice sounded young. Even so, she was taking everything at her own speed, the same as always.

I stepped out into the street a little, falling in line beside her. Then, lips trembling, I tried to say her name. "Ms. Y-Yuki."

"Nope. Say it right."

"Yuki."

When I could finally say it without feeling self-conscious, Ms. Iwato—no, Yuki—nodded in satisfaction. Then she said: "All right. From now on, we're friends."

I have no idea what my expression looked like just then. For a moment, I didn't feel a thing; it was like being in the eye of a typhoon. Logically, though, I understood. Before the sadness hit, while my head was still working, I needed to brace myself somehow—

"I'm sorry. The thing is, you're a good person."

I wasn't a good person, nothing like it, and I wasn't the sort who needed to be apologized to. Yuki was getting further away. Even further than she'd been all winter, when I'd felt such a vast distance between us.

"I knew I couldn't go out with you," she said.

I couldn't speak, and I didn't know where to look. My gaze was drawn to the ground.

"I'm the worst, aren't I?" Yuki went on quietly, as if she'd expected my reaction. "I'm going to say one more awful thing." She gazed at me with eyes that were even more serious than before.

I was dazed, but I managed to make sure my ears kept working.

"Until tomorrow, pretend we're dating. Starting the day after that, I swear I'll be a good friend."

"Why would you ask me to do that?"

"Because I'm worried about my mom, I guess."

Yuki tilted her head apologetically.

It was the best smile I'd seen her make all day.

When we got back, the house was filled with the aroma of stewing vegetables. Yuki stuck her cane into the umbrella stand, crouched down at the entryway ledge, took her shoes off, then looked up and held out her hands. "Help me."

"Sure."

I touched Yuki's palms. Her fingers were as cool as freshly changed sheets. When I pulled her up, her knees buckled and she lost her balance, falling against my chest.

"I'm sorry."

"It's fine, seriously." I heard the sound of my heart twisting. "Please don't keep apologizing."

Touko was cooking up a storm in the kitchen. Yuki grabbed an aluminum walking stick from where it hung on the edge of one of the metal shelves, then sat down on the sofa. I took a seat next to her and caught the fresh scent of deodorant mingled with Yuki's sweet fragrance.

"Welcome back," Touko said. Then her eyes shifted to me. "You too, Natsuki," she added. "You didn't fall, did you, Yuki?"

"I'm fine, Mom. Natsuki helped me. He's really reliable." Yuki smiled at me.

"Yeah, actually, I'm the one who almost walked into a telephone pole."

Touko laughed, and it made me feel just a little better.

"What are you making?"

"Cream stew. I just need to add the milk, grated cheese, and mushrooms, and then it's done."

"I'll look forward to it."

I was doing what Yuki said so faithfully that it was funny, and I felt pathetic. If I didn't do it, though, what place did I have in this house?

"The party starts at seven."

"Oh, you mean the ritual?"

I'd spoken casually, borrowing Fuyumi's word. However, Touko tilted her head, repeating "Ritual…?" dubiously. "That's odd. Why would you put it like that?"

"Um, well…" I hadn't been expecting that question, and it startled me a little. My eyes strayed to Fuyumi, who was at the kitchen table, tearing apart pieces of chicken breast.

Touko noticed. She'd been opening a pack of mushrooms with a kitchen knife, but she set it down, went over to Fuyumi, and spoke in a low voice. "Did you tell him that, Fuyumi?"

Sighing openly, Fuyumi went on shredding chicken breast. "Yes. Why?"

"It's just an ordinary party. You'll make him think it's strange."

"It doesn't matter what we call it."

"When did you talk about that? You'll make Natsuki worry for no reason."

Fuyumi's hands stopped moving.

Then she tossed the shredded chicken fragments into a bowl.

"Make him worry…? Up until a week ago, our whole family was acting like we'd hit rock bottom, but we're supposed to flip a switch and be fine the moment Sis wakes up?"

Touko's face went pale as I watched. She grabbed Fuyumi's arm with a hand that was still a little wet. "Come here," she said, taking her into the hall. "You know we promised not to tell Yuki about that."

The argument filtered in to us through the closed door, seeping into the living room like a cold draft. I casually got out my earphones, gazing at the picture of the convenience store that hung on the wall.

When I'd gotten through one stand-up comic video, a rumbling shock raced through the room, and I turned around.

"Why must you blow it out of proportion like that? What happened in her second year of middle school—that only happened once. She's been stable ever since. And look! She's even brought her boyfriend to meet us, just like a normal girl."

Touko's voice pierced my earphones. Fuyumi stomped loudly into the kitchen and grabbed the carton of milk out of the refrigerator.

Yuki was still watching the TV screen as if this was nothing. However, I couldn't keep pretending I wasn't seeing it.

"Like I care!" Fuyumi shouted. The rims of her eyes were bright red. "I don't, I don't, I so don't care! All of this can just go to hell!"

I couldn't just sit by and watch. I stood up and tried to calm Fuyumi down.

Her response was like a string of icicles. "Why are you here, hmm? Why? It's not like there's a damn thing you can do. It's not like you aren't just going to leave my sister."

Fuyumi headed for the stairs, but Touko stood at the door, barring her way.

Yuki leaned forward and put her head between her knees.

"Enough," said Touko. "Don't be rude to our guest. And don't pretend you're beyond reproach."

"Did I say anything of the sort? No, I didn't. What I'm saying is… What I'm saying is, why do you always take Sis's side?!"

"That isn't true. I'm thinking of you, too. But listen, act normal, at least when Yuki's home."

"Nothing about this is normal!!"

Fuyumi swung her arm back. The next instant, something shot over my head and crashed into the window looking onto the yard, dyeing the biggest area I'd ever seen pure white.

"Sis…isn't normal at all, and you know it," Fuyumi gritted out. Then she disappeared upstairs.

Touko just stood there for a little while. Then, suddenly, she looked at me. "I'm sorry about my daughter."

She bowed her head low, as if she was deeply embarrassed, and kept it there for quite a while.

I tried to get up, but Yuki caught my arm and held me back. "Just leave her. Mom's doing this because she needs to."

Bam. A thud echoed from the ceiling, and more followed for some time.

To clean up the milk that had splashed everywhere, we first used rags and a bucket to mop it up, then wiped it down with hot water, then dried it with more rags. When Yuki tried to help, she got sent back to the sofa. Touko and I worked on it together, and even then, it took us more than half an hour.

Finally, when it was close to seven, a fragrant aroma began to fill the room.

Yuki was sprawled across the whole sofa, watching the commentary on a game. I sat in a chair, watching Touko cook.

I'd realized that the more I tried to talk to Yuki like a boyfriend, the less real our relationship became, and so I'd learned to keep a certain distance. Apparently, that actually made us look more like a couple to Touko.

I heard a noise in the entryway, and Touko's face brightened. "Your dad's home."

Those words made my heart jump. I heard the hollow *clop*s of shoes hitting the ground, and then the door opened to reveal a man in a suit. He wasn't all that tall, but he was well built. Behind his spectacles, his face looked intellectual, and half of his close-cropped hair was white.

I stood up and bowed. I'd never bowed so politely before, not even at my university entrance interview.

"You're Natsuki?" The man set his briefcase on a chair and held out a hand to me. "It's good to meet you. I'm Reiji, Yuki and Fuyumi's father."

His mild voice and gentle eyes relieved me a bit, and some of the tension drained out of my back.

"I'm glad you came today," he continued. "This may be the first time we've met, but all of us talked about you a lot, even before Yuki woke up."

That was the first I'd heard of it. Controlling my surprise, I said, "I see."

"They tell me you're a hot-blooded young man who came all the way from Tokyo because he was worried about Yuki."

Immediately, I felt my face turn red. I couldn't just avert my eyes, however; all I could do was let them drift down a little and apologize. "I'm really sorry about that."

"You didn't know anything about all this, and the matter's fundamentally between you two anyway. Still, there were probably a few things you should have done before leaping into action like that."

"...I really can't apologize enough."

I bowed very deeply. Reiji laughed and said, "Maybe I went a bit too far there." He really seemed to be enjoying himself. "As long as Yuki isn't mad, you're welcome here. As far as I'm concerned, that's what's most important."

Reiji glanced at Yuki, and she smiled bashfully, then looked away. It was a perfectly balanced gesture: She wanted to brag about me to her parents, but she was also embarrassed.

Immediately, I lost all sense of what to do with my face.

"Well, I'll go get changed." Reiji disappeared upstairs, and then Yuki stretched, popping her neck. I heard light cracking noises, and her belly button appeared in the gap between her fleece jacket and sweatpants.

Noticing my gaze, Yuki put on a mischievous smile that could have come from a completely different person than the one who'd just made that gesture for her dad. For that one moment, the air around us felt like a summer night.

Once Reiji came back, now wearing a tracksuit, Touko put the resting pot back on the stove and stuck a big heatproof plate in the oven.

We sat at the table. Reiji, who'd been glancing at Yuki and me, asked, "Where's Fuyumi?"

The air grew heavy. Taking my cue from the other two, I kept my mouth shut.

"I think she's in her room," Touko told him, in a slightly subdued voice.

"Studying?"

"…Probably. She might be procrastinating, though."

"I see. It's about time for the ritual, so we'll need to have her come down." Touko tensed up.

Without looking the least bit dubious, Reiji opened the evening paper.

For my mom— It made me remember Yuki's wish. She hadn't said why, but having the guy she'd dumped pretend to be her boyfriend wasn't normal.

To this family, this ritual—or rather, this party—was simply that—

"Um."

My back was trembling. It felt like all I'd been doing lately was shake. The family's eyes turned toward me, and I forced my shrinking throat open. "Is it okay if I go check on her? On…Fuyumi…"

Folding his paper in half, Reiji peered out from behind it, seeming mystified. Touko, who'd put on an oven mitt, gave me a bright smile. It was as if a weight had rolled off her shoulders.

Folding the paper up with a swish, Reiji exchanged a look with Touko. After a short silence, he nodded a few times. "Certainly, if you don't mind," he murmured.

I stood up and started toward the door. Behind me, I heard Yuki's cold voice whisper, "You don't need to bother."

I didn't turn back. Instead, I made a beeline up the stairs, past all those pictures.

8

Like Yuki's door, Fuyumi's room had a log nameplate hanging on it. FUYUMI was written in clumsy English letters, as if it had been scribbled.

"You're in there, right?"

I knocked twice. No answer.

"I'm coming in."

Behind the door, I heard a heavy thump. I grabbed the doorknob and turned it, but the door stopped at forty-five degrees, then started to force itself back toward me.

"Hey— Come on, let me in."

"No...way."

The doorknob and the hinges creaked. Childishly, I shoved back with both hands, but Fuyumi was pushing pretty hard on her end, too.

"Why aren't you coming down? Everybody's waiting for you."

"They...don't...need...me."

"That's not...true."

"How...would you...even...know?!"

I won the arm-wrestling match with the doorknob, and the door swung inward.

The room was totally dark. Fuyumi had fallen on her butt, and I tripped over her left leg and lost my balance. My knee landed between her thighs with a thud, and all of a sudden, our heads were close enough to touch. A stifled scream flew into my ear.

"I'm sorry!" I shouted.

"Shut it!"

"What?!"

"That, *that*!"

Fuyumi was pointing at something. Finally figuring out what she meant, I shut the door, then crouched down. The room was almost pitch-black, and we couldn't even tell where the other was. All I could make out was Fuyumi's breathing.

Even if that had been an unavoidable accident, I still thought she might hit me. Or, considering our positions, would she kick me in the stomach? That sounded more likely.

She didn't attack at all, though.

"We need to get the lights on," I said. Standing up, I groped my way along the wall, but I couldn't seem to find the switch. Then Fuyumi crept up behind me and reached toward a spot that was right below where I was touching. There was a click, and the room filled with light.

"Wow," I said.

Fuyumi looked up at me, her expression mocking. "It's my room, so it wasn't very hard."

Aside from a study desk and a bed, the only thing in Fuyumi's room was a bookshelf, and it was jammed with books. The top shelf held a long row of red entrance exam workbooks from famous public universities; under that, there were some tough-looking med school texts. I didn't see any of the art materials or pictures I'd seen in Yuki's room. Not only that, but there wasn't so much as a hint of any stuffed animals, manga, or game consoles.

There was a CD rack, which was pretty rare these days, a pair of thick headphones hanging on the wall, and a single *K-On!!* poster. That was it.

"Quit ogling everything," she warned me. "And? Why are you here?"

Fuyumi seemed to have recovered completely. She sat down on the bed, looking irritated. There was a chair, and I assumed she'd left it empty for me, but when I tried to sit down, she said coldly, "Don't even think about it."

"You're telling me to stand?"

"No. Sit wherever you like."

I took another look around, but there was nowhere to sit except that chair. I pointed at the floor, thinking that couldn't possibly be what she meant. Fuyumi nodded.

I wasn't happy about it, but I knelt on the cold floor.

"So who put you up to this?" she asked.

"Nobody. I'm here of my own free will."

"Your own free will? Wow, Natsuki, you're a comedian." Fuyumi cackled, looking down at me with a sneer. "You get close to my sister even though you don't really care about her. Then you pretend to be her boyfriend. You know you only wanted to sexually harass a cute girl."

Should I have fallen for her at first sight, then? Would it have been better if I'd known her for ages and ages?

No. There was just one fact here: the fact that I had no comebacks for any of this.

"Then as soon as you find out she's abnormal, you start acting like a hero and want to save her. You think you can. Even though you can't do a thing. That's hilarious."

"Abnormal…"

"Of course she's abnormal!" Fuyumi's agitated voice echoed through the room. "A girl who hibernates? Don't pretty this up with fantasy vocabulary. She's a vegetable all winter long. She can't even eat or pee properly. She's completely dependent on other people to keep her alive. That's the sort of person my sister is. Why, you ask? Because her brain is abnormal. Maybe it's her hypothalamus, or her pituitary, or her frontal lobe."

Fuyumi jabbed an index finger at her temple, spitting out the words.

"No one knows that yet," I countered.

"'Yet'…?" Her gaze ran me through with a mixture of hatred and contempt. "Exactly what are you basing that assumption on? Do you think my family hasn't done anything? We tried every university hospital that does clinical research on persistent vegetative states. Even I helped check into things. No matter what so-called authority looked at her, none of those doctors could put a name to what she's got."

Fuyumi seemed to be speaking the language of some other world.

I'd thought I was the only one in this house who'd been left behind, but that had been an arrogant misunderstanding. Nobody had "left me behind." After all, I hadn't taken a single step forward since the day I met Yuki.

"Do you understand what I'm saying here?" Quietly, Fuyumi rose from the bed, setting her feet down right in front of me. "My sister is never going to get better!"

Then she leaned over and toppled onto me.

"Whoa! What in the—?!"

Fuyumi's thigh wedged itself between my legs. It was the opposite of our situation earlier.

I could feel her breath on my chest, hotter than anything else in the room.

I stared. Lit from behind, her expression of stifled shame seemed to surface like a red star.

I could feel her racing heartbeat across the twenty centimeters that separated us.

"Pick me instead." Her voice was trembling. "If you're going to sexually harass someone, I'll do, won't I?"

Slowly, the shadow she threw over my vision grew bigger. Fuyumi had her eyes squeezed shut, like a child who was about to eat something she didn't like.

I anticipated the sensation of her soft lips, but before anything could happen, I set my hands on her shoulders and pushed her back gently. She didn't seem to have expected me to refuse. She didn't struggle, and she wound up in a half-sitting position, so far beyond embarrassment that she seemed stunned.

"No. That won't work," I said.

"Why not?"

"It's simple."

"No, it's not. I don't get it. I mean, it doesn't really have to be my sister, does it?!"

"It didn't at first."

Startled, Fuyumi looked at me.

I had to say it. All this time, I'd been looking for someone to confess to.

"At first, it was just how things played out. I thought I could make it work, so I went for it. But then Yuki disappeared, and I got all strange. I couldn't take it. I wanted to see her again, even if once was all I got. That solitary winter hurt so much I thought I'd die."

Yuki Iwato wasn't "my" anything. She hadn't walked into my life; I'd known for ages that I was just an extra passing through hers. However, the cold of that winter had frozen me to the core, and now I couldn't ignore it.

"I'm just… Without Yuki, everything's so much harder. A little while ago, she told me we should just be friends. In other words, we'll act like we're dating until tomorrow, and then that'll be it, forever. I know I don't have a chance anymore. But I'm still clinging to hope because I just can't give up."

"……"

Fuyumi's expression passed through anger and came out the other side. Her eyes looked damp and fragile. "That doesn't make it okay to be a stalker…"

"Yeah, everybody tells me that."

Fuyumi sank back, slumping onto her behind. I pushed myself up and turned to face her.

"I'm sorry," I said.

"No, I'm sorry…" Fuyumi gave a shallow apologetic nod.

Tick, tick, tick. The sound of the clock echoed through the room. It was already half past eight.

"Mom won't be happy until her daughter is normal." Fuyumi was the one to break the silence. "She's always looking forward to the day my sister finds a normal partner. By *normal*, I mean a relationship where they shop together on the weekends, and go for walks holding hands, and have their meals together… A regular person. Not somebody who'll camp in my sister's room all winter and swear he'll take care of her for the rest of their lives."

Fuyumi's eyes were dark and shadowed, as if there had actually been someone like that once.

"It would have been so much better if my sister were a guy, or if you'd been a girl."

Yuki was fairly good-looking, and that attracted men. That should have meant having a "normal relationship" was an achievable goal, but as soon as they found out about her handicap, they ran.

"We can't change our bodies or our gender identities. There's no helping that. Frankly, if we were the same sex, I might not have been drawn to Ms. Iwato. I might not even have met her. I think having the male me meet the female Ms. Iwato was the only option there was."

"At least you're honest." Fuyumi looked up at me through her lashes.

"I hate lies," I told her, and her eyes softened slightly at the corners. "For now, come downstairs."

"Why? I won't be any use down there."

"Even if that's true, come anyway."

Fuyumi refused weakly, but I took her arm and stood up. When I pulled her to her knees, she grudgingly rose.

"Wait a second."

Just before we reached the top of the stairs, Fuyumi stopped. She fiddled with her smartphone, then held it out in front of me.

It showed a complicated black-and-white pattern. A QR code.

"My contact info," she said, then looked down and added, "Just in case."

"It's all right for me to contact you?"

"Um… No. I initiate all contact."

This conversation wasn't going anywhere. I used my smartphone to read the code.

Her icon showed a foreign guy with slanting, angry-looking eyes and a mask that covered the lower half of his face. Although it was partly cut off, I spotted the red star on his shoulder. "*Captain America*'s good, isn't it?"

Still scowling, Fuyumi shot me a glance. "So you know it. That's impressive."

"Your icon's the Winter Soldier, right?"

As I thought back over the movie I'd seen some time ago, I grew increasingly certain. When I told Fuyumi he was a lot like her, she looked away and fell silent.

The Winter Soldier was a physically enhanced, hard-boiled assassin who lived in a frozen land. However, deep down, he was always thinking of his good friend Captain America.

When we got downstairs, we couldn't see the table for the food.

There were two wooden bowls, one mounded high with turnip salad, the other with potato salad. A basket was filled with croissants and baguettes, and a large plate held an array of meat pies and roast beef.

"I thought you'd be coming down soon," Reiji said, glancing from his watch to us and back.

"I'm going to bring the pot over. Would you clear a space in the center?" Touko asked. Fuyumi grabbed a potholder and shifted the plates around, making a landing site for the pot in the very middle.

"Was it a productive conversation?" asked her father.

"That's a good question," I said. "I think Fuyumi and I get along just a little better now, though."

"Is that right? I'm glad to hear it."

The pot went down, and the lid came off, revealing a clear soup with potatoes and carrots in it. Reiji peeked in, then cocked his head. "Hmm? Weren't we having stew?"

Touko exchanged a look with Fuyumi, and they both forced smiles.

"I thought pot-au-feu would go better with everything else."

"Huh? But this has chicken in it."

"That's the sort of pot-au-feu we're having today," Touko said firmly, and Reiji nodded reluctantly.

When Touko and Fuyumi took their seats, all eyes converged on the one empty chair. In the living room, Yuki slowly got up from the sofa.

"Yuki, let's get started."

She came over, walking a little unsteadily, and pulled out the chair. The day's guest of honor: Sleeping Beauty, now awake.

"All right. Let's begin the Good Morning Ritual."

At Reiji's signal, the others applauded, and I joined in a little late.

Outside the window, the world was pitch-black.

"I'll go first," said Reiji. "Thank you for waking up. They said we had the biggest cold wave on record this year, so it's still chilly, but it's only going to get warmer and warmer. I hope a warm future is waiting for you as well, Yuki."

When Reiji finished his speech, he added, "Good morning."

"Me next." Touko raised her hand, so Reiji passed her the baton. "All else aside, I'm relieved that winter is over. Last year was a bit chaotic, so I'd like to move things along more smoothly this year. I'm glad you've grown up normally, Yuki. Good morning."

Touko gave her a motherly smile, and the baton passed to Fuyumi. I sensed a weak resistance from her, but she quickly rallied. "Good morning, Sis. Now that you're awake, I'd like to talk to you more. My college entrance exams are this year, so I want your advice on all sorts of things. I'm going to cause you just as much trouble over the summer as you caused me during the winter, so don't get mad about it."

For once, Fuyumi's smile seemed genuine.

So this was the ritual... *What a curious family*, I thought, watching with a certain sense of distance. Then, without warning, I got pulled in.

"And finally, Natsuki."

"Huh?! Me too?!" Startled, I looked at Reiji. He nodded casually, and there was a trace of heartless mischief in it. "But what should I say...?"

"Just tell Yuki what you're thinking. 'I like you' is fine. So is 'I love you deeply,' or 'I want to marry you'..."

"Dad?!" Fuyumi shrieked, her forehead wrinkling incredulously. Reiji didn't add anything else.

"Um..."

My chest constricted.

This was a love that would die on the vine, just a sham. I'd never been Yuki's boyfriend, not once. My feelings for her might get in the way and keep us from even being friends.

Still, no matter what, I couldn't ruin this ritual.

Act. For Yuki. For this family.

"Ms. Yuki. Good morning."

"Didn't I tell you?" Yuki interrupted. "I'm not your upperclassman anymore."

"Huh?"

"I got held back. We're in the same year now."

"I...I see."

This was probably depressing for Yuki, but it made me a little happy. I hated myself for that.

Slowly, I looked up.

"I'm in love with you."

The atmosphere in the room froze.

Even I didn't understand why I'd said it.

This was a mistake. We were supposed to be dating already. That meant this wasn't the—

"I think I was probably drawn to you from the moment we met at the new students' event. I was scared to admit it, though. After all, I'm not a good match for you. The people around me don't think so, and neither do I."

I swallowed and caught my breath. Then I took another, much deeper breath. "And so I kept my guard up, bracing for the day when you'd dump me."

Even now, the sight of Yuki Iwato standing there against the night was branded onto my brain. Everything about the din of chaotic Shinjuku, Tokyo, had been at her service. All this time, I'd actively avoided calling that sensation *love*.

"But when you actually did it, I felt wretched and sad, and in the end, I had to accept my feelings for what they were. Oh... That's, um, extremely ironic, isn't it?"

Slowly, Yuki looked up. I kept my eyes fixed right on hers. "And so, um... Th-that's it. Yeah."

Silence. No one spoke. Fuyumi looked conflicted. At that point, the thin whistle of the electric kettle cut in, announcing that the water was boiling.

Touko got up hastily. Reiji was gazing at me with a smile. Yuki was staring, her mouth hanging open slightly as if I'd startled her.

"Will that...do?" I asked.

"Great, that's good!" Reiji announced, giving one sharp clap.

When I glanced back at her, Yuki looked down uncomfortably. However, just before she did, I thought I saw the corners of her lips rise ever so slightly in a satisfied smile.

9

Most of the grand dinner disappeared into Yuki's stomach with astonishing rapidity. Her body's functions had been on pause for four months, but they'd hit their stride again over the past week. Her organs seemed to have remembered their proper roles, and they were all demanding nutrition at once.

After dinner, on Touko's instructions, we all started to take the dishes into the kitchen. Yuki moved slowly; at first, Fuyumi helped her, but then Reiji called to them. "You rest over here, Yuki."

Touko, who was running a sponge over a platter, glanced at Reiji.

"You know the drill, Fuyumi," he said.

Fuyumi nodded once, then took over her sister's job as well, briskly carrying dishes.

Having lost her place in the dining room, Yuki went into the living room and lay down on the sofa, as Reiji had instructed. She'd stuffed herself at dinner, and her belly bulged slightly; when she lay on her back, she reminded me of a seal.

Once I'd finished wiping down the table with a wet cloth, I started to head for the sofa, too, but Reiji beckoned to me from the veranda. He'd stepped out for a smoke.

I pulled on my down jacket, went out onto the veranda with a cup of hot tea, and sat down on the edge. I'd thought Reiji was having a cigarette, but I didn't smell smoke. The glow I'd seen wasn't a flame but a flame-colored LED.

"I'm a little surprised," I said. "Today felt like a party; I didn't expect to be invited to something like that."

"Did we startle you?" A puff of dense water vapor left his lips, which were beginning to show their age.

"Yes. To be honest, I still don't really understand why you invited me."

"Long ago, Yuki hurt somebody. It was our fault, too, though. There was a young person who wanted to be someone's supporter more than anything in the world, and we failed to understand those innocent feelings. So this time, I wanted to have a proper talk about it."

My brow had furrowed without my realizing, and I forced out the wrinkles, temporarily swallowing any questions I had about that word, *hurt*.

"In the end, maybe it all worked out for the best," he said. "Things might yet improve, after all."

"I, um… I see." I hugged myself to ward off the cold.

"This is how our family has adapted." The white smoke of his e-cig escaped into the deep, dark sky. "It wasn't always like this. Before the year Yuki turned five, when her symptoms manifested, we were more of a 'normal' family. When she started elementary school, though, the situation changed a bit. She stopped going to school entirely in winter, so people thought something must be wrong. The first person to check into it was her homeroom teacher.

Yuki was called to the guidance office and asked why she didn't come to school during the winter. She was honest and told them she slept. The next day, the teacher called our house. I answered. At the time, though, even I didn't really have a handle on the ill effects of Yuki's symptoms."

Reiji broke off, looking pained. He set a hand on his forehead, then pushed it upward, raking his fingers through his hair.

"The teacher suspected us of neglect."

He pulled out his smartphone and showed me a photo. Fluttering cherry blossoms, brickwork, and a sign that said CONGRATULATIONS, NEW STUDENTS. It was a photo from Yuki's school entrance ceremony, showing only Yuki and Reiji.

"Where's Touko…?"

"Touko was very busy at the time. She's a nurse, so she'd been busy to begin with, and then she was made assistant head nurse at a young age. I worked for a midsize company that ran on the seniority system, so it was often easier for me to go to school functions. Looking back, that may have been one of the reasons they suspected us."

"That's…awful."

"Touko and I thought about how to explain this to the teacher. We talked about it for three full days. I felt we should tell the truth. However, Touko said the woman would never believe us, so we should just try to gloss things over somehow until Yuki graduated."

"Wasn't there a medical certificate or something you could use as proof?"

"The thing is, as far as the numbers are concerned, Yuki's perfectly normal." Reiji sounded as if he'd been waiting for this question. "It's only that her 'normal' and our 'normal' don't match up. That means what she has isn't acknowledged as an illness, and there was no medical certificate for us to submit. Even so, after talking it over, we decided to trust her homeroom teacher, so we met with her and told her the truth."

Reiji exhaled a puff of smoke, and the orange light of his e-cig began to blink.

"I have a vivid memory of the look of utter contempt that teacher gave us. She seemed to pity Yuki for being born to parents who didn't deserve a child. However, the one who was really hurt wasn't Touko or me. It was Yuki. At the time, the fact that she was different from everyone else frightened her terribly. She developed anxiety even in the summer, when she was healthy. We learned we couldn't spread the truth around casually, and that's been our family policy ever since."

That was probably what had caused Touko's near obsession with normalcy.

It might not have been a real solution, but they'd tried to keep things normal as a sort of therapy. If they couldn't cure her completely, they'd at least wanted to do something to keep Yuki's heart from breaking.

They'd used the framework of "being normal" to protect her.

A little eddy of wind blew, whipping up the dry leaves that blanketed the garden. I wanted to listen to Reiji for a while longer, so I forced myself not to shiver.

Reiji put his e-cig into its charging case, then spoke in a low voice. "I'm just going to be blunt and ask you: What do you think of Yuki?"

The words were casual, but the intention in them was deep. It wasn't a question I could answer carelessly, and I struggled to find the words.

"My wife says Yuki is normal. However, although I think we should interact with her normally, I believe we need to acknowledge that some things are not normal. What about you?"

"I…"

Another gust of wind blew through, strong enough to push all the dead leaves in the garden ahead of it.

What I needed to say had been clear all along.

"I don't know yet. Whenever I have to make a choice, though, I want to talk it over with Yuki first. I'd like us to make all our decisions together, as a team."

Reiji looked me straight in the eye. "Thank you for being honest with me. I'm really glad you came."

They put me up in the storage room on the second floor.

The room held an easel, the IV stand and heart monitor that had finished their work for the winter, and a set of drums Reiji had once played. It was pretty cramped, but much better than having to sleep in Yuki's room would have been.

By the time I got my futon laid out, it was well past midnight. I rummaged through my backpack, looking for my toothbrush, then realized I'd forgotten to bring one.

I pulled on my down jacket and went downstairs, trying to walk as quietly as possible. Most of the lights were off, but I could see a faint glow from the living room.

Touko was all alone at the table, gazing at the pale light of the TV. Noticing me, she asked what was wrong.

"It looks like I forgot my toothbrush."

"A toothbrush… I'm not sure we have an extra. If we did, it would be under the washroom sink, but…"

"No, I'll go buy one. Is there a convenience store nearby?"

"Yes. Turn left as soon as you leave the house, then go straight for a while. At the second traffic light, you'll see a pharmacy with that cute little frog mascot character outside it. Turn right, and it'll be on your right."

"Left, right, right. Is that it?"

"Yes, left, right, right." There was fatigue in Touko's smile.

"Are you feeling okay?"

"Yes, I'm fine. It's nothing. I'm just a little tired."

"Today was an awful lot of work, wasn't it?"

"Yes, it was quite draining. Still, my daughter is precious to me, and it was her party. This is nothing…"

Touko's eyes were on a picture sitting on the aluminum shelf. It showed a rather odd convenience store that seemed to rise out of the darkness, drawn in colored pencil.

It was a curious picture. The store was taller than it was wide, like a lighthouse, and the magazine racks, the registers, and the parking lot sign were all drawn in detail. Yuki's pictures tended to be dark, but in the light of the TV, this one seemed to emerge from the shadows. The fact that it was surrounded by blackness made the light of the convenience store really stand out.

"It's a good picture, isn't it?" Touko had noticed what I was looking at. "She likes places like those."

"Convenience stores?"

"She says that because they never sleep, they light the way for solitary

people out on the road at night, like shelters. She's a strange girl, isn't she?"
Touko chuckled.

As it stood there in the darkness, the convenience store in the drawing really did look like a lighthouse illuminating the road.

"She draws when she's lonely. That means there are as many pictures as there are times she's felt alone. Even so, I like this one."

I did, too.

I didn't know much about art: composition, concept, shading, use of color. But I could sense something behind this picture. How Yuki had looked as she drew it. An urgent message, as if she were rising toward the water's surface, desperate to breathe. The certainty that she had to draw.

"So you see, I have to do my best, too."

Touko was beginning to nod off; her head sank between her folded arms. The living room heater had been turned off ages ago, and the accumulated heat in the room was fading fast. I couldn't shake her to wake her up, so I took a jacket that was hanging on another chair and draped it over her rounded back. Before turning off the TV, I took another look at the picture.

Yuki is amazing.

To my great embarrassment, that incredibly vague word was all I could come up with.

No, I was looking at this the wrong way. My reaction had been normal.

There was no way anyone could understand the depth of someone else's creation right from the start.

I see... So those weren't lies?

In other words, when Atsushi spoke proudly of my dream of being an author and Tomomi supported my writing, none of that had been false. What had made it a lie was my own fear of taking on the challenge, and my weak, embarrassed heart.

I'd told people I was going to write novels, and yet I'd just kept lowering the bar to protect myself.

"I'm so pathetic." I said the words aloud, but quietly, as I tiptoed out the front door.

Left, right, right. I was chanting the words in my head as I walked when, just past the first traffic light, I was struck by an intense feeling of déjà vu. Up ahead, I saw the bewitching back of a woman who seemed about to melt into the darkness.

It was the same back I'd followed out of that smoky pub. I'd taken my first step away from the me who couldn't even breathe without comparing myself with others. Without her, I wouldn't have ever been able to face my own work. I wouldn't have even made it to the starting line.

It was all her.

Thanks to her, right now, I was—

"Ms. Iwato."

My voice echoed across the midnight street. The woman turned, glossy black hair fluttering. "Natsuki…"

Yuki was fully dressed, with a coat and muffler. Her expression clouded as if she felt guilty.

"You went out."

At this hour, most people were fast asleep. A frightening amount of silence hung along the sides of the damp street. I jogged up to Yuki and asked if she'd walk with me for a while.

She nodded. Her face was buried in her muffler.

I walked as slowly as I could along a green-painted road marked with signs giving cyclists the right of way.

"So you really were planning to disappear, weren't you, Ms. Iwato?" I realized I'd unconsciously reverted to addressing her politely. Still, for now, it felt like the most natural option. "Why didn't you tell me?"

"……"

Yuki shoved both hands into her pockets, then pushed her arms down, stretching the bottoms. Her felt coat creaked a bit, pulling taut. "You know why," she said recklessly.

Yeah, I knew. She'd had no way to tell me. How was she supposed to explain it? If she'd said she had a unique constitution that made her sleep all winter, I'd almost certainly have refused to listen. I could see myself doing exactly that.

"Even so, I wish you'd tried." I heard one of us grit their teeth. "Or…could you really not trust me?"

"I never said that."

Two gleaming eyes glared up at us from the gutter. A cat with dark fur bounded into the road, running right past me. Many people had passed Yuki by like that: not getting in too deep, taking all they could get before they actually started to care.

"Then why?"

"I told you: I wanted you to be happy."

"I never asked for that."

Our voices echoed through the quiet night, and the cat dashed off, vanishing into the darkness of an alley.

"So what? You wanted me to be happy, so you ignored me? What is this, some old movie? That sort of mediocre self-sacrifice makes me sick. Seriously. It's boring. 'I did this for you'? Quit running away, all right?"

What was I saying? It wasn't like I could talk.

Even so, I was going to say it. This was probably my last chance.

With a rustle of feathers, several crows took flight one after another, and the power line they'd left swung with a taut hum. Yuki crossed the road, putting it between us, then glared at me, her lips set in an irritated line.

"Oh yeah? What was I supposed to do? Tell you everything and say, 'On that understanding, I look forward to our continued relationship'? What, you're that reliable? Are you supposed to be my hero or something? Look, I can't afford to trust somebody and get betrayed all over again!"

"Then why did you tell Fuyumi to let me in?"

She clammed up. Yuki's expression floated in the darkness, silhouetted against the glow of a cigarette vending machine outside a beauty salon. In the light of the streetlamp, her eyes were damp and glittering.

"Why did you let me near you while you were asleep?"

"……"

I didn't know even a tenth of the burdens Yuki was carrying. What's more, I'd never know all of them, no matter how hard I tried.

Even so.

"Your heartbeat was so slow, Ms. Iwato. Once I heard it, it was too late to turn back."

"......"

I held out my hand. There were two and a half steps between us. If Yuki didn't take it, my arm would just hang there in midair, looking stupid.

Yuki swallowed hard, working the muscles in her throat. Her lips opened slightly, white breath escaping from between them.

"It might hurt, you know," she murmured. It almost sounded like a cough.

"That's fine."

"I don't want to end up alone."

"I'll stay with you."

"It might be really rough."

"Even so, I'll stay."

If everything before had been a lie, we could simply start from here. For now, at least, I could still say such things, though I knew that wouldn't last for long.

"Ms. Iwato, let's—"

I relaxed my throat, opening it up, and looked her in the eye. One syllable at a time, I told her exactly what I wanted to say.

The next thing I knew, we were in front of the convenience store. Just like the one in Yuki's picture, it cast a warm glow, like a lighthouse guiding the lost.

I held Yuki's hand tightly so that I wouldn't lose out to that light. Desperately, I tethered her to me so that we wouldn't get separated on gloomy, late-night roads ever again.

There's a small lantern in my hand. Its flickering flame
is a whispering voice.
I have no map, no shelter. My shadow is the only thing
that walks beside me.
I've been left behind in this stretch of time, all alone.
I've been flung into an ocean of darkness, and I breathe as
if I'm drowning, crawl as if I'm swimming. To keep the light of
my lantern from going out, I count the hours until I'm free of the dark.
Even though I know that only time will bring an end to this,
my restless body carries me off somewhere.
I'm waiting to wake up.
In order to wake up, I cross a distant river of silence.

1

When I woke up, the curtains were open and early summer sunlight was streaming down over me, from my forehead to my chest. The sun wasn't that high yet, but I could feel myself starting to sweat under my clothes. On reflex, I covered my face with both hands.

Something got up onto the bed; I felt myself sink a little under its weight. As I rubbed my sleep-dazed eyes, the summer coverlet I'd been clinging to was stripped away.

Squeezing my lids shut, I curled up into a ball, fighting all of it. I groped around by my pillow for my earplugs and put them back in. As if in protest, the bed rocked violently. Left with no choice, I opened my eyes to see Yuki Iwato in shorts and a hoodie, bouncing on the bed.

"Aha!"

Once my eyes were fully open, Yuki stopped jumping and dived on top of me. The impact crashed through my guts, and I felt my stomach twist. "Oh, Yuki…"

When I said her name, dazed, she nuzzled me with her head like a cat. "You finally woke up," she purred, almost literally.

Through the space between her shoulder and neck, I could see the blue tarp hanging from the second-floor loft. I thought I remembered her holing up in the loft studio the previous evening, saying she was going to paint.

My mind still felt vague and hazy. I wrapped my arms around her slim body and pulled her to me. Then I realized I wasn't hearing my alarm, and anxiety fizzed up my spine. "What time is it?"

Yuki didn't answer. I craned my neck to see the analog clock hanging behind her. "Uh... Seven...thirty?" I grimaced. "It's still way early."

Yuki looked at me mischievously. "I was bored," she said.

"Our first classes aren't until second period today... That's ten thirty."

I'd been up working on my novel until three that morning, so I'd set my alarm for nine thirty. This was a lot earlier than I'd planned to wake up.

"You were sleeping in too long, though."

"You wake up too early, Yuki."

Somewhere in the distance, I heard a rapid-fire electronic beep. Yuki pushed herself up and went off toward the kitchenette. Last year, I'd bought a cheap kitchen timer at the hundred-yen shop; I'd assumed it wouldn't last, but it was still in active service. Yuki shut off the timer, took a pot over to the sink, and poured steaming hot water down the drain.

"What are you making?" I asked.

"Soft-boiled eggs."

"For breakfast?"

"Sure, if you want. I just thought we'd use them if we had them."

While I was in the washroom, I heard the sizzle of something cooking. When I got back out, Yuki was just bringing over our breakfast plates.

"You always wake me up, and you always make breakfast, too. I feel bad."

"Don't. I'm doing it because I want to."

Yuki had gotten almost everything ready, so I made a token contribution by taking out two glasses and filling them with milk.

"Thanks for the food," we said in unison.

Crispy bacon, toast with soft-boiled eggs on top, and a bowl of salad dressed with olive oil and salt.

Yuki took a swallow of milk, then picked up the remote control and turned on the news. The morning show was monopolized by talk of the earthquake swarm we'd been having. A stammering seismologist was saying that the Japanese archipelago would sink to the bottom of the ocean within the next century.

"There really have been a lot of earthquakes lately, huh," Yuki said.

"Have there?"

"You think the world might end on us?"

I munched on my toast. I ate the white of the egg first, carefully, making sure I didn't break the yolk.

"Well, if it happens, it happens."

At the news desk, a staff member from the Meteorological Agency mentioned that there had been a magnitude 5 earthquake in Setagaya Ward last night.

"I didn't even notice. Were the dishes and everything okay?"

"They were fine," Yuki said. She was about to take a bite of bacon when she paused and hastily added, "I checked this morning."

I set down my toast, which had only the yolk on it now, and started in on the salad. "Now that I think of it, your hair's grown out."

I could see Yuki's bob-length hair out of the corner of my eye. A little before her Good Night Ritual half a year ago, on the day before we went back to her parents' house, we had visited a little-known hair salon in Jinbocho to get it cut. That was when I'd heard, for the first time, that Yuki chopped her hair short so she wouldn't develop bedsores while she hibernated.

"Yeah."

Yuki nodded, stroking her hair with her fingertips. The glossy strands were such a deep black that they never went translucent, even in direct sunlight. As her fingers pushed the hair back, it slipped behind her ear and fell to her shoulder.

"Do you like longer hair?" she asked.

"No, that's not what I meant. I like all hairstyles."

"That's cheating."

Her hand was playing around with my knee, and when I caught it and squeezed it, her face blossomed into a smile.

In May, we'd moved into a rather spacious studio apartment with a loft and brought in some of Yuki's things. Her boardinghouse contract renewed in March of next year, and until then, she was leading a double life. We used the loft as her studio and for storage, while the first floor held a bookshelf, a table, and a semidouble bed.

I opened my mouth wide, trying to eat the egg yolk in one bite, but ended up dripping some of it onto my plate. Mopping it up with a bit of bread, I turned to Yuki. "How's the picture coming?"

We'd tacked a blue tarp to one wall of the loft, and leaning against it were a folding easel and a canvas about 117 by 91 cm. The canvas was covered by an enormous, gusseted, sack-shaped cover, which she kept from sticking to the still-wet paint by nailing small pieces of scrap lumber to each of the canvas's corners. Yuki had already repeated the year three times, so she had to be pretty close to getting expelled, but she looked away, acting like she didn't know what I was talking about.

"Yuki, you're submitting that to the competition, right? Shouldn't you be putting more work into it? All you did yesterday was play around."

"Oh, so you're worried about me?" With a mischievous smile, Yuki bit into a piece of bread. "The thing is, while I still can, I want to spend as much time as possible with you, Natsuki. So it's fine."

That was nice of her to say, but I didn't think it meant she needed to slack off on her project.

Instead of pressing the issue, I started cleaning up our dishes. I set the salad bowl on top of the stacked plates, then headed for the kitchenette. Out of nowhere, a ferocious stabbing sensation ran through the sole of my foot. The unimaginable pain almost sent me to my knees.

"What's the matter?!"

Yuki ran to me. I'd managed to set the plates down on the floor, but the bowl had slipped off and was bouncing away, scattering leftover dressing as it went.

When I looked at the bottom of my foot, there was a Lego brick embedded in it. It was almost the same cream color as the floor, and it had blended right in.

I picked the Lego off my foot, then got up unsteadily and set the brick by the *Millennium Falcon* model that was on display in the entryway. The box and the instructions were both long gone, and at this point, I had no idea where the piece went.

"Sorry," I said. "There was a spaceship part on the floor."

"Are you okay?"

"Yeah. I'm fine. I just got olive oil all over the entryway."

"I'll grab some rags."

"No, I'll do it."

Still wincing from the sharp, lingering pain, I was checking through the cupboard under the bathroom sink when a soft weight pressed against my back. Two arms descended to wrap around my neck like a muffler.

"C'mon, pay attention to me," Yuki whispered sweetly.

I kissed her soft cheek. "After I wipe down the entryway."

"That's fine. It can wait."

She clung to me, and she wouldn't let go. Carrying her piggyback, I relocated to the kitchenette, then grabbed some rags from under the sink there. "I need to do it now."

I gently caught Yuki's arms and pulled them away from me, then wiped the entryway down with water and went to start on the dishes.

2

Six months earlier...

As I waited at the south gate of Shinjuku Station, searching for the person I was supposed to meet, my smartphone rang. It was Atsushi, inviting me to a New Year's Eve party. I decided to hold off on replying and resumed my search.

My smartphone rang again. This time, it was from the man I was looking for.

When I glanced over at the pillar he'd indicated in his text, I saw a man a little shorter than my height holding a bag in one hand and waving at me with the other. His solid build was encased in a trench coat, and he had a black muffler wrapped around his neck.

"Long time no see," said Reiji Iwato in his usual husky voice.

"A long time indeed, sir." Heedless of the people around me, I bowed deeply and stayed that way for longer than usual.

"Ah-ha-ha. Don't be so formal." Reiji's eyes went to his watch. It was still only seven. Pretty soon, the crowd would swell, and most of the people would head for the neon lights of the major streets.

I almost never went to pubs, so I chose the one place I knew was good. The bright-red letters spelling out TANGIER rose up in front of us, bringing with them memories of another, previous night.

"Good atmosphere," Reiji said after he'd stepped through the shop curtain. I followed him, and the scent of countless spices promptly tickled my nostrils.

"Yuki actually took me here, way back when."

"Oh, yes, of course. I had a feeling. When she chooses restaurants, for some reason she's never wrong." Reiji took another, more impressed look around.

We took our seats. We were sitting at the bar this time.

"Well, what'll it be?" he asked. "Beer?"

"I'm sorry; I'm not great with beer. I'll have a grape sour."

Reiji smiled, then ordered our drinks, along with those numbing cucumbers and some salted spicy fish guts.

For a little while, we talked about the winter weather, school, and the novel I was writing.

"I see," he said. "So that picture of Yuki's…"

"Yes. Compared with that, I thought I was embarrassing—I mean, I thought having been embarrassed about creating something was the most embarrassing thing of all. That's why I submitted it to a contest. I'm not confident at all, but…"

Our drinks and snacks appeared, and Reiji and I quietly clinked our glasses.

"To a young man who's taken a step forward." Reiji's toast made me self-conscious, and I forced a smile.

"By the way, how is Yuki?"

I took a bite of the numbing cucumbers. I'd lived a highly spiced life with Yuki over the past year, and these no longer hit me the way they had the first time. Apparently, my tongue had gotten used to pain.

"She's doing well. All thanks to Touko and Fuyumi," Reiji told me, downing about half his beer in one go.

The morning and evening IV drip and sterilization. Changing the collection pouches for urine and feces. Washing her body. Exercising her limbs so that her muscles wouldn't atrophy. All these things needed to be done every day so that Yuki stayed healthy.

That burden lasted more than a hundred days.

They called a nurse and a physical therapist to check on her once a week, but Yuki's coma was expected to last only four months in total. Just once, between her second and third year of middle school, she'd stayed asleep for a year and five months. After the fact, the family had petitioned and were awarded a first-class disability pension, but it had been applied to only that period.

As far as contemporary medicine was concerned, Yuki was the picture of health.

Insurance wouldn't cover any of it. In other words, she'd fallen through the cracks of the welfare system. Japanese medicine was said to be among the world's finest, but there were countless people even it couldn't save. That was why her mother and sister had been forced to become Winter Soldiers.

"But doesn't Fuyumi have her college entrance exams this year?"

"She gives more thought to Yuki than anyone else. Her mother and I told her we'd divide the work between ourselves, but she wouldn't listen. She's a tough, responsible girl. Granted, that's a problem sometimes."

Reiji used the serving chopsticks to dish himself up some salted fish guts, then brought a big clump to his lips.

Oh, crud. Too late, I realized I should have warned him.

"Wow! That's really something…," Reiji muttered, then washed it down with beer. In no time at all, his mug was empty.

"Yuki really does like spicy foods, doesn't she?" I said.

"Yes, she does. Poor kid."

I took a swallow of my sour, then glanced at Reiji. "What do you mean?"

"I'm sure you know this already, but before she falls asleep, her heart rate drops. That slows down her metabolism, and her senses grow dull. Of course most of that goes back to normal when she wakes up in February, but there's one thing that never did."

At first, I had no idea what he was talking about. However, after I gave it a little thought, it was pretty clear what hadn't come back.

Reiji took advantage of a pause in the conversation to order a highball.

"The winter she was thirteen, her sense of taste went out of whack, and it's never corrected itself."

"……"

"Touko cooked lots of food that spring, too. Beef stew and squid-ink spaghetti. Octopus carpaccio. A mountain of mashed potatoes. Garlic French bread. Unusually, though, Yuki didn't want to eat any of them. We thought she'd done too much rehab during the day and wasn't hungry, but that wasn't it. She said none of them tasted right."

He accepted his highball from the server and promptly drank about a third of it.

"Even when she had chicken ramen or her favorite—boiled meat dumplings—she said they all tasted strange. They should have been delicious, and yet they tasted bad. Water seemed sweet to her. That made it gross. She ate less and less, and we rushed her to an ENT doctor. The doctor told us it was idiopathic and we'd just have to keep an eye on it; however, an acquaintance who was a registered dietitian told us that we should try making the flavors as extreme as possible until she could eat again, so we tried it. Too much salt would have been dangerous for her health, so we tried adding lots of pepper first. Then we tried vinegar. Neither of those worked, so finally we ended up with cayenne pepper."

I hesitated with my mug halfway to my mouth, then set it back down on the table. I turned to look behind me. It had been there—right over there, on that padded bench—that she'd told me as much. *It's just how I'm wired*, she'd said.

"Is that what it was?" I murmured, as if breaking the words down for myself. "But why didn't she... I mean, why didn't Yuki say anything about it?"

"Probably because as far as she's concerned, it's nothing special."

Nothing special? That couldn't be right.

Those words couldn't possibly cover it.

"Maybe she didn't think telling me about it would do any good?"

"It's closer to the reason you don't tell people why you have two arms."

Was that what "living normally" meant?

No, it was the opposite: If she'd been obsessed with normalcy, she would have told me why her sense of taste was abnormal. She'd accepted the way she was now as "normal." In other words, she was acknowledging that she was abnormal.

"I should have asked her properly."

"I'm not so sure. Unfortunately, I doubt she would have told you if you had. She doesn't want people worrying about her."

How could I not worry? What was the point of us being together, then? I wanted to understand her better. Whatever problems we faced, I wanted us to overcome them together.

But then, how was I supposed to get through this winter without her? How should I live in order to keep myself on track?

"I really have to get my act together, don't I?"

"You've changed, Natsuki," said Reiji, before adding, "You mustn't feel too responsible for this."

The first round of our meal arrived, filling the table. Most of the items were grilled. Divvying up the food little by little, Reiji and I started to eat.

"Last month, we spoke with an SI consultant. We've done that several times before, but..."

"You mean a social insurance consultant?"

Reiji took a bite of pork cutlet, then reached for the pickles with his chopsticks. He nodded, crunching away on them. "Yuki's been examined by all sorts of doctors, but none of them have been able to pin her symptoms to a specific illness. We thought it had to be an issue with her brain, so we'd limited ourselves to brain surgeons and neurologists."

I'd heard that from Fuyumi as well.

"Last January, we had her hospitalized for testing for two weeks at a place called Fujiwara Internal Medicine."

"Two weeks? That's quite a long time."

"Yes. They acknowledged that she was clearly in a coma and advised us that if the cause wasn't down to brain activity, we should suspect a mental disorder. Fujiwara Internal Medicine is a psychiatric clinic, you see."

"And how did that go?"

"We don't know yet. However, we decided to try applying for a disability certificate."

I was squeezing my chopsticks too hard; they started to creak. My eyebrows pulled together so tightly that they felt like a big, hard lump right above my nose.

"Touko approved."

When I heard that, I got a very odd feeling. Was I happy, or did I feel as if there was no going back from this? No matter what category anyone put Yuki in, I wanted to be with her. Would she be able to accept that, though?

No, that wasn't right. The issue wasn't all mine or all hers. It was whether Yuki and I would be able to deal with this as a couple.

"It's taken twenty-five years, but we've finally gotten this far." Reiji's expression was somewhere between pride and embarrassment.

Knowing it was presumptuous of me, I leaned forward a little. "Tell me one thing."

"What?"

"If Yuki agrees to this and gets that certificate…will her life change?"

Closing his eyes, Reiji shook his head slowly. "There's no life that doesn't change."

I'd hoped talking with Reiji would help me feel a little less starved of you, but of course it didn't. I was alone. Still, this loneliness existed for the sake of our springtime reunion.

I woke at an awkward time, around dawn, and shivered at the coldness of the room. At the same time, the empty feeling of being left behind in winter swept over me… And so I went into the kitchen, took a cardboard box out of the upper cupboard, and had one of the two dozen Mouko Tanmen spicy instant ramen cups I'd stockpiled.

I wrapped myself up from head to toe in a cheap black terrycloth blanket and slurped my noodles in the glow of the table lamp. I felt as if this red cup of instant noodles still held a little of your essence, Yuki.

Yes, I'll send you off on your long journey into dreams. I'll wave good-bye to your sleep-dazed face every year from now on.

And I'll never be able to live through the same time as you.

After all, in winter, you leave me behind.

The next morning, I opened the mailbox for the first time in quite a while, and a mountain of paper avalanched out with a *whump*. In among the countless flyers was a manila envelope. *From the Selection Committee*, it said. I took it back to my apartment and tore it open.

I'd placed in the Toshiki Miki Literature Prize. Apparently, all winners got the judges' comments and a five-thousand-yen prepaid card.

I set the paper down on the desk and took a deep breath.

During winter, while you weren't here, I'd taken another step into adulthood.

I glanced over at the semidouble bed. I'd sleep there again tonight, between the botanical-patterned sheets you picked out for me. Then, with my back to the bookshelf you'd put together—the one that was all art books—I'd choose a TV show to watch the next day, one we hadn't already planned to watch together.

I could see your outline there, as clearly as a cookie-cutter shape, even though you were gone.

I wasn't the only one. This room was also waiting for you to come back.

"So listen, Yuki. Wake up properly again this year. All right?"

That was important, so I said it aloud.

Over and over, I'd imagined winters that didn't end, versions of you that never woke. Every time, fear would start to rage inside me, and I'd dose it with anesthetic: *It's going to be okay; it will, it will.*

Imagination was not my friend.

Only the things that were real led to you. The air in this room, a single speck of dust suspended in the morning sunlight, the premade meals for one I'd stocked the fridge with, the "Thanks for the food" I said every evening—all these things were votive offerings to the day you'd come back.

I got out my smartphone and turned down that invitation to the New Year's Eve drinking party. Atsushi promptly responded with *Why?* I told him I wanted to focus on my novel.

I didn't ever want to make you uneasy again, so I couldn't make mistakes. To greet you with pride, I needed to be unwaveringly "correct."

"Just placing in a contest isn't enough. I need to get acknowledged in a bigger way."

Writing was all I could do right now. That meant I had to do it thoroughly and sincerely.

I had to support myself with enough unshakable correctness to conquer my hesitation and unease.

3

My eyes were constantly shuttling between my watch and the way ahead. My other hand was pulling Yuki along by the wrist. As we emerged from the gloom under an overpass, the wind from a car that had just passed through clung to my back.

"Wait." Yuki's arm resisted slightly.

"We can't. It's already ten thirty-two."

My conversation with Reiji last winter came back to me. My mission was to support Yuki.

"I know, but…" Yuki puffed her cheeks out petulantly. Looking at her made it hard to remember why I was in such a hurry.

"This is your class, Yuki, not mine. You need to get it together."

On Thursdays, my classes started with third period, in the afternoon. The second-period class we were headed to, History of Abstract Painting, was one Yuki was retaking. She'd failed it last year due to lack of attendance.

"Professor Kanzaki is picky about tardiness, isn't he?"

"Pssh. Him. He's done a lot worse than be late."

"This isn't the time for that! Not after they decided you could earn credits even if you didn't attend during the winter."

Only if she had zero absences and was on time for every class during the fall and spring terms, though.

"Come on, walk faster."

Her wrist was so slender it felt like it might break if I squeezed it… Or so I'd thought, but when I did squeeze it, it was surprisingly sturdy. I could pull as hard as I needed to.

I hadn't been able to do things like that at first. Now that I'd been with her for more than a year, though, I'd realized Yuki's easygoing ways weren't helping her academic career.

I had to do this. Right now, I was the only one here with her.

Yuki tugged on my arm. I turned around; her face was twisted in pain, and

I hastily let go. As she rubbed at her wrist, looking bewildered, a deep voice called to her. "Hey, Yuki." It came out of nowhere, and I jumped a bit, looking around for its owner.

There was a bar down in a half basement, its exterior decorated with rugby balls and tennis rackets. A big man was just pulling down its shutter. He seemed to be waving in our direction.

"Headed to school? Have a good trip."

I did a double take, startled. Yuki put on a sociable smile, went over to the man, exchanged a brief greeting, and came back.

"What was that…?" I asked.

"I guess he remembered me."

I glanced at the sports bar, then my mind flashed back to our immediate problem. In the distance, I saw the green light turn yellow. Urging Yuki on, I started to jog. The moment we hit the crosswalk, the signal turned red. It wasn't that far to the other side.

I was about to ignore the light and start across when Yuki pulled on my arm. "That's not safe."

Cars started passing in front of us, and I gave up. The university was right there. I wanted to think we'd be fine now that we'd made it this far, but the fine arts building was in a weird spot toward the back of the campus.

I almost glanced at my watch, but then my eyes went to Yuki's face. She looked a little worn out. Wasn't she sleeping at night? When I woke up that morning, she'd already made breakfast and was waiting for me again.

"Hmm?" Yuki glanced at me curiously. As I was trying to figure out what to say, she made a guess: "Oh, is this about that man?"

I nodded vaguely. I'd been in a hurry, so he hadn't really stuck in my mind.

"He's an acquaintance."

"What sort of acquaintance?"

"I worked there part-time."

The next thing I noticed, the signal had turned green. I took Yuki all the way up to the College of Art's campus, then released her.

"Thanks! I think I'm gonna make it!"

Yuki waved and trotted off. I watched her go, then stopped by the convenience store, bought a rice ball for lunch, and entered my own campus through the rear gate.

Since my class didn't start until third period, I still had two and a half hours left. Now that I was paying attention, I noticed it was a brisk, clear autumn morning.

As I walked toward the library, I saw a man and a woman in suits walking together; they reminded me I'd gotten a mailer from Aoyama Suits a few days ago.

I kept my head down, doing my best not to look their way, but for some reason, the couple started toward me. When I tried to detour around them, they flagged me down. "Hey. When somebody's calling you, at least notice."

It was Atsushi, and the woman next to him was Tomomi. I wasn't used to seeing them in suits. I felt a little daunted but said "Hey. It's been a while," trying to sound as unfazed as I could.

"It sure has! How are you?" Tomomi seemed a little shy. She was wearing a two-button jacket and a tight skirt that clung to her thighs. It made her look like a completely different person.

"What's the matter? You look surprised," Tomomi said. She seemed mystified, and there was no malice in her smile. Atsushi, who was wearing his suit jacket unbuttoned, leaned in, holding up a hand to screen his lips, and whispered something in her ear.

Tomomi suddenly turned to face me again. "I'm sorry!" she said. I had no clue what she was apologizing for; all I could do was look from her to Atsushi and back.

"You know. Back in our first year," Atsushi said. "We didn't tell you we were going out, did we? I felt bad about that."

"Um, the thing is! I sort of thought you'd figured it out. Besides, I thought we might break up pretty fast...," Tomomi added. She was blushing faintly.

"Geez, why?" Atsushi asked, grinning casually and elbowing her in the side.

I hadn't heard what had happened with the two of them after that party at Atsushi's. We hadn't talked about it at all last year.

"So I figured we'd tell you right away the next time we ran into each other." Atsushi sounded oddly formal.

"We're—"

"The two of us—"

Their words overlapped, and they looked at each other and laughed. Apparently, the more they synchronized, the funnier it was to them.

"We're doing really well now," Atsushi said, summing up.

I nodded a few times and told them I'd thought they probably were.

Since we hadn't seen each other in a while, the three of us decided to talk in the cafeteria. Atsushi sat next to Tomomi, and I sat across from him.

"It really has been a long time," Tomomi said, nibbling on a cupcake. "Since we talked like this, I mean. I think it's been since our first year."

"Actually, yeah," said Atsushi. "We didn't see each other much last year."

"Really?" I said, but I was looking out the window. A guy was standing with one knee propped on an outdoor table, playing an acoustic guitar and busily writing in a notebook by turns. Was he composing or something?

"Everyone was busy, what with this and that. I had the club, and Atsushi, you had your teaching license stuff, didn't you?"

Tomomi had risen through the ranks to become president of GTR, while Atsushi had opted against the welfare route and was still taking classes toward his teaching certification, even though he'd thought he would quit right away.

"The homework's a slog, but it's a job that lets you work with people, so I think I'll be okay."

"I see, I see."

Tomomi nodded several times, then squeezed Atsushi's left hand. He squeezed back.

The guy outside strummed his guitar a bit. Then he yanked out the notebook he'd tucked into his waistband and flipped through it madly. The pen fell out; he picked it up, then started writing again.

I looked back at the other two. Their perfectly coordinated outfits made them look as if they'd grown up all at once.

"So you're writing novels."

I'd told them I'd submitted a full-length book I'd written over the summer to the Gantosha Fantasy Literature Award.

"C'mon, man, if you were writing stuff, you could've let us read it." Atsushi stretched exaggeratedly. His spine cracked and popped, and he leaned back far enough that his chair bumped into the one behind it.

"You want to be a writer, Natsuki?" asked Tomomi.

"That's right." I nodded emphatically.

"I see. That's really cool." In the dimly lit cafeteria, Tomomi's carefree smile was dazzling.

"Yeah," said Atsushi, "people who stick with writing are in a whole different league."

I let my gaze crawl over the roughened white tabletop.

At this point, I understood that reactions like "cool" and "a whole different league" were both 100 percent genuine and 100 percent a wall they used to separate themselves from people who lived in another world.

That was what let me speak from the heart. "You two are tackling job hunting head-on. I think you're the cool ones."

Two years ago, we'd been just college students—anonymous young people. We'd been nothing more than a group: No one had stuck out, we hadn't had to be nervous about how someone else had grown, and we'd been protected by the thin membrane known as "friendship."

It wasn't like that now.

The time had come to take the reins of respect and split ourselves off from the group.

"I don't know if I'll be able to make it or not, but I don't have any other dreams. Right now, I think this is the right thing to do."

Atsushi widened his eyes and looked at me as if he was deeply impressed.

I glanced out the window again. Guitar Guy was gone. The notebook was wedged into a groove in the table, the wind swirling around the buildings fluttering its pages.

"Are you two here for a seminar or something?"

"Yep. Different ones, though. Once third period's over, we'll walk part of the way together."

Apparently, Atsushi had teaching practice, and Tomomi was attending a music publisher's lecture.

Atsushi got up to hit the bathroom. He had to take a dump, he explained, though nobody wanted to know.

Once he was gone, the noisy cafeteria suddenly seemed quiet. I took another look at Tomomi; she gave off a totally different aura in that suit.

"You look really legit now, somehow," I said.

"Is that supposed to be a compliment?"

"Yes, it's a compliment."

"In that case, thanks."

Tomomi smiled and meant it, and I found myself smiling, too. Gradually, I stopped caring about what was outside the window.

"Listen, Natsuki, how've you been?"

"What do you mean?"

"You know. You're living with her, right? I heard from Saori."

"Well…"

"The thing is, there's something I need to tell you." Tomomi's gaze fell to her lap for a moment. Then she looked me straight in the eye. "I'm sorry for trying to stop you from seeing Ms. Iwato back then." She bowed so low that her forehead touched the tabletop.

I didn't know what was going on, and I tried to protest.

"I told you I have an older brother, didn't I?" she continued.

I nodded. I was pretty sure she'd said he dropped out of university a long time ago.

"He finally started going to a trade school."

"That's great."

Tomomi shook her head. Then, as if making up her mind, she went on. "His name is Haruto. He was in the Film Department next door, at the College of Art. He belonged to GTR, four years before me. They still made lots of films back then, and people said my brother was going to be their next representative."

"Your brother went to the College of Art?"

"Yes. And that's where he met Ms. Iwato… I've only heard this from other people," she added.

I couldn't tell where this story was going. I found myself chewing on my thumbnail.

"To tell you the truth, I know about Ms. Iwato's situation. My brother told me… It sounds really rough. She was two years below my brother at the time, and he fell in love with her. They were both artists, and they both loved comedy movies, so they hit it off."

It was true—Yuki loved all types of comedy, not just movies. An image of her profile in a movie theater, laughing so hard she was crying, rose in my mind's eye.

"The two of them got closer and shared their worries with each other, and they started going out. He collaborated with Ms. Iwato, using her paintings in his films. It was going well. Then one day, she disappeared."

"Hibernating…"

"Hibernating, yes, that's right. That's it exactly!" Tomomi nodded several times, as if she'd finally heard an expression that seemed to fit. "So my brother followed her. He went to Nagoya… All the way to her parents' house. He saw Ms. Iwato there, asleep."

My words deserted me.

I hadn't been Yuki's only one.

But come to think of it, something Fuyumi had told me had seemed to imply—… And if Touko wanted a "normal boyfriend" for Yuki so badly because she'd had one before who didn't fit that description—

"He'd made a promise, you see. He'd promised Ms. Iwato he'd protect her forever. Just like some middle school–aged boy. Ridiculous, isn't it? But my stupid brother seriously thought that was what going out with somebody meant."

That's wrong, I thought. That was just forcing an arbitrary label onto Yuki.

Tomomi's eyebrows knit with worry. "My brother said he'd take care of Ms. Iwato while she slept. The whole time. Unbelievable, right? That's what he said, though. Ms. Iwato was crazy for agreeing, too. She must have known what would happen if she asked that of somebody, but she didn't turn him down."

It wasn't Yuki's fault. It was Haruto's, for treating her like she was broken. For posing as a hero.

I swallowed hard and felt sticky strings of saliva spin down from the roof of my mouth.

"My brother dropped out of school."

Tomomi glanced at me. I suspected it was the exact same look she'd turned on her "stupid brother." With a start, I realized that the coolness she'd directed at Yuki up till now hadn't been because she was concerned about me personally. She'd been seeing her brother in me.

Everything she'd done suddenly made sense.

"What happened then...?" I asked.

"My brother the dropout moved in with some strange woman's family. That was how it looked to me anyway; I knew nothing about the situation. That wasn't the worst of it, though. He threw away everything—his university studies, his club friends, his hobbies—and devoted himself to Ms. Iwato. After that, he went all strange. He started following her around, and finally, her family called our place and said they didn't want him seeing her again. Then my parents kept my brother under house arrest, basically, until the spell wore off..."

Long ago, Yuki hurt somebody.

I remembered what Reiji had said. So that had been Haruto?

The huge ventilation fan spinning above our heads seemed to be getting louder and louder.

I remember almost nothing about what Tomomi's face looked like then.

"So did the spell wear off?"

"Probably. I highly doubt he's still in contact with her."

Tomomi heaved a deep sigh. That meant I finally had permission to sigh, too. The mood had been like that the whole time.

"So—"

"What are we talking about?" Atsushi had brought over a tray with three teacups on it, but we hadn't noticed him until he spoke.

"Nothing," Tomomi said, smoothly covering for us. She glanced at me. "So anyway, I was worried, but... At this point, I'm cheering for you!"

"Like I said, what's this about?"

"It's nothing to do with you, Atsushi."

"Huh? Keeping secrets from your boyfriend? Geez, don't be mean." Atsushi reached for the teacup he'd set in front of Tomomi and pulled it back. Tomomi promptly resisted, putting some muscle into it.

After we'd talked for twenty more minutes or so, I said good-bye and got up. I left the cafeteria and walked for a little. Once I was sure they were both out of sight, I worked on getting my breathing back to normal.

Why was I so shaken up about this? I'd known all along that I wasn't Yuki's first boyfriend.

Deliberately putting it out of my mind, I hurried to the library.

4

When we stepped through the venue gate, the aroma of cayenne pepper and other spices filled the air, making it immediately clear we were in a different world. The weather forecast had said that night would be cloudy with rain here and there, but that hadn't thinned the crowd at all.

Although the sun was down, a few last traces of light dyed the sky blue, and glaring spotlights lit up the site from all directions. Yuki pulled me along by the hand, as giddy as a little girl.

"Have you been to this before?" I asked.

"Nope, it's my first time! Nobody else would come with me."

"What about Ms. Shimoki?"

"Spicy food is the one thing Ena can't handle."

She talked as if I was particularly good with spicy food. Now that I thought about it, I hadn't heard from Ms. Shimoki in a while. She'd said she wanted to be an editor; had she managed to find a job? And something about Yuki's phrasing tugged at me a bit.

"'The one thing'? What does that mean?"

"She does all sorts of things with me, even though they don't interest her personally. Like Lumine the Yoshimoto comedy theater, or art exhibitions, or midnight camping."

As we spoke, we reached the ticket vendor. Apparently, we were supposed to buy food tickets we could then use at any stall. I put our conversation on hold and checked the number of tickets with Yuki. Ten. *That many?* Cringing, I pulled a five-thousand-yen bill out of my wallet.

"Wait. Midnight camping…?" I turned back to Yuki. She looked nonchalant, as if that were a perfectly normal thing to do. "What's that?" I asked.

"Oh, just what it sounds like. You go to a park late at night and camp. You take a collapsible cooking stove and roast marshmallows or grill sandwiches."

"People do that?"

I started to tell her I'd never seen anyone trying it, then realized I actually had. Ms. Shimoki had been doing just that two years ago, on that semicircular stage. It seemed she'd caught the habit from Yuki.

"But why?"

Yuki frowned and thought for a bit. "...Because you get hungry?"

Right after she said that, we were handed a strip of bright-red tear-away tickets and a pamphlet with a stamp bingo sheet. Stepping out of the line, we opened the pamphlet. Our pale shadows, cast in several skewed layers, mingled on the paper.

"Hmm. Where should we start?"

From what I'd heard, this was a collection of thirteen famously spicy restaurants from around the city; they'd won their spots here through a tournament. I'd spotted Tangier's name on the participants list.

Yuki raked her hair back from her face as she leaned in closer to the pamphlet. September had begun. She'd talked with Professor Kanzaki—who was also the department chair—and had settled on the day she'd leave for home. Her hair fell past her shoulders now; we'd have to get it cut before we left.

The red was rapidly fading from the sky. *As the night deepens, you grow lovelier.* I reached out for those ten centimeters of accumulated time, which were about to be lost.

"Help me figure this out, Natsuki."

"Okay."

"Were you looking at my hair again?" Yuki sounded a little disgusted. I retracted my hand, but she shot me a rather scornful look before I had a chance to make excuses. "Boys do like long hair, don't they?"

She swept her hair aside with the back of her hand, making it flutter. She had started to look like a magazine model to me. Her frighteningly perfect features, her blessed limbs. If Yuki didn't hibernate, I was sure the one here with her wouldn't be me—

"No, you're wrong. That's not what I meant. I'll love you no matter what you're like, Yuki."

I meant that. I was prepared. So there was no way I could ever fall for somebody else.

"Really?" Yuki leaned to the side slightly, smiling mischievously. "What if I fall asleep and never wake up? Will you still love me then?"

I wasn't the type of guy who'd take advantage of Yuki's disability to ingratiate myself with her.

But what if she developed more symptoms than she already had? What if she stayed asleep for nearly a year and a half, the way she had ten years ago? Or what if, like her lost sense of taste, some other, more important sense vanished and never came back…?

"Are you planning to fall asleep and never wake up?" Perhaps fear had made my voice softer. Yuki was gazing into my eyes, her mouth open as if she were dazed. That wasn't something I could say a second time.

"U-um." I pleaded with her vague, wavering eyes.

"Huh? What did you say?" she asked, looking startled. I told her it was nothing.

Among the throng of cayenne pepper specialty shops, Taiwanese food, and Moroccan cuisine, our first stop was a Nepalese place called Tenjin Sherpa.

One after another, plates of food were handed out from the long rows of box-shaped temporary kitchens. There were long lines at every restaurant, but the crowd at Tenjin Sherpa was comparatively thin. When I handed over two tickets, a brown-skinned man served up two plastic bowls of green curry and added super-spicy sausages.

We sat down in a corner of the tent-covered seating area.

"Bell peppers in curry… For something super spicy, that seems pretty tame."

"Those aren't bell peppers. They're green chilis."

I looked at the large green chilis floating in the gentler green of the curry and felt a shiver run through me.

"Yuki, about your sense of taste…"

"I know. My dad told you, didn't he?"

"Yeah…"

I looked down slightly, and Yuki prodded my head with her index finger. When I looked up, she shoved a sausage dusted with bright-red powder into my mouth.

It was surprisingly tasty. Just as I was about to tell her so, a heat that made it feel as if the depths of my throat had caught fire blasted through my mouth, and I ended up hyperventilating for a while.

"I told you it was how I was wired, not a hobby." Without rice or naan or anything, Yuki quietly started in on her green curry. "I lied, though."

I gazed at the bottom of my already empty cup.

"I actually got to like spicy things. I mean, of course I would. If I didn't like them, I'd have to live with a screwy sense of taste forever." Yuki's spoon kept shuttling smoothly from her bowl to her mouth and back. She even ate the green chilis without hesitating.

"That's why I started liking them."

Yuki smiled. She probably really did like them now. What she'd just said didn't seem like a simple attempt to hide her embarrassment.

Even though she'd put most of her green curry away, there wasn't a single bead of sweat on her forehead. Not only that, but she looked as if she wasn't quite satisfied. "This is a little mild."

"Is that even possible?"

"Yes. Try it." Yuki scooped up some of the curry left in the bottom of her bowl and held the spoon to my mouth.

Managing to eat half of the sausage had made me careless. The curry caught me completely off guard. That one bite made me break out in a full-body sweat, and I opened my mouth as wide as it would go, my face twisting.

"What's the matter?" she asked.

"It's *hot*."

"Really?"

"Do I look like I'm lying?"

Yuki's cup still had plenty of water in it, and I stole it and drank it down. Yuki finished her remaining sausage, then started to get up. She couldn't seem to get her legs under her, though; she tipped backward and almost slipped off her chair. I put a hand behind her to catch her, and she looked up at me, puzzled. Even she didn't know what had happened.

"...Are you okay?" I had Yuki sit down again, then looked her straight in the eye.

Yuki nodded and reached for the empty bowl that had slipped out of her hands. "Maybe I'm a little dehydrated. I'm thirsty."

Thinking back, I realized that even though Yuki ate extremely spicy stuff, she didn't drink much water during meals. I could think of one possible reason: Since her taste buds had gone strange, water tasted weird, even though it shouldn't have a flavor at all.

To her, meals were a battle. They were the first step in accepting her new, strange self.

"I'm sorry. I shouldn't have taken your water." Gently escorting Yuki, I bought two chai teas at the same restaurant. Then, plastic cups in hand, we searched for our next stop.

We ate our way through spicy-savory chicken wings, Taiwan *mazesoba*, and mapo tofu. Our strip of tickets steadily dwindled. About the time the crowd had started to thin out a bit, we joined the line for the place that had really jumped out at us when we first looked around: Salaman, an Indian restaurant from Ikebukuro. Since these were temporary facilities, the restaurants all looked more or less the same, but Salaman had an enormous bunch of string-bound cayenne peppers hanging out in front, like those bunches of a thousand paper cranes.

"One 'Spiciest Curry in Japan,' please."

I handed over a ticket and accepted a dish with an extremely literal name in return. The second I took hold of it, the unmistakable aura of a "final boss" crossed the distance from my hands to my face and thrashed me.

Yuki started eating as soon as she sat down, as if she couldn't wait. Just like that, her glum expression was gone. Every time her spoon rose and fell, an eye-wateringly pungent aroma drifted over to me.

"Whoa. They used ghost peppers," I said. "According to this, they're four hundred times spicier than cayenne. Isn't that hot?"

Yuki shook her head. Apparently, this one was a winner: She shoveled the thick, deep-red curry into her mouth almost as if she were bolting down a beef rice bowl. "Is it good?" I asked her. With an artless smile, she told me it was.

"Listen." When she'd eaten about half the bowl, she put her spoon down and looked at me. "The thing is, I didn't know if you actually loved me."

Her abrupt confession shut me right up.

"Wait, don't look like that," she said. "I'm talking about a long time ago."

"How long ago is 'long'?"

"Last year... When was it? Anyway, up until some point last year." Yuki seemed to feel a little guilty; her gaze skated away behind me, then came back. There was heat in her eyes.

I uncrossed my legs so that both my thighs were pressed flat against the seat of my chair.

"It's different now, though," she continued. "You put a lot of thought into it, and you kept a healthy distance so we could survive as a couple. And so, you see, I decided I'd stay in love with you forever."

Those were the words I'd been waiting to hear all along. The very fact that I'd been waiting made them seem somehow unreal. I felt dazed.

That was how much I loved this woman.

"Natsuki, I love you. Stay with me forever, okay?"

Yuki's words threatened to go right over my head, but I managed to catch and process them, then hastily nodded.

When we got to the Keio New Line platform at Shinjuku Station, we still had a little time left before our train. We sat on a bench, glancing up at the electronic signboard every now and then, and talked about that evening's date.

"You barely ate anything, Natsuki." Yuki puffed out her cheeks a little, scolding me.

"Don't ask the impossible. My tongue's normal."

"Mine's normal, too. It's just a little insensitive to flavor."

"The stuff today wasn't just 'a little.' Seriously, that last one wasn't fit for human consumption."

Yuki took out her smartphone and played a video. It showed me as I writhed in pain after attempting a mouthful of the "Spiciest Curry in Japan."

"Fine, I get it. Just put that away. The train's coming."

For Shinjuku Station, there weren't many people on the platform, and we managed to snag the very first spot in line. How many more dates would we be able to fit in before Yuki went home? I was visualizing the calendar in my mind when Yuki tugged on my sleeve. "I'm thirsty."

She looked wistfully up at me through her lashes.

"It'll be here any minute," I said.

An announcement about the train's arrival played overhead. Seeing two headlights shining in the distance, I started to feel a little anxious. However, Yuki was giving me a flirty, petulant look.

"Argh. Fine. Geez."

"Real Gold. If there isn't any, then something sour and fizzy."

"Okay, okay." I turned around and ran to the vending machine. I scanned the plastic case for a yellow bottle but didn't see one. *Soda, soda*, I thought, getting out my wallet, and then I heard a rush of air behind me. I had to hurry; the train was on its way in.

"Hey, Yuki, there's no soda in this one."

Stressing out, I tried to shove a hundred-yen coin into the slot but fumbled it. The coin bounced back and slipped out of my hand to roll around at my feet.

"C'mon, what do you want instead?" I stomped on the coin to stop it, then picked it up. Out of the corner of my eye, I saw Yuki's back and the approaching train.

If I didn't like them, I'd have to live with a screwy sense of taste forever.

Out of nowhere, Yuki's words skimmed through my mind. To her, meals were a fight. She hadn't freely chosen her preferences; she'd been forced to choose them, in order to live her life. But hadn't she gone a bit overboard earlier? After eating that super-spicy curry, I'd developed a dull pain in my stomach.

Yuki hadn't just been fine; she'd said it was mild.

That couldn't be right, could it?

"Hello?" I called.

Yuki's back seemed a little smaller. I thought it was probably my imagination, but then I saw it, and a chill ran down my spine. The wind lifted her long hair, her heel came up, and her head sank down—toward the tracks.

"Yuki!"

Flinging my wallet aside, I sprinted.

As Yuki was drawn down toward the rails, I reached out for her. Just after that, the light from the train blotted out the right side of my vision.

5

In the dim corridor, an alarm like a mechanical whisper echoed at fixed intervals. Other than that, it was nearly silent. I sat in a chair against the wall, breathing as quietly as possible.

Then the sound of the elevator asserted itself. I heard hasty footsteps, and then Fuyumi strode in, carrying her guitar case. Ignoring the eyes of the nurses stationed in the treatment room, she tossed her guitar case away and grabbed me by the shirtfront. The case hit the ground and slid a little, then collided with a fire extinguisher and stopped.

"Hey!" Her violent voice and gaze stabbed into me. I lifted my head, trying hard not to avert my eyes from her scowl.

"I'm sorry," I said.

"Do *not* give me that…" I could feel her hands trembling just below my neck. Every time they shook, she pulled harder, and it got tougher to breathe. "Why exactly are you with my sister? What is your purpose?"

"It's my fault."

"It very obviously is. Not one little thing about this is my sister's fault. Those are the stars she was born under, that's all."

Releasing me, Fuyumi took a couple of steps back, her expression fading to icy blankness. She looked down at me coldly. "Cover for my fragile sister. Help her be stronger. You know that's your role."

Abruptly, anger welled up inside me. I knew Fuyumi's feelings were justified, but somehow it felt as if she were making fun of Yuki through me. "What do you mean, my role? I'm not dating her because it's my job."

"This when you're lucky to have a role at all!"

Fuyumi's voice thundered through the corridor. A startled nurse emerged from the treatment room and asked if we were all right. We were the ones who really wanted to ask that question, though: Yuki was on the other side of that door. Was she smiling right now, or—?

Just then, the door opened. Light spilled into the hall, and an elderly man with round glasses and a lab coat with pens in the breast pocket stuck his head out. He beckoned to the two of us. "Please, come in."

Yuki was inside, lying on a stretcher, under a blanket.

"Yuki!"

"Sis!"

Coming from opposite directions, we went right up to her. Her head was sinking into her pillow. There was a gauze pad on the back of her skull, held in place with a bandage. She was lucid, and she looked from me to Fuyumi and back, seeming puzzled. "Well, Fuyumi. What's the matter?"

"Don't give me that! As soon as Natsuki told me what happened, I came running."

"But you won't make the last train."

"Who cares?!" Fuyumi was agitated, and the attending nurse checked her. Yuki gave her a kind, big-sisterly look; Fuyumi had been living in Tokyo on her own for only two weeks. Then Yuki turned to me.

"I'm sorry. I got a little dizzy."

"No, I'm sorry…"

Yuki shook her head, which earned her a warning from the nurse: She was supposed to keep her head as still as possible.

"Are you a family member?" asked the doctor.

Fuyumi nodded. "I'm her little sister."

The man looked startled. "So you're the one Ms. Touko was pregnant with back then? You've gotten so big." He smiled at her.

Fuyumi gazed at the doctor blankly, but then her tension eased. "It's good to meet you," she said. "You're Dr. Amano, aren't you?"

"Yes, that's me."

"Oh, I see. You hadn't met him, Fuyumi?" Yuki asked, keeping the back of her head glued to the pillow. "I think it's been about twenty years now. We traveled to hospitals all over Japan, but none of the tests they ran turned up any abnormalities. Finally, we found Dr. Amano. He was the only one who took an interest in my symptoms."

Ever since, Yuki said, he'd been her regular doctor in Tokyo. I remembered seeing his name on her smartphone, in the app displaying her emergency contacts.

"I'm not sure *interest* is the word. I merely thought it wouldn't be impossible. However, modern medicine can't put a name to it, and there are no model cases. Yours is the only known example."

Dr. Amano's brow furrowed with concern. He looked between the two sisters, comparing them, then put a hand over his mask and gave a phlegmy cough. There was only one chair in the exam room, and Fuyumi took it.

"Your sister has a concussion caused by physical trauma." Dr. Amano opened a CT scan result on a vertically oriented monitor. Yuki's brain was up there, sliced and on display. "When you called us, you said she'd struck the train tracks."

"Yes. I thought she was in danger, so I impulsively pulled…"

"In all likelihood, she hadn't made contact. There are no abrasions. Her concussion was caused by a blow to the back of her head. Aside from that, there are…no issues."

The doctor pointed at the darker area of the image.

Back then, as Yuki was falling toward the tracks, I'd caught her arm and hauled on it as hard as I could. As a result, I'd fallen over backward, and I'd ended up pulling her down with me. I hadn't let go the entire time, so her head had crashed into the platform.

She'd been unconscious for two minutes or so.

"I'm told she lost consciousness, but it was temporary. She was already able to converse without any real issues in the ambulance. She's fine. Or, well, I'd prefer to believe that's the case. There is a possibility of lingering aftereffects, though, so I'd like to have her hospitalized for testing."

Fuyumi fixed me with a steady, chilly gaze.

"For how long?" Yuki asked.

"Three days should be enough," Dr. Amano said promptly.

"Doctor, listen…" Out of the corner of my eye, I saw Fuyumi scowl. So this counted as meddling, huh? Still, before I could retract my question, Dr. Amano encouraged me to go on.

"Why do you suppose Yuki had that dizzy spell?" I continued. "Actually, there were several times today when I thought her senses seemed to be blunted. She should still have a month left before she begins hibernating, though."

The doctor's forehead creased, and he frowned a little. "Hibernating… I see. Medicine hasn't yet elucidated the mechanism by which she only sleeps during the winter. That means that what I'm about to say is mere speculation, but…" As he continued, the doctor gazed at the CT scan. "One of the initial triggers of ordinary sleep is a drop in core temperature. If this is true of Yuki's sleep as well, it's possible that the record-setting cold waves we've had during the past two winters have affected her body's rhythms."

It had gotten colder, so her hibernation was beginning earlier? That was refreshingly intuitive, but on the other hand, something in the doctor's words nagged at me.

Last year at some point, I'd told Yuki we should go see real snow. She had never seen any before, since she slept straight through that season. Snow wasn't a seasonal thing everywhere, though. We'd joked about going to Hokkaido or touring lands even farther to the north. However, if we carelessly flew to Hokkaido, Yuki would—

"Then are you saying she'd get sleepy in the summer if she used the air-conditioning to cool herself off and got a chill?"

"I'm not sure. I really doubt…"

"What about cold-water baths?"

"Erm, it's possible Yuki detects the change in temperature over a fairly long span of time. Just like an ordinary human day, only much, much longer." The doctor paused frequently as he spoke, adjusting his glasses multiple times. "However, we don't know that for sure yet."

"That's all you people say."

The words were out of my mouth before I knew it.

Silence fell.

"'We don't know.' 'We can't say for certain.' That's all you say. Isn't saving people a doctor's job?"

"We're doing everything we can. It's only that—"

"'Only' what? That Yuki's special? That's why you can't diagnose her?"

"I understand how you feel. That's why—"

"You don't understand a thing!" I yelled, undeterred. "You don't have any idea what sort of problems Yuki's up against right now!"

I told myself I was being someone's weapon.

"Natsuki." A gentle, firm voice stopped me. Yuki was sitting up. Her straightforward eyes bored into me. "That's how it is."

Those resigned eyes were persuasive. They belonged to someone who'd seen this same scene play out a thousand times before.

That voice seemed to paralyze me, and I couldn't get any more words through my throat.

After Yuki was taken to a hospital room on the fourth floor, Fuyumi and I were given the choice of sleeping on cots in Yuki's room, seats in the waiting room, or beds in the treatment room. In the end, we both spent the four hours until the first train on benches in the waiting room, which was illuminated only by the floor lighting and the glow of the vending machine.

When I lay down, the bench was wide enough for only one person, and if I stretched my legs out, my feet and ankles hung off the edge no matter what I did. The astringent smell of the leather didn't bother me that much, but the metal fittings of the backpack I was using as a pillow were rough, and they hurt.

"Are you awake?" asked Fuyumi's hushed voice.

I sat up a little. On the bench farthest from my own, I could make out the back of Fuyumi's head. "Yeah, I'm awake."

"That was something else back there. You've got a lot of nerve." She heaved a small sigh. "...But thank you. You told him what I was thinking."

"I didn't say it for you or anything."

"I am thanking you. Act like someone who's being thanked."

I forced my body onto its side and covered my head with an arm. The faint, humming vibration of the vending machine was keeping me awake. "You don't have to stay here. Have them let you into her hospital room; you're family."

"My sister doesn't like to be with other people at night."

Really? Up until now, Yuki had always spent her nights asleep in the bed with me. I recalled the weight of her head on my upper arm. She slept deeply, like she was sinking into the abyss.

And very soon now, that deep sleep would swallow her up.

"What about the treatment room, then?"

"What are you talking about? We aren't patients, you know," Fuyumi said flatly. After getting to her feet, she came over to my bench, smacked my outstretched legs carelessly out of the way, and sat down next to me.

Even in the gloom, her eyes caught the light of the fire alarm and shone with a red cast. "Natsuki." Her voice was tense. I thought she was going to tell me off again. "I like my sister's pictures."

The angle of her cross eyebrows softened. I sat up straight and turned toward her.

"We're six whole years apart, so even in my earliest memories, there were already lots of pictures."

"Your house is the only place I've ever seen one of Yuki's finished pieces."

Looking triumphant, Fuyumi said, "Oh, really?" and flashed me a half smile. "She says she sees them in dreams. Things like a rainbow river floating in the darkness, or a mountain of light that swallows people, or a silent, deserted town."

For a few moments, Fuyumi's gaze was fixed on something far away.

"They're vague topics, but my sister paints these completely indescribable, brilliant pictures from them. I wanted to watch her do that forever."

"And that's why you have to protect Yuki?"

Faintly, in the darkness, I saw her nod. "I was supposed to save my sister. That's why I was born."

"I'm pretty sure you're overthinking that."

"No. I'm really not. It's in my name... Don't you think it's strange?" Fuyumi laid a hand on her chest, gazing at me steadily. Fu *as in* fukanou, *"impossible."* Yu *as in* yurai, *"origin."* Bi *as in* bijin, *"beauty," but read* mi—she'd taught me how it was written when we first met. Fu *as in* fukanou, *"impossible."* The intensity she'd put behind it at the time had buried the impression the character had made on me.

"People don't normally use negative characters like *fu* in names. You can't ask my origin. Therefore, I have no meaning."

All I could do was nod. I'd never asked why my parents named me Natsuki, and I'd never really thought about what the name meant.

"Besides, I heard them talking. I think it was in my second year of middle school. My sister had decided to go to a university in Tokyo, and the whole family was scrambling. We had worked long into the night, getting ready for her move, and I'd gone down to the first floor to get a drink. Mom and Dad were arguing; Mom told Dad she was too nervous to let my sister go, but Dad said it was necessary. And then Mom said it was my job to stay with Yuki, so why not send me to Tokyo with her."

"......"

"I know things were hard back then. It's just…I'm empty, a substitute for my sister. I was born to perform that role…but I can't actually do it, so…"

"Why do you say you can't do it?"

"You must know that, Natsuki. You of all people."

I squinted, gazing at the array of items in the vending machine, even though its light nearly erased them.

"Because I'm family, and you're a stranger," she said at last. "Being a stranger means you can be her life partner."

Life partner.

Before the impact of that term could really hit me, Fuyumi went on. "Sometimes I think about where this road might lead. However, way up ahead, the road forks and heads off in different directions. We sisters were originally one road, and we can't merge. You, though—"

Oh, I see… Both the distance I'd felt because I was a stranger, and my irritation at not knowing Yuki more deeply—to Fuyumi, both of those had been something to be envied.

Because we were strangers, we could choose to travel the same road.

Since Fuyumi would have to live her own life someday, she had no choice but to entrust this to someone else.

"So…you were jealous?" I asked.

"Th-that's an extremely blunt way to put it."

"I'm sorry; I really didn't know. I just assumed you hated me."

"I do hate you!" Fuyumi said loudly, then added, "I have all along." She looked down slightly, then raised her eyes to look straight into mine.

"I am grateful to you, though."

She bowed, then got to her feet and went back to her original spot.

This time I couldn't see the back of her head.

When I woke up, faint, hazy light filled the space above me, and my whole right side was sliding off the bench. When I moved my fingertips across my face, I could feel a dried track of drool from the corner of my mouth all the way to my chin. The realization that I'd genuinely fallen asleep hit me, bringing with it a rush of anxiety.

Hastily, I checked my smartphone. It was six AM sharp, and I had six texts.

Three were from online news sites, one was from Tomomi, and two were from Yuki. Yuki's texts were already an hour old. She said to go buy her orange juice and some breakfast.

"Orange juice."

I jumped up, pulled my crumpled coat back on, grabbed my backpack, took a look at the floor map on the wall, then hurried to the hospital's shop.

In the morning, the hospital seemed completely different from the way it had at night. The whole place felt refreshing and clean.

The big windows let in plenty of morning light. Through them, I could see an enclosed courtyard with a modest botanical garden and a wooden deck. Consultation hours hadn't begun yet, so the lobby was deserted.

The shop wasn't open yet, either, of course, so I tried the vending machines in the lounge instead. I saw grape and even peach juice, but no orange. In the fifth vending machine, I finally found a tangerine drink that was 20 percent fruit juice. I got that, grabbed a curry roll from the food vending machine next to it, and went up to the fourth floor.

The ward was already bustling with enormous carts loaded up with breakfast trays; the nurses were visiting patients' rooms, starting with the lower numbers and working up. I saw an elderly man walking laps around the hall, pulling along an IV stand.

As I was looking for Yuki's room number, a nurse came up to me and asked if I was visiting. When I told her about the night before, she took me to room 438.

It was a private room instead of the usual four-bed kind. That meant no nurses had visited yet, and Yuki's breakfast hadn't arrived.

When I quietly opened the door, I heard voices inside. "Sis." Moving even more cautiously, I slipped in through the gap I'd made. "Enough. Just stop this."

The voice belonged to Fuyumi. I held my breath, just the way I had when I'd come in, and softly closed the door. There was a pink curtain right in front of me, and I couldn't see behind it.

"There, see? You've been talking so long the nurse got here, Fuyu."

"Don't turn this into a joke." Fuyumi's tone grew rough.

The two of them were silhouetted against the curtain. They reminded me of a mother and daughter.

"He's a good person."

"I know. I know that better than anybody. What happened, Fuyu? You spent all that time hating him, remember?"

"I—! I just…"

"Just what? You were just lonely because he was taking your big sister away?"

There was a mischievous smile in Yuki's voice. It made me feel as if something were tickling the inside of my rib cage.

"Look, forget about me. We're talking about you right now."

I could visualize Fuyumi's scowl.

In the cramped space between the curtain and the door, I leaned back against the sink, half sitting on the rim and resting my gently closed fists on my knees.

"I knew it," said Fuyumi. "This won't work."

Yuki didn't respond. The only sound was the rattle of a serving cart out in the hall.

"He hasn't done anything wrong," she continued.

"Fuyu, listen. To me, he's—"

"You fell for him. I know. I know that far too well. That's why you can't do this. How far are you planning to drag him in?"

"But this time, I'm sure—"

"You *always* say that. You say it, and then you do this stupid, stupid stuff."

I had no idea what they were talking about. I hadn't even noticed that my butt had slipped off the edge of the sink. All I could do was stand there motionless in that in-between space.

"Please. I'll make this the last time." Yuki was pleading. It was her voice, but the words sounded like they belonged to someone else. "This will be the last one."

Fuyumi's voice seemed to smack away her fragile entreaty. "Right. You said that with Haruto, too, Sis."

Haruto Oujiro. Tomomi's brother, the one who'd dropped out of university. The man who'd loved Yuki so much it had sent his life off the rails—or that was what I'd heard, anyway. What had actually happened?

"Haruto has nothing to do with this."

Yuki's voice, saying another man's name. It was oddly sexy and alluring, and I gulped.

"Well, sure, Sis, you were just sleeping. So yeah, it had nothing to do with you!"

Clang! I heard one hard object strike another: I'd flinched and knocked the green liquid-soap bottle into the sink. *Clunk, rattle-rattle-rattle.* The bottle rolled onto the drain, tripping the sensor and sending water gushing out of the faucet.

"Huh? Something's weird. The nurse is taking too long," Fuyumi said. She stalked over, and before I had time to open the door, she'd ripped the curtain away.

"Whuh?!" Her eyes flew open, and her pale cheeks gradually flushed pink. "Eavesdroppers suck!" She smacked a hand into my chest, shoving me away, then walked out and headed toward the elevators.

I couldn't bring myself to go after her, so I turned back, excused myself, and went through the curtain.

"Hey, the orange juice has arrived." Yuki sat up slightly, pointing at me with an expression as bright as a flower in bloom.

"The shop wasn't open yet. It's not one hundred percent what you asked for."

"I forgive you anyway."

"Thanks," I said, and I sat down on the folding chair. It was a little warm, as if the hostility of the person who'd just left it was still clinging to the seat.

"You like orange juice, don't you? Even though you hate oranges."

"I just can't do oranges." Letting her hand dangle limply, ghostlike, Yuki shook her head.

"People usually bring whole fruit when they pay hospital visits, though."

"You're lucky, then. You know what I actually want."

Just as Yuki took the curry roll, a nurse's assistant in aqua scrubs pulled a plastic plate out of the serving cart and set it on top of the overbed table. Rice, pale-looking miso soup, something like steamed bacon, a cabbage salad, and yogurt.

Setting the curry roll beside the plate, Yuki started in on the rice and soup. "I haven't eaten since yesterday. I was hungry."

Early sunlight shone through a gap in the curtains, pouring down over her jet-black hair. Out of nowhere, I felt my chest constrict.

Yuki cocked her head. "What's wrong?"

I couldn't seem to find the right words. Her left hand was resting on top of the table, and I squeezed it tightly.

"Ow!"

"You really could have died."

I bent down and pressed my forehead to the back of her hand. She patted the back of my head with her free palm. "There, there," she said.

"You could have died..."

"You're overthinking it."

Hearing a noise behind me, I raised my head. With light clattering sounds, a nurse was wheeling in a silver instrument trolley. Wiping my eyes as naturally as possible, I stood up. "Okay, I'll...head to class. I need to stop by the house first. I'll tell the professors why you're absent. I'll be back this afternoon."

I pulled out my smartphone and took a full-body photo of Yuki and her hospital bed. Even then, Yuki was wearing a radiant smile.

6

I waited on an eggplant-shaped chair in the first-floor lobby of the fine arts building until I heard the click of approaching hard-soled shoes. They belonged to a bearded middle-aged man in a green business suit. When I stepped forward, he stopped with a rather startled look and asked if I was Mr. Uzume.

"That's right. It's been a long time, Professor Kanzaki."

"Ah, I knew it. Remembering faces gets harder as you get older, you see. I'm glad. We spoke about Ms. Iwato before, didn't we?"

The professor still didn't sound sure of himself. When I told him we had, he nodded several times in relief. "And? How can I help you?"

"The thing is, Yuki's in the hospital." I held up the smartphone photo I'd taken that morning.

Turning pale, the professor stared at the screen. "Is she all right? What's her condition?" He sounded worried.

"She just bumped her head yesterday. She's probably fine. They told me she could leave in two or three days."

"I see. Thank you for going to the trouble of delivering the message in person."

"I thought it might be a little while before you caught an e-mail. Your History of Abstract Painting class is during fourth period today, isn't it?"

The professor nodded. There was a tight knot of people standing behind him. I'd probably registered their presence while I was waiting, but I hadn't really noticed them until just now.

"So, um, the thing about how she can't miss a class if she won't be attending in winter..."

"Oh, of course she should attend, but after seeing a photo like that..." Professor Kanzaki shifted his leather satchel from one hand to the other. He had no idea he'd leaked a student's personal information from that very bag, way back when. "Bring proof of her hospitalization to the office. Tell them Kanzaki sent you."

"Thank you very much, sir." I bowed.

Just then, although I hadn't been paying attention, my ears caught several hushed voices. People were saying Yuki's name and kicking around groundless rumors.

"I won't be able to visit her in the hospital, though," the professor continued. "Tell her I said to get well soon, if you would." Then he walked away, shoes clicking.

Left behind, I took a look around the fine arts building. Everyone in here except me was probably a College of Art student.

"Hey, isn't that Yuki's...?"

"The one who's hung in there for more than a year?"

"That's the longest anybody's managed since Haruto."

Before I knew it, the gossip had come to focus on me, and words were coming at me from all sides. Five guys in particular were staring at me in a way that obviously crossed a line. It was the group I'd run into in the sketching room once, when I was going around asking about Yuki.

"Hey, Ryuutarou, knock it off." His friend with glasses tried to talk him down, but Ryuutarou kept right on glaring.

I started to get scared; I wanted to get out of there as fast as I could. I turned my back, pretending I couldn't hear them, and began to walk away.

"So she gets a pass and doesn't have to come to school, huh?" Ryuutarou's grumbling sank its claws into my back. "The class is a yawnfest to begin with, and then they had to make it a friggin' required course. Kanzaki's shit, but that bitch isn't much better. You know what this means? She's sleeping with Kanzaki, too."

It was the first time I'd ever clenched my fists so hard my nails jabbed into my palms. Gritting my teeth, I took a step. Once I'd managed the one, another followed naturally.

"It ain't fair," he said.

"What's not fair?"

Before I knew it, I'd turned around. Not only that, but I'd walked right up to the guy called Ryuutarou.

He turned a smile loaded with sarcasm on me. "Well, it ain't, is it? Due to some real fuzzy 'family circumstances,' she doesn't have to come to school all winter. You think it's okay to allow individual exceptions like that?"

"Yuki didn't ask for things to be this way."

"So what? What I'm saying is, it's not fair."

Not fair. I wanted to throw those words right back in his face. How much better would it be if this guy were the one who slept all winter, instead of Yuki?

"Listen, that girl has it all. She doesn't have to come to class; she doesn't have to turn in her homework. Her life's way too easy."

Something in my head exploded. "You don't know a damn thing!"

For the first time in my life, I hauled somebody up by the shirtfront. There was less to grab than I'd expected, and I couldn't get his head locked. My hand slipped, and I basically ended up pulling on the right side of his collar. "You have no clue what her family's going through, or what Yuki's feeling! You've never even thought about it, so quit running your mouth!!"

"Who the hell cares about that stuff?" Ryuutarou grabbed my arm and squeezed it. My bones creaked, and my grip gradually weakened. "If she put a little effort in, it'd work out somehow, right? There are people from single-parent homes who work a ton of part-time jobs, and they're still giving a hundred percent. There's even a guy who comes to school in a wheelchair, every day. She's just not trying hard enough, that's all."

When my hand slipped off his collar entirely, the belligerence in Ryuutarou's eyes shifted to pity. "I feel real bad for you, pal."

He yanked on my arm, pulling me in close to him, then grabbed the back of my head and squeezed.

"You're just being used."

"Seriously, *enough*," the guy with glasses cut in. "Just drop it." He shoved Ryuutarou's chest, pushing him away, then looked back and jerked his chin at me. "And you, my friend. Don't throw your weight around over here too much. This is the third week in a row you've dropped by."

"I only came to pick her up."

"Yeah, maybe so, but I don't think you should do too much of that," he said simply. Then he yanked on Ryuutarou's arm, and their group walked away toward the corridor.

I let my right arm fall. Pain ran through my wrist; it felt as if I'd been wearing handcuffs. I took one more look around, then headed for the campus gate.

When the elevator arrived at the fourth floor, the family who'd ridden up with me got off, too. As they did so, a man wearing a windbreaker over a hoodie traded places with them. There was still some time before the night shift took over. Was he on his way back from visiting someone?

"This is going up," I told him, mostly just to make myself feel better.

Beneath his hood, the man's face came up sluggishly. "Th...th...th...," he stammered; it took him a little while before he managed to say "Thank you." Then he turned away so hastily that the thing he was wearing on a cord around his neck smacked into my shoulder.

"You've, uh, still got your visitor's card."

"Oh!"

Startled, the man looked up again, revealing a round face with a five-o' clock shadow. Putting on a pathetic smile, he said, "Eh, ex-excuse me," and bowed.

When I told Reception I was visiting, they handed me a piece of paper. Bracing it on my Boston bag, I took out my pen. There were columns for the date and time, my purpose, and a list of options for my relationship to the patient. *Family, Friend, Other...* Those were the only options available, and my pen hovered uncertainly for a little while.

Finally, I wrote *Boyfriend* in the parentheses by the *Other* option and turned in the form. The receptionist took it, looking a little puzzled. I heard her whisper, "Boyfriend...?"

Were my looks that much of a problem?

The visitor's card the man from the elevator had just returned came right back to me. I put it around my neck, then started for room 438.

When I opened the door, the pink curtain had been pulled back. Through the windows, I could see the deepening blue of the sky and the hazy lights of the city, which were just beginning to come on. As if she were drawn toward the view, Yuki sat on the edge of the bed with her back to me. She was wearing a hospital gown that wasn't much different from a paper apron.

"I brought you extra clothes and things," I said.

Yuki's shoulders jerked, and she turned around. "Th-that was fast!" She was resting an elbow on the C-shaped overbed table and drummed her fingertips against its surface.

"Really? I was about to apologize for being late."

"Oh? I guess you have a point. It's still early, though. The days have gotten so short."

Her gaze went to the window again.

I set the Boston bag down beside the bed, then pulled a folding chair over and took a seat. Oddly, it still seemed faintly warm. "Huh? Was somebody just here?"

Yuki's fingertips stopped moving. "A friend."

"How about that. So you have a friend besides Ms. Shimoki, huh?"

"They took X-rays and an MRI today. MRIs are incredibly loud. I wish they'd do something about that."

Annoyed at getting shut down, I opened the Boston bag and laid out the clothes and game device I'd brought on the bed.

Yuki finally turned back and started inspecting the clothes. "Thanks!"

When I looked up, I spotted a large basket containing two big bottles of orange liquid. Each bottle had a different label; there were medallions at their necks wrapped up with gold ribbons that seemed to indicate they'd placed first in some competition.

"Did someone bring you a gift?"

"Huh? Oh, yes."

It was the frank, solid color of orange juice. I picked one up, and it was so much heavier than I'd expected that I almost dropped it. The bottles themselves were high quality, and very thick. More than anything, though, I could imagine the juice's refreshing taste—a perfect balance of acidity and sweetness—just from that rich, intense color.

"Usually, people put fruit in baskets."

"Yes, um… Yes. My friend is odd, huh?"

A few books sat in a careless stack on Yuki's side table. I counted seven volumes. No matter how much free time she had, I really didn't think she could read all those books over three days in the hospital. Not when they were running tests, too.

"Were those…?"

I hadn't quite figured out how to ask when a nurse came in, pushing a wheelchair, and told us it was time for Yuki's tests.

"I'm sorry," she said. "I have to go."

Yuki stood up. On reflex, I reached out to support her shoulder, but almost no weight came to bear on my arm.

Yuki went over to the nurse, grabbed the armrests, and slowly lowered herself into the chair. The nurse bowed slightly to me, then pushed the chair away. I followed them out into the hall. In front of the elevators, Yuki looked back once and smiled, and I waved.

Once she was out of sight, I went straight to the reception desk.

"Excuse me. Do you leave baskets in the private rooms?"

"Baskets…? Do you mean as part of the service? No, we don't."

That meant Yuki's visitor had brought it. And they'd gone out of their way to pack the basket with bottles of orange juice instead of fruit.

The receptionist looked up at me blankly. After bowing to her, I returned to the hospital room.

I folded the pajamas I'd laid out and put them in the closet. Then I sat down on the edge of the bed and flopped over sideways to lie on the mattress. I caught the faint scent of the fabric softener Yuki used on the pillow and coverlet.

Just then, I heard five muted buzzes in a row. Yuki had a habit of leaving her smartphone under her pillow. I sat up, looking at the stack of books.

Another buzz. I picked one up. The topmost volume was a collection of poems by Chuuya Nakahara. *Corrugated iron's eating rice crackers / Twilight on a spring day is...* I kept reading the same line over and over, getting nowhere.

The phone buzzed a few more times. Unable to endure it, I yanked the pillow away and grabbed the smartphone as if I were snatching up a shore crab I'd found clinging to the back of a rock. It was faintly warm, and its screen showed the most recent three texts.

But that has
No additives, so
I hear it's good if you drink it hot, too.

They were all from somebody named Haru.

I tossed the smartphone onto the bed, then slumped into the chair. Dropping my head into my hands, I sank my fingers into my hair and grabbed fistfuls of it. My bangs poked the spot above my nose, prickling my forehead.

When I got home, the main lights and the lights in the kitchenette were on. Even though I knew nobody was there, I hesitated in the entryway, looking around restlessly. Then I took my shoes off as quietly as possible and shuffled silently in. I must have forgotten to turn the lights off that morning. I didn't remember it, but I'd been in a hurry, so it was definitely possible.

I checked under the bed, in the closet, and in every single space on the first floor that could conceivably count as a hiding place. Then I climbed the ladder and stepped into the loft.

It was filled with the smells of oil and ink, and with Yuki's scent.

Stooping, I picked up the canvas leaning against the wall—cover and all—to make sure there was nothing behind it. Then I set my hand on the ladder again. I could feel the chill of the iron rungs under my fingers.

Abruptly, my brain synthesized the image of a tall, clean-cut man, then kept right on expanding it. My limbs locked up, and I stopped partway down the ladder. Then I started back up.

In the loft again, my eyes went to Yuki's things, which were packed into the narrow space where the roof angled down to the floor. There was a small aqua-blue carry-on suitcase and a camping backpack. Aside from her clothes, most of her stuff was here.

I reached for the zipper on the backpack. It held oil paints and poster paints, unused palettes, fine-line pens, and varnish, plus sketchbooks and university lecture notebooks. I picked one up and opened it. It was filled with dense writing, notes on a lecture peppered with technical terms, and I couldn't make any of the information stick in my mind.

My smartphone rang. It was hard to get my hand into my pocket while I was stooped over like that. The caller was Tomomi. I let the phone ring six times, and then she gave up.

The carry-on suitcase lay on its back on the floor, secured with a combination lock. The lock was the type you could buy at stationery supply stores, the sort that had only three number wheels.

I hadn't known that Yuki locked any of her things. I pulled on the lock, but it just rattled. I let go of it for a minute.

You're just being used.

I knew that couldn't be true, and yet...

March 9th... I tried Yuki's birthday, just once, assuming it wasn't going to work. With a click, the lock released. Instantly, I felt the pit of my stomach go icy cold. I didn't even need to touch it: The combination lock fell to the floor, all by itself.

I pulled on the zipper, then lifted the top. The first thing I saw was a makeup set in the clear accessory pouch. The bag was further partitioned with an *Indiana Jones* tin we'd bought at Universal Studios during a trip that summer and a can of fried brown-sugar crackers, a souvenir from Kusatsu. Inside the can was a bankbook and a personal seal.

What was I doing?

As I was about to close the bag back up, my smartphone rang again.

"Hello?"

"Are you by yourself…?" Tomomi's voice sounded a little shrill.

"Yeah."

"Oh, good. I'd heard you were living together."

"Is this something you couldn't say if Yuki were here?"

A staticky noise like a rush of wind hissed in my ear. In the distance, I heard a voice say, *"Yoshikawa, could you go make a delivery?"*

Then I heard Tomomi inhale deeply.

"Listen, I wasn't sure whether I should tell you about this, but… Natsuki, were you with Ms. Iwato on September fourth?"

"I'm pretty sure I was."

Just then, something slipped out from the mesh netting on the underside of the suitcase top and fell to the floor. It was a bright-red envelope embossed with gold and silver foil. It had the words *Merry Christmas* written on the front, and there was a sticker in the shape of a green tree.

"It was just a coincidence, but we had a club graduation party on September fourth, and I was late starting home. I ended up hanging around the area in front of the station until the first train. And then, you know that bar near your place, the one decorated with rugby balls and things? Ms. Iwato was there, and…"

My phone vibrated. Tomomi had sent me a photo via a messaging app.

After switching the phone to speaker mode, I opened the photo.

"Of course Ms. Iwato told you about this…right?"

Two days later, Yuki was discharged from the hospital. Her consciousness wasn't impaired, and they'd found no abnormalities in her brain. She came home fresh and new, in a condition that should have delighted anyone.

7

As I was lying in bed watching late-night TV, propped up on pillows piled against the headboard, Yuki's head tilted and began to thunk lightly against my right shoulder. I glanced up at the clock; it was half past midnight. Come to think of it, she always started to get sleepy then.

"Should we turn in?" I asked.

Eyes moist beneath her creased eyelids, Yuki nodded.

Even if Dr. Amano had certified that there were no abnormalities, we were already into October. I walked Yuki to the washroom, sticking close and making sure she didn't fall.

After picking up the blue cup from our matching set, I poured water into it, soaked my toothbrush, then loaded it up with toothpaste. Yuki was reaching for her toothbrush as well, so I scooted over, toward the adjoining bathroom.

The mirror over the sink was clouded with limescale, and the bottom half was unusable. Yuki's reflected expression was hazy. What had I been doing on Christmas last year? I remembered drinking with Reiji.

I scrubbed roughly with my toothbrush, right and left, up and down.

"You shouldn't brush so hard," Yuki told me. Her bright-white mouth was wide open, and her own brush had fallen still. I rinsed with the water in my cup, and when I spat it out, there were pink swirls in it. "There, see?" she said, shooting me a reproving look.

"Why?"

"Hmm?"

"I was doing it right."

The water Yuki spat out washed the pink down the drain. She might have been trying for that on purpose. After she'd rinsed two or three times, she dried her mouth on the back of the hand towel, then turned to me. "If you do it right but go overboard, you're not still 'doing it right.'"

"That can't be true," I said. I'd spoken at a volume pretty near the upper limit allowed at night in rental housing, and my muffled voice echoed in the bathroom behind me. "I've been doing it right the whole time."

"Yes, but it's probably best not to brush until you bleed."

Yuki left the bathroom first. The second I was alone, the overhead light started blinking.

"I've been doing it right…"

The guy in the mirror glared at me.

When I left the washroom, Yuki was already lying on the bed, kicking her legs lazily into the air. The bed was against the wall, and she was lying on the front edge, so I tightrope-walked across the unsteady terrain of the mattress to get to the back, careful not to step on her slim legs.

Yuki always liked sleeping at the front. She never tried to move back.

"Good job on all the writing you did today," she said.

I'd started the morning by polishing what I'd written the day before, then added another two thousand characters. That was pretty good progress. I cradled Yuki's head and said "Thank you" right above her ear.

The night was the same as always. So was the bed. The only thing off was me, and I really wanted all of this to be paranoia. Keeping that thought hidden in the depths of my heart, I switched the overhead light to night mode, then curled up under the covers. My spine bumped into Yuki's, and I felt her flinch. At this time of year, the summer futon was still enough, but sometimes the cool night air slipped into the spaces between our pillows and backs and made me shiver.

After that, I counted in my head to keep myself awake. Once I'd counted from one to a hundred, I went back to one and started over. Sometimes static like *Is forty-one a prime number?* got mixed in. When I stopped counting, I started plotting my novel.

I breathed in and out as naturally as possible, trying to keep my shoulders from tensing. I'd recorded myself sleeping and listened to the audio, so I knew what I should sound like, and I think I faked it well. I didn't just breathe evenly; I took a deep breath here and there, and sometimes I groaned a little.

The whole time I did this, I was listening to Yuki breathe next to me. The way she slept made her seem very content. Sometimes she'd roll over or cling to my back. The thought that Yuki was next to me always let me sleep more soundly than I ever managed on my own. I never woke up at weird, in-between times when she was there. That was how reassuring her warmth was to me.

What am I doing?
This is ridiculous…

One hour passed, or maybe it was two. Yuki had been clinging to me, one hand on my neck, the other on the small of my back. She rolled over again, and abruptly, the soft murmur of her breathing fell silent. Slowly, I felt something move across the bed.

There was a slight tug on the coverlet, as if a cat had crept out. The gap behind my back gradually widened, letting in more air.

Then, like some kind of magnificent jailbreak, Yuki was out on the side of the room with the entryway. A ninja couldn't have managed it more efficiently.

I could hear her feet pad away, sticking to the floor slightly. Swallowing down the call that threatened to spill out of my throat, I poured all my focus into my ears.

Her footsteps receded, and then there was a creak. That was definitely the closet opening; that door stuck a bit. The sound of rustling fabric went on for a while, and then I heard another creak.

The *click* of a door opening and closing, as muffled as possible, finished up the sequence.

With a brain that was suddenly wide awake, I thought.

My heart was throbbing violently. Pressing a hand over it, I curled up under the covers. I hugged my knees, trying to be as small as possible. I counted from one to a hundred, went back to one, and counted up again. The whole time, I was waiting for the hands of the clock above my head to crawl forward.

If she'd gone to the closest convenience store to buy something, it would take her only ten minutes. When I was sure that much time had passed, I threw off the covers, stood up, and used my smartphone to light up the hall. The closet door stood half-open. Inside, Yuki's pajamas were folded up neatly, still warm.

"Yuki…," I said to the night that had infiltrated every corner of the apartment. Finally, I opened the front door, barefoot. The moonlight slipped in, and I shut it immediately. She'd been wearing her favorite beige pumps during the day, so I realized right away that they were the ones missing.

For a while, I gazed at the darkness in a daze. Then I got my key and went outside. I locked up, put the key in the rear pocket of my tracksuit, and sat down on the stone steps outside the front door. Then I slumped over sideways and waited for time to pass.

Someone was shaking my shoulder. I could hear a voice, too. I'd been dreaming that Yuki was missing, and I was searching for her. The dream had ended with me being questioned by two detectives in an underground bar that was covered with graffiti.

"Excuse me."

I opened one eye. Pale light crept in, so I covered my head with an arm. I saw a human figure in the light. "Yuki…"

"Huh?"

By the time I could tell that the voice belonged to an elderly woman, the silhouette had cleared up—it was dumpy and pear-shaped.

"Hey. Hey, son."

The shaking got more intense.

Ignoring my weak protest, the woman raised her voice. "You can't sleep here. I really don't think the residents of 104 would appreciate it."

"Oh, one-oh-four… That's my apartment."

"What, it is? I'm sorry; I'm new. We can't have this, though. If word gets around that people are sleeping in front of the apartments, the owner will yell at me, and I only just got this job."

"I see. That wouldn't be good, huh?"

When I stood up, unbelievably sharp pain shot through the back of my head, plus the shoulder and hip that had been against the ground. My back popped and cracked with a noise like countless small twigs snapping.

I arched my spine, releasing a huge yawn. That raised my line of sight over the manager's head, and all of a sudden, I saw Yuki standing there, frozen.

I felt just a little triumphant. But her eye-catching appearance—that bright-red dress and the white cardigan—left me speechless.

Yuki started to say something.

"Save it." I thrust out my palm, cutting her off.

The manager looked from me to Yuki and back. "Well, be careful, all right?" she said, and she walked away.

Yuki's eyes were skimming the area around our front door, around and around, with the blazing morning sun behind her. In my pocket, I gripped my smartphone. Behind Yuki, two bicycles whirred past.

I heard the click of a door closing: The upstairs resident had left their apartment. Next, footsteps crossed the iron deck above me. Particles of rust sifted down over my arms.

"Welcome back," I said, lowering my hand. Tension had made my expression icy, but it softened a bit, and the muscles around my eyes relaxed. "Let's talk inside."

I took the key out of my rear pocket and went in first. While I rinsed out my gritty mouth in the washroom, Yuki removed her shoes in the entryway. As I left, she stepped in to take my place. Then I sat down at my desk, and she took a seat on the edge of the bed.

"Let me explain," she said.

"Explain what?"

"Well, what just happened."

"What do you mean, 'what just happened'?"

The blue tarp was hanging down from the edge of the loft, falling over the clock. I'd moved the ladder, so now my desk was partially under it. Yuki was looking down, and I tried to make out her expression through the ladder's rungs.

"I'm the one who's going to explain," I told her, as if I were handing down a death sentence. I took the red envelope out of the second drawer of my desk and tossed it over to the bed where Yuki sat. It spun like a throwing star, then stopped vertically, one corner stuck into the bedclothes.

"I found that. It was in your stuff. Inside the carry-on bag. Don't worry; I didn't read it. The name of the guy who sent it really concerned me, though."

"The thing is—"

"Haruto Oujiro. He's your ex, isn't he?"

"Yes...but..."

"Look at the date," I told Yuki, attacking while she was already down. She was hanging her head, looking as if she was about to cry. "Look at the date!"

"I did..."

"Read it out loud."

"December twenty-fifth, 2019."

"That's last year."

That year had been my second winter.

How many winters had it been for Haruto?

"Did he come?"

"Yes, he did… But there's nothing like what you're thinking, Natsuki!"

"I would really rather have heard that before I saw you come back home from spending the night somewhere else."

Yuki glanced down at her cleavage, then wrapped the coverlet around herself as if she was embarrassed. The red Christmas card flew through the air and fell somewhere behind the furniture.

"One more thing," I said. "I need to tell you what I found out. Yuki, I've got this friend, Tomomi. She's the little sister of Haruto Oujiro, the guy you drove crazy. She was worried about me, so she sent this over, though it sounded like she was really hesitant to do it."

My smartphone was hot. I took it out of my pocket, opened the image file, and shoved it at Yuki. I could see the circles in her dark eyes shrink down tight, transforming into tiny points. She was even holding her breath. I could probably have heard her heartbeat.

"That's you in the photo, isn't it?"

"Yes, but…"

"And you're with two men. It looks like you're drinking with them."

"It wasn't that sort of—"

"That's not what I'm talking about."

I gritted my teeth, my forehead twisting. Not looking at her made me uneasy, but looking hurt. Gradually, the girl in front of me no longer seemed like Yuki Iwato, but someone else entirely.

"Please listen," she said.

"No, you're the one who's going to listen," I yelled, and I hurled the phone. It put a small hole in the wall, and the phone's screen cracked. For good measure, I slammed my palm onto the desk. I wasn't demonstrating that I was mad. I'd used that dirty hand to shove proof at her and threaten her, and I wanted to get rid of it right this minute.

"I'm a real idiot, aren't I?"

Actually, I didn't need any of my limbs. I couldn't forgive myself for thinking that meeting her had been a miracle. I wanted to get rid of everything that made me "me."

"What exactly do you think it feels like for me while I'm waiting? Those four months when you're not here. It feels like holding my breath in the desert. Seriously. Ever since I decided to face this with you, I've tried to do it right. I always thought I had to be practical, to keep it together."

"I swear, Natsuki, I haven't done anything to betray you!"

For a moment, I thought, *That might actually be true.*

With a hiss, that thought melted on the hot steel plate of my heart, like fleeting snow.

"But in the winter, you leave me behind!"

When I yelled that, Yuki's face abruptly went calm, all its confusion evaporating. Her eyebrows, which had risen with worry, went completely flat, resting quietly above her large eyes. Her cheeks hollowed a little, and I glimpsed darkness between her slightly open lips. It was as if her emotions had retreated to some distant place.

"If we stay together, no matter how happy we are, again and again, you'll leave me behind in the winter. How am I supposed to breathe when you're gone?"

All that was left in Yuki's emotionless face was an emptiness so vast she hardly seemed human anymore.

Even so, I kept pushing her.

"Those four months without you hurt. You can sleep just fine when you're alone, though. You leave me here, and you sleep like a rock on your own!"

My voice thundered through the room. As I stood there motionless, Yuki passed me like the wind. She ran up the ladder, taking it three rungs at a time, and dropped the blue carry-on bag down. Then she dashed past me again, not caring how she looked.

We seemed to repel each other like magnets. Without turning around, I listened to her fling the door open behind me. Then I collapsed into the chair, put my feet up on the desk, and crossed my legs.

8

The skin of my back was so tight it hurt. When I raised my head, there was a tense, creaking noise from the nape of my neck. My right arm was numb and prickly, and my shoulders were unnaturally cold.

I'd been dreaming.

I could barely remember any of it, but in the dream, I'd been much older than I was now, caring for a woman who lay in bed, asleep. Day after day, I changed her IV drip, wiped her body with warm wet cloths, and changed her clothes. She never woke.

I shivered. When I got up from the chair, my butt smarted and stung. On creaking legs, I tottered over to the bed and fell onto it. The window glared with broad daylight, and I set the shutter to lower and closed my eyes, planning to go back to sleep.

Vrrrrr. A sound approached from overhead, little by little, descending to the height of the bed. As it did, the room gradually sank into darkness. I didn't need the morning sun. Night could stay forever.

My ears rang, but I told myself it was because of the shutter. Something was smoldering in the depths of my eyes, and I clenched the muscles around them, forcing my eyelids to stay closed. I smelled something moldy, and my eyes came open.

When I woke up my smartphone, there was a message from Yuki. I meant to ignore it, but my fingers were numb and clumsy, and I accidentally opened the chat.

Natsuki,
I know I'm selfish. Thank you for staying with me this long.
When I met you, I started to think life might be worth something after all.
I guess it was still too soon for me, though. I've decided to quit school.
I'll leave here by the end of the day.

Yuki Iwato

"'Thank you,' she says. Don't give me that. Could she get any more self-centered?" I griped out loud. I wasn't talking to anybody, just to the dark ceiling. The more I ran Yuki Iwato down, the less I wanted to break stuff, and the calmer I felt.

She should just commit a crime or something.

I turned on the lights and went to the entryway to get a garbage bag. I pulled out the biggest size we had—the ninety-liter type—took it up to the loft and started stuffing all of Yuki's things into it. Her backpack, her sketchbooks, her half-dried paint cups, her easel… I went clear across the loft, from one side to the other, tossing in everything I could grab.

Finally, all that was left were the blue tarp, a big blue cushion, and that huge canvas under its cover. I could put the cushion into a different bag, but the canvas was wood and cloth. Did that make it recyclable waste?

My grip on the garbage bag loosened. A palette spotted with purple, black, and navy blue tumbled out, and I sucked in a lungful of the stink of oil and paint thinner, like poisonous gas. When I tried to put the palette back in the bag, thick black oil paint clung to the hem of my white shirt. Once, when I'd gone to Yuki's department to pick her up, I'd seen her busily running around in brown coveralls splotched all over with paint in every color of the rainbow.

I shook my head.

The canvas stood vertically, so it came up almost to my chest. I remembered discussing how to get it up into the loft with Yuki at a neighborhood café, almost half a year ago. I'd gotten black coffee; she'd had cocoa with whipped cream. We'd put together a detailed plan, bought cargo rope at the home center, tied the rope over the cover, and tried to hoist it up. The rope had caught on the edge of the loft, though, and we'd gotten it only twenty centimeters off the floor.

In the end, we'd had to slide it up the ladder. Even then, both my hands had been chafed raw, and we'd dinged up the loft railing a bit.

When I looked down at my hands, the pain came back to me, and I squeezed them into fists.

She'd bought that canvas at the Sekaido art supply store, intending to submit it to a big contest someday.

She'd never told me anything about the picture she was painting on it.

I touched the cover. The fabric was rough under my fingertips. As I let them glide over the hard frame, they hit a few splinters, and one that was thicker than the rest jabbed me. Red pigment dripped down.

"What, 'Don't touch me'?"

I retracted my hand, but then touched it again.

"I don't want to touch you, either."

The canvas clung heavily to that space. Looking at it made it impossible to stop the voice welling up inside me.

Yuki's lack of motivation had been reassuring to me.

"It wasn't that I didn't know about her work. I just never tried to find out. I was relieved that she wasn't trying, because it meant I could see her as less than me."

Yuki Iwato had always been out of reach. When we'd started dating, even when we'd moved in together, I'd always felt like I wasn't a good match for her somehow.

What joker had said *I'd like us to make all our decisions together, as a team?* I'd only said things that would help me out, and only when they were convenient.

Deep down, I'd just wanted to be her equal. That was why I'd wanted her to stay careless. Not only that, but I'd been trying to use her apathy to cancel out my own wretchedness.

"I suck."

I forced a good, solid laugh, then ripped off the bag-shaped cover.

It was a portrait.

The background was jet-black, like the darkness at the deepest part of the night. The landscape was dreary, without a single star in the sky. In its midst stood a figure cloaked in murky light, wearing a simple traditional Japanese outfit.

Something crept up my spine, and the underside of my chin prickled as though a bug were crawling over it.

I was 172 centimeters tall. That made this an accurate half-scale portrait of Natsuki Uzume. Looking at my own face in the mirror weirded me out, but the face in the painting, while it certainly wasn't handsome, didn't upset me.

When had she drawn this?

That question was what started it.

After all, she spent most of the time I was home lying on the bed gaming or watching videos or listening to music.

I'd thought the art supplies she'd brought in here were just to augment her work hours at school. In fact, I'd seen her several times sketching on smaller canvases she'd brought home in a tote bag. This canvas was too big to take to school easily, though. Especially if she was in the middle of painting it.

The sensation was like an oncoming sneeze that didn't happen. Like knowing where the itch was, but not being able to reach it.

I climbed down the ladder and paced around the apartment, eventually extending my route to include the entryway.

The gray cockpit of the *Millennium Falcon* was looking at me.

Sensing something, I went closer.

A small Lego brick sat beside it, sticky and covered with dust. It was the piece that had once detonated under my foot like a land mine.

For some reason, it seemed as though it shouldn't be here.

I picked up the block and tried to return it to the spaceship—but there was no place to put it. The only cream bricks were around the pilot's seat, inside the cockpit. However, once I'd built the *Falcon*, I'd never taken it apart.

There really have been a lot of earthquakes lately, huh.
You think the world might end on us?

Yuki had said that as soon as I turned on the TV. What if we'd had an earthquake the previous night? What if the spaceship had fallen and broken apart, and she'd fixed it, but she'd overlooked that one brick and left it on the floor?

It hadn't just been that night. Yuki was always up earlier than I was. Every single morning. The earlier in the day, the more affectionate she was, and she never got tired of making big breakfasts.

"Yuki Iwato, you…"

When I'd met her, I hadn't been able to process what I was seeing. In my attempts to understand it, I'd organized my thoughts around the term *hibernation*. But now that I thought about it, no one else had ever used that word.

"She wasn't hibernating. She was…"

I put a hand on the wall and pressed my other hand to my temple. The smell of oil hanging in the air was making me dizzy. The fact that Yuki had been here just a little while ago, and that now she was gone, made my arms shake.

Why had I simply decided it was hibernation?

Had I been struggling to understand something incomprehensible and thought that would get me closer to it?

"That was her normal, wasn't it?"

As if in answer, the apartment creaked.

"Then what is this painting? Was she working on it the whole time I was asleep? And she hid it from me? Why? Why would she do a thing like that? Why—?"

I gripped the canvas's splintered frame, and my fingers brushed something powdery. I hadn't noticed when the cover was on it, but when I looked, my fingertips were smudged with something that looked like red chalk.

I turned the canvas over, and I found it.

When the world around me grows cold, my body starts down a dusky street. Traveling as I'm led, I'll dance with the streetlights and play with the night wind. In this solitary, isolated place, until morning comes, I'll offer a ceaseless prayer shaped like my breath.

I'm waiting to wake up.

In order to wake up, I leave on a little journey, taking only myself.

It was written on the back of the canvas, in several lines of what was clearly Yuki's handwriting: a song of lonely nights spent wandering in order to awaken.

The words had been here all along. Here in this apartment, the whole time. I just hadn't noticed.

"Yuki…," I called, but she wasn't here.

Yuki Iwato wasn't in this house anymore.

She'd disappeared from my life. I'd erased her.

All because of a stupid misunderstanding.

I jumped down from the loft without bothering to use the ladder. The bed sank under me with an unpleasant groan, and I tumbled off and hit the floor on my feet. I snatched up the first coat I saw, then left the house with only my wallet.

I called her phone, but it didn't go through. The announcement I got instead wasn't one I'd ever heard before. I tried over and over, but the results were the same. I leaned against some railing, trying every social media account she had, but none of them worked.

Just inside the gate that opened onto the street, the apartment manager was talking with a man in work clothes. She shot me a probing look through the space between the man's neck and shoulder.

Managing to calm down a little, I searched my contacts. She'd told me I wasn't allowed to call her, but this was my best available option. I hit the call button as though saying a prayer.

It took ten rings. Just when I was about to give up, a "00:00" call time appeared on the display.

All I could hear was a noise like blowing wind right by my ear. *Ffhooo, ffhooo...* It was the sound of someone breathing.

"Oh, thank goodness. Fuyumi. Thank you."

Fuyumi was definitely there. The fact that the call time kept counting up the seconds was proof.

"Yuki left home—I mean, I was stupid and chased her out."

"......"

"Has she told you where she is?!"

Fuyumi sighed. Her breath blew over the mic, making a noise like a sandstorm.

"I wasn't sure whether I should even answer this call."

"But you did." My smartphone had grown hot, and I squeezed it, pressing it to my ear. "I have no idea where Yuki's gone, but if I don't look for her, it feels like I'll never see her again."

Fuyumi just listened to me impassively. She loved her big sister, so she was sure to be worried after hearing she left, unless...

"Fuyumi... Do you know?"

"......"

I cursed my own foolishness. She was family. Of course she knew. She also knew I hadn't been able to believe Yuki, and that I'd never picked up on her biggest secret.

"The Hikari 599, departing at eleven thirty-two."

"Huh?!"

"If you're calling from home, I'd give up."

"Wait."

"But if you're even one step outside your house…"

"Fuyumi, you're—"

"Then hang up the phone and start running, you stalker bastard!"

A discordant noise echoed in my ear: She'd ended the call.

I tumbled out into the road with my coat half-on. After that I just sprinted. I already knew the shortest route to Meidaimae Station.

Just as I was about to hit the main road, I heard a car rev its engine behind me, and I whipped around on instinct. "Geez, what?!"

I saw an *L* logo on a wide front grille. A silver Lexus was rapidly closing in on me, and I hastily plastered myself against the stone wall like a crab.

I'd never seen a car slide like that up close before. The Lexus slammed on its brakes near my apartment, then skidded ten meters or so before coming to a stop a little ahead of me. In the distance, I saw the manager and the man in work clothes stick their heads out of the gate, stunned.

The glossy door opened, nearly connecting with the wall. Out stepped a figure in a deep-black overcoat and sunglasses, dressed like one of the Men in Black—although judging by the high heels, it was probably a woman.

"Get in!"

"Huh?!"

The woman shouting at me had short hair and ruby lips. I had no idea what was going on, and I closed the distance warily, one step at a time.

Impatiently, she tore off her sunglasses. A cold wind blew through, carrying the smell of decay and dead leaves, and fanned out the tail of the woman's long coat.

"Ms. Shimoki?!"

The heels she was wearing made her a head taller than I was, but that commanding expression couldn't have belonged to anyone else.

"What are you doing here?" I asked.

"You're in a hurry, aren't you? Get in. Then we can talk."

Her gaze, like a straight sword, pierced through my confused thoughts. "Okay," I said simply.

Ena returned to the driver's seat, then moved a manila envelope from the passenger seat to the back. I could see a manuscript peeking out; it was marked up with red pen and fastened with a big silver clip. The moment I shut the door, Ms. Shimoki released the side brake, put the car in gear, and stomped on the accelerator.

Steering fearlessly, she sped us down the narrow, winding lane and onto the main road. The GPS already showed a blue line on the map with a flag at our destination.

"Destination… Tokyo Station? Why…?"

The car swung right, pitching me to the left. Though this was technically a main road, this whole area was a student neighborhood dotted with institutions like Meiji University. Cars were invariably stopped in front of the convenience stores, and cargo trucks blocked the roads nearly every day.

"Because Yuki's going home to Nagoya. Or I suppose saying 'She's attempting to go home' would leave you a bit of hope."

"How did you know?"

"Oh, I know everything. 'Knowing' is all I do, though. In the end, I'm a coward who was unable to act. More importantly, your seatbelt isn't fastened all the way."

When I glanced at the instrument panel, I noticed a red alert to one side. I unfastened my seatbelt, then refastened it with a click.

I took another look around the car's neat interior. I could smell the classy scent of leather from the seats. It smelled like a car in its natural state, without the intrusion of an air freshener. On the steering wheel, Ena's hands were sheathed in fingerless gloves. She looked as if she'd been born for this, although part of that could have been the sunglasses.

"So you can drive, huh?"

"I've discovered that my job is going to require transportation. I just got my license last month."

"Huh?!" I shouted, unconsciously leaning forward. The seatbelt went tight around my chest, yanking me back against the seat.

"There's no cause for alarm. I come from a farming family in Akita. My granddad was the union president, and he often had me drive tractors when I was a child."

I could see her deep-black eyes through the side of her sunglasses. Their expression softened slightly—maybe she was homesick.

"I see… But why did you bring the car to—?"

"No matter how well you navigate public transportation, the trip would take you thirty-four minutes at the very least, and that's only from station to station. If you drive, you can get there in sixteen minutes. That difference is crucial."

"No, I meant why did you bring the car to my place?"

Just then, the signal up ahead turned red, and the car slowed. As it shifted from motion to stillness, Ena's all-black upper body and short hair swayed forward and back slightly.

"You sure ask a lot of questions, and this is hardly the time. Why not just accept everything? Or rather, you must. If you don't, you'll never manage to bring her back."

Truck after truck cut across the complicated intersection. It was hemmed in by skyscrapers on all sides, and above those, a huge construction crane was slowly turning its head.

"I was contacted."

"By Yuki?"

"No, her little sister. It was about two hours ago. She said Yuki had made up her mind to go home. However, she hadn't notified me. It was patently odd."

"So you knew how to get in touch with her."

"Yes. I knew…"

The GPS issued directions in a mechanical voice, and the car started moving again. Ena changed lanes with a smoothness that seemed unthinkable for a beginner, and her sunglasses gleamed darkly.

"There once was a student." She spoke in a beautiful alto, as if she were reciting the opening lines of a play. "An inconsequential thing who'd failed to reinvent herself in college. When that student met Yuki, the image of herself that she'd believed in was shattered; she's liked Yuki ever since. The student would have done anything for her, and so she kept Yuki company in whatever she wanted to do. Then, eventually, she went to her house."

I forgot the stifling sensation of the seatbelt and, instead, clung to the bundle of black fibers as if it were a lifeline.

"However, someone had beaten her there. It was a man whose heart Yuki had stolen, like the student's. A man who hadn't been able to give Yuki her true spring. His feelings for her were even stronger than the student's, and so the student chose to withdraw."

With terrifying speed, the top of the windshield swallowed a yellow signal. We were already going twenty kilometers per hour over the speed limit.

"So, um, this student…"

"And so she decided to be her friend. Even if it meant casting her own longing aside, it seemed like the best alternative. She was a coward. And so—I know. I know everything."

"Then you knew about 'that,' too?"

"The fact that Yuki doesn't sleep at night, you mean?"

Ena's response made the glowing embers of my regret blaze up with a roar. That large canvas. The early mornings, the breakfasts. Where the Lego block had come from. And that photo from the sports bar Tomomi had sent me, of her drinking with male customers. All those things had pointed to it.

As a rule, Yuki Iwato didn't sleep. It wasn't that she woke up early. She wasn't a night owl. She never slept a wink. It was a second unique trait for the girl who was fated to sleep all winter.

No, that wasn't right.

It wasn't a second trait. It was the flip side of her winter slumber.

In other words, anytime I'd seen her sleep during the rest of the year, she'd only been pretending.

"It's such a curious thing. They say people spend a third of their lives asleep. Yuki sleeps all winter, so during every other season, she never does. Or rather, she can't. However, she's merely sleeping that third of her year all at once. That's why she only sleeps for four months. On the whole, it's a dreadfully normal cycle."

"Dammit…"

Words welled up inside me, bringing stomach acid with them, then seemed to stick in my throat like needles.

Normal.

Yuki had always lived in a way that was normal for her. It was just that the university, and human relationships, and society—all the concepts that served to frame people's lives—had concluded that her normal was abnormal.

"I can't forgive the guys at school who talk smack about Yuki, or the people who arbitrarily get things wrong and stereotype her, or the doctors who can't put a name to her illness—but most of all, I can't forgive myself. I helped her decide she was abnormal. I saw her symptoms, arbitrarily called them 'hibernation,' deluded myself into thinking I knew what I was talking about, and said I'd protect her just to make myself feel good. I'm hopeless."

"Don't blame yourself," Ena said, twisting the wheel sharply. "It's the most pointless thing you could possibly do. It creates nothing."

"But—"

"In your case, realization came late. Not too late, however. There's still something you can do, and I'm here to help you do it."

"Why are you helping me, Ms. Shimoki?"

As a third-year in college who still hadn't gotten my driver's license, I found her dignified profile the most reassuring thing in the world.

"That's a good question. Even I couldn't say. Yuki did need you, though. Having been betrayed over and over, she keeps a certain distance between herself and others so she won't be hurt again, and yet she tried to believe in you. I'm sure you're her last partner."

"Her last...?"

"She's planning to give up on everything. Her paintings, university, even connecting with society. Whether that decision is right or wrong isn't the issue. If she goes home, that's it: She'll never come back to Tokyo."

Twenty-two minutes later.

Dump trucks and steamrollers were stopped in front of the imperial palace for a road maintenance project. Their bulky yellow shapes had closed off the southbound route as well; cars were being forced to pull U-turns, and traffic was piling up. Ena told me to run, before the cars in front started to move. It was 11:20. I eased the door open and forced my way out under the October sky.

Between its four rows of ginkgo trees, Gyoko-dori Avenue was carpeted with spent crimson leaves. One block down, I saw a red brick building.

It was Tokyo Station, looking just as it had a hundred years ago.

Close to ten years earlier, a ceremony had been held to celebrate the station's completed restoration, and the building had been illuminated with countless small lights. I remembered seeing it with my mother.

In my head, I chanted, *It's going to be fine. There's no problem. As long as you see her, it'll be fine.*

My phone and wallet bounced in my trouser pockets. I got winded and had to slow down. Still, whatever else I did, I knew I couldn't stop. No matter how much speed I lost, I kept running.

My coat got in the way, so I ripped it off and hugged it to my chest with one arm. I couldn't wait for the cold air to fill my lungs.

I reached the Marunouchi south gate. As I ran through the arcade at full tilt, the ticket gate area with its dome-shaped ceiling came into view. People were coming and going every which way, as if this were an obstacle course.

Turning myself into an invertebrate, I dodged and wove, pressing forward, until finally I pushed my smartphone against the reader and passed through the ticket gate.

Overhead, an electronic signboard displayed the names and arrival times of inbound trains. At the very top of the list, in red letters, was HIKARI 599, 11:32, BOUND FOR SHIN-OSAKA.

I woke up my smartphone. The time had just switched from 11:28 to 11:29.

I headed down the south corridor, hung a left, and made for the middle of the concourse. The Nagoya-bound Tokaido-Sanyo line was at the south transfer gate. Last October, to make sure Yuki's trip home went safely, I'd drummed the map of Tokyo Station into my head, all the way down to the fourth basement floor.

By the time I got to the transfer gate, the time on my phone read 11:30. In my head, I could hear clock hands ticking away. Sweat broke out on my palms, making the phone's screen slick.

When I pressed my right hand to my chest, my heart was pounding fit to break; it didn't usually get worked this hard. Down the corridor and up the stairs, on a platform swarming with people, I had to find just one person. She'd probably gone back to her boardinghouse before coming to the station, and I couldn't even guess what she'd be wearing now.

All the hair on my body stood on end.

The ticket barrier up ahead seemed to be conspiring to keep me from getting any closer to Yuki. I didn't know how else to describe it.

"It's no use."

Everything had been too late. Going any farther was...pointless.

9

I was in the basement Gransta mall at Tokyo Station.

An hour ago, I'd put anything in the fridge that seemed remotely perishable out as burnable trash, packed the bare necessities in my carry-on bag, and left my boardinghouse. By the time I'd reached Tokyo Station, my heart was set.

I felt a little sick, but I hadn't eaten anything since the night before, so I didn't have much choice: I went to Starbucks and ordered an orange-ginger tea and a grilled tuna sandwich. The chic, bitter-brown interior of the café teemed with cross-legged businessmen typing away on their computers, and with girls in neat, tidy clothes that showed a generous amount of skin. I really didn't belong there.

I slid my garbage into the trash, then left the café. At that point, warm air seized me and told me where I needed to go.

Four years ago, this place had seemed like a labyrinth to me, but now I could walk through it fearlessly. I'd made five trips to and from here. I didn't think it had all been a waste. This time last year, Natsuki had shown me around Tokyo Station. He hadn't had the map down at all, though, and we'd both gotten lost. He always tried hard, but sometimes he ended up bluffing.

I inserted my ticket and passed through the gate.

Leaning against the tiled wall beside the Kiosk store, I opened the very top contact in my phone's list.

She picked up before the second ring.

"Hello?"

On the other end of the line, I could hear my mom's anxious breathing. Almost immediately, she said *"Yuki"* in a gentle voice. Then, *"Are you all right?"*

"Yes."

"What you told me earlier was true?"

"Yes, it's true."

Office workers came and went, buying bento boxes and cans of beer, then dashing onto express bullet trains as if racing against the clock. I was sure society existed for people like them.

I shielded my mouth with a hand. "I'm sorry; I know this is sudden. I couldn't do it."

"Mm-hmm." My mom's voice held a warmth that was different from usual.

"So I'm coming home."

"All right. Come on back. That's what family is for. You've made up your mind, haven't you?"

"It's not really about making up my mind, though."

"Yes, I suppose you're right. Still, he did face you in earnest, didn't he?"

Leaning against the wall was making my back and butt go prickly and numb. My heels were bearing all my weight, and they were slowly starting to hurt. I didn't want to go up to the platform yet, though.

"I think he did. Face me, in earnest. But you see..."

"It's all right, Yuki."

"Uh-huh... Of course, there were a few misunderstandings, but...I think he decided we should break up because he'd faced me squarely."

"Mm-hmm."

Who knew putting words together was so hard? I'd forgotten this feeling ages ago. Back in middle school, the first time a boy confessed to me, I was genuinely happy. And yet, I suspected we might both be attempting something we couldn't handle. When we finally broke up, behind the unending sadness, there was always a wavering sense of resignation: *I knew it would be like this.*

"I...I haven't... There's so much I haven't...told Natsuki yet... Oh, that's no good; I know I can't be like this."

Wiping my eyes roughly on my sleeve, I shook my head. I was desperate to keep the sobs from escaping my throat. It felt a little like struggling not to throw up.

I heard a rustle from the speaker.

"Yuki, listen." The noise went on for a while, and then there was a *clunk*, and it fell silent. *"Did you tell him about...you know?"*

"......"

The footsteps and voices of the people passing through the station, the souvenir shops calling to attract customers, the noise of arriving bullet trains—all of that vanished, leaving only my mom and me. After a little while, my mother murmured, *"Yes, I see, I see... You weren't able to tell him, were you?"*

I choked again and again. It took a very long time to get my next sentence out.

No. In the end, I wasn't able to tell him.

Even though it was the first thing I should have explained.

"Natsuki is...you know. He's nice. If I told him the truth, I'm sure he wouldn't have been able to sleep at night anymore. He'd try to...stay awake, all the time, and then..."

"You thought he might start hating you."

"He works really hard. He's the type who'd sacrifice himself. If I'd caused any more trouble for him, we'd never have been able to build an equal relationship."

No—

In the depths of my heart, I knew that was an ugly excuse.

We'd decided to talk everything over, to think about it together, and yet I'd held this in and ruined things for myself. I hadn't been able to say it, simply because I was a coward.

And now here I was, still trying to make that Natsuki's fault.

"It's hard, isn't it? Accepting it is frightening. It scares me, too. I'm the one who had the hardest time admitting you weren't normal. I'm sorry." My mom's voice cracked. *"Yuki, I'm sorry. I'm so sorry."*

She apologized again and again. Her crushed voice gradually grew watery and tearful, and I began to hear sniffling as well.

"No, Mom, it's not your fault… It's not Dad's, either. In the end, it's me. It's all my fault. I was waiting for Natsuki to ask about this. I couldn't bring it up myself, so I made it his problem."

I wouldn't cry anymore. The moment I made that silent vow, I got an intense flashback of that night in Nagoya last spring. The warmth of his right hand as he'd taken mine. The solitary ray of light that had lanced into my endless, lonely nights… His persevering smile had been almost too dazzling, and I'd imagined a future where he'd pull me along forever.

From the moment he'd said he would protect me, my heart had been protected.

I was the one who'd thrown that future away.

"I…betrayed him. I was working a part-time job at night, and I didn't tell him. I didn't mention I was corresponding with Haruto, either—"

In the past, my whole family had rejected Haruto. Two years ago, I'd begun getting letters from him. He said he'd started going to a trade school and apologized for having forced his feelings on me.

That was wrong. He hadn't done a thing to me that required an apology. And so I'd had to respond. I was atoning for the mistake we'd made together.

If I'd told Natsuki about all of this, he might have understood. In the end, I'd been afraid—that was all. I'd wanted to look good in front of him.

And now, he'd found out all on his own. At this point, the whole business was just a bunch of ugly excuses.

"When you said you were going to work a part-time job at night so you could pay your own medical expenses, I was against it. I didn't think it was wise to let my daughter work alone at night, even if it was at a sports bar. But now, everything you do to help keep yourself focused on the future makes me proud."

Maybe my mom had changed a little. Come to think of it, she was the one who'd named my sister Fuyumi, meaning "someone who's beautiful without reason." I was the only one who'd been warped. I hadn't changed, and the results were no more than I deserved.

"You did well. It's all right. Your dad and I are here. Come home, Yuki."

At the sound of an announcement, I looked up at the electronic sign. My blurry eyes picked up the word HIKARI in red letters.

"I'll see you soon, Mom. The train's almost here."

"Be careful on your way back."

"I will. Thanks."

I ended the call, then slid down the wall into a crouch. Burying my face between my knees, I let my sobs escape into the gap. Once I could hear the sound of my own heart, I got to my feet again.

A shot of air skimmed past right in front of me, blowing away the residual tears that had pooled in the corners of my eyes. A memory of my fall at Shinjuku Station skimmed through my mind, and I stepped back a little from the white line near the edge of the tracks.

Countless windows with countless people behind them. Their figures flowed past me from right to left, too fast for my eyes to register, and every one of them seemed to be criticizing me for being a despicable person. People left the smoking booth and got up from the waiting room benches to form a line behind me. When I took a step forward, the person behind me did, too. I circled around to the very back of the line, then leaned against a vending machine.

The white-and-blue bullet train gradually slowed, then stopped completely, sounding an alert. People with lots of luggage disembarked in fits and starts. Once they'd thinned out, office workers in overcoats and old men with backpacks started entering car 14 as if they were racing each other. They were followed by a group of high school girls in sportswear who carried racket cases on their backs, and a family with seven kids.

A rectangular door, like a section expertly carved out from the fabric of society, inhaled people, refilling the cars that had just emptied. I glanced down at my ticket. Car 14, seat 14C. Since I'd bought it at the last minute, I'd only been able to get the aisle seat in a three-seat row.

As I stood there, travelers jogged past me on both sides.

I took one step forward, then another. That brought me to the bumpy yellow tactile paving. Out of the corner of my eye, I caught sight of a man in a grungy knit cap having trouble finding the right coins at the little shop on the platform. A woman in a Gothic Lolita outfit stood behind him, stern-faced, hugging her shoulders and shivering.

Why had I come to this city in the first place?

Was there a dream I'd wanted so badly to chase that I'd simply had to go to a university that would let me paint?

This place was dirty, noisy, and cold. There wasn't a single good thing about it.

The Gothic Lolita woman hurried toward the bullet train. A station employee had begun performing the preliminary safety checks.

"I'm getting on!" I shouted, raising my hand.

The employee's eyebrows arched dramatically. He came over and set his thick white-gloved hand on my back, pressuring me very slightly. "Hurry up, then. The train's departing soon."

"I know. I'll hurry."

I pushed in the handle of my carry-on bag, then turned it so I could hold it by the side strap. It was light. I'd had no idea my life weighed so little.

Wait!

A voice called from behind me, gently embracing me, holding me in place. It wouldn't let me go one step farther. I'd known this was how it would be, really. I just didn't know what face to wear.

The station employee's eyes had gone wide. I gave myself the space of a breath to rearrange my expression. Wearing as much of a smile as I could manage, I turned back.

"Wait! That one's going to Osaka. We're headed the other way."

At the sound of a big man's voice, a woman stopped. She looked from her ticket to the bullet train, then turned around and ran back to the man, laughing to hide her embarrassment.

I'm such a fool.

Of course I wouldn't hear that word.

The man and woman who'd been involved in mere seconds of my life walked away. I could hear a murmuring noise like the rain, and then there was nothing but the bustling currents of people, flowing left and right.

My ears rang, and I twisted to face forward. The train's departure melody urged me on.

The staff member gave some sort of sign, and the closing doors opened again. He pushed my back, harder this time. To get away from that pressure, I stepped forward.

It was just a few steps—much shorter than I'd thought.

It would be easy, as long as I didn't turn back.

"It's fine now. I'm getting on."

The staff member nodded with a smile, then stepped away from me. Through the gap between the train and the platform, I saw a sliver of track and the slightly spinning wheels. Just as I began to step up, the gentle alert that signaled a station announcement played above my head.

"Attention, all passengers. This is a lost-child alert. The child is a thirteen-year-old girl wearing cayenne pepper–colored clothing, and her name is—"

What color was cayenne pepper? And a thirteen-year-old girl, huh? That was the age Fuyumi had been when I'd decided to come to Tokyo. I remembered her standing at the ticket barrier in front of the Silver Clock at Nagoya Station, looking terribly sulky. She wouldn't wave to me.

"—Yuki Iwato. If anyone has seen…"

In spite of myself, I retracted my foot from the train step.

Huh?

"If anyone has seen Yuki Iwato, her brother is looking for her. Please contact the Lost Child Center. If you happen to be nearby, come to the center in person."

The doors shut right in front of my face, this time for real. As I stood there in a daze, the staff member pulled me back, away from the train.

"W-wait!"

"Stand back, please. It isn't safe."

With a disconsolate *hissss*, my reserved seat started to lurch away.

"If you've seen Yuki, please contact the Lost Child Center. If you happen to be nearby, come to the center—"

For a little while, I gazed after the receding bullet train, forgetting about the one that was on its way in.

10

The Lost Child Center was sandwiched between the Japan Rail ticket office and the Kiosk store. Yuki trudged toward it, pulling her aqua carry-on bag. I'd braced my arm on the shelf outside the ticket office, crouching down and pressing my free hand to my chest. When she saw me, Yuki looked dumbstruck. She fumbled the handle of her carry-on, and it fell over with a *thump*.

I straightened up and turned to face her squarely. She was standing stock-still about twenty steps away. At first her forehead was creased with bewilderment, but gradually, her eyebrows came down, and her lips trembled.

"I'm the one who called you."

A startled Lost Child Center clerical worker was staring at us through the window. Glancing from me to Yuki and back, she tilted her head as if she were watching some sort of bizarre phenomenon.

"This was the best I could do. I didn't have time to buy a ticket."

Yuki's lips were pressed together tightly.

"I wanted to talk to you," I said.

It might have sounded like a threat. Because of me, her train had left without her, and the next one wouldn't arrive for eleven minutes. I'd taken advantage of that to tether Yuki to this unstable no-man's-land.

"I wanted to apologize, no matter what."

"There's nothing for you to apologize—"

"I made you into a person who hibernated."

The clerical worker had gone back to working on her computer, but at that, she widened her eyes.

I took ten steps forward, then stopped, looking straight at Yuki. "On some level, I thought I was special. That I got left behind in winter, all by myself, like a tragic heroine or something. That's why, when I first saw you asleep at your parents' house, I decided you must be hibernating."

Back then, I'd thought I'd found the answer. I'd seen something preposterous, and I was desperate to put a name to it. The idea that I'd been caught up in some sort of story excited me. However, all I'd done was make an out-sider's random assumption. I'd acted as if I wanted to understand, but I'd been about as far from understanding as you could get.

"I left you behind at night, too, didn't I?"

Yuki's face crumpled.

I desperately hardened my expression; I was determined not to cry before she did. "I acted like I hated the prejudice people focused on you, but I was the most prejudiced one there."

A soft, cool wind blew down toward the concourse, rumpling my hair and coat as it passed.

"Then that picture...," she began.

"I saw it."

Yuki broke into a tiny smile, then pulled herself together again. "That's embarrassing," she murmured. "Is that how you figured it out?"

"Yeah, but I should have noticed sooner. I wound up doubting you."

"I see."

Even now, crowds of people were climbing up to the bullet train platforms, but none of them cut between Yuki and me. Although our surroundings must have been loud, the noise seemed distant. Only Yuki's outline stood out, illuminated by pale light.

Her plump red lips moved slightly. She'd started to murmur something, then swallowed the words instead.

"So I'm sorry—"

"That's no good," Yuki said, cutting me off. She looked away guiltily. "It's no good. We can't do this. I thought I'd listen to what you had to say and that would be the end of it, but then I was glad to hear your voice. Just a little." Holding her skirt down with one hand, she crouched and scooped up the handle of her carry-on bag. The dampness that had been in her eyes a moment ago was gone. Now there was firmness and a deep shadow there; her eyes reminded me of Fuyumi's.

"I've already made up my mind. I'm sorry."

When she bowed, her black hair tumbled forward, hanging down. It was a flawless, ninety-degree bow, and people started to stare.

"Thank you for everything."

Those words opened a rift right in front of me. My vision warped, and something hot welled up from the depths of my stomach.

"I need to be careful not to miss the next train."

Straightening up, Yuki glanced at me, then walked away. I stood there petrified as she started toward the ticket adjustment counter. Her back looked the same as it had the night I met her: distant and unapproachable.

She was close enough that I would have touched her if I reached out, but I couldn't do it. Yuki walked through the counter's automatic doors and called a staff member. My feet wouldn't move; I knew if I tried to keep her here by force, I was bound to screw up. I was still missing something crucial.

What was I missing?

I wanted to be with her. I wanted to be near her. I loved her. I wanted to protect her. And yet my way was clearly barred by something those childish arguments were powerless against.

What was it?

What was she most afraid of? Being alone. She knew she'd be closing the book on her relationship with me if she went home now. She was aware that she'd end up alone. Above and beyond that, though, she'd sensed that we'd hit our limit.

The adjustment counter's door opened, and Yuki came back. Slowing down in front of the ticket barrier, she looked my way, just once.

In that moment, I finally managed to identify that beautiful, ephemeral darkness in her eyes.

"You did it to survive, didn't you?!"

Yuki stopped moving.

I sucked in a lungful of air. "It was all so you could live, wasn't it? I was wrong. You…you always had your life on the line. I mean, obviously. While you're asleep, your life is completely out of your hands. Someone always has to take care of it for you. But who? Your parents? Your sister? None of them can do it forever. Didn't you always have a vague fear of death when it came to ending up alone?!"

I felt dizzy. I couldn't have hated myself more for not picking up on it, for being so oblivious to someone else's pain. I ground my teeth, and my fingernails bit into my palms.

"If I did…" Her small back and rounded shoulders began to tremble. "If I did, what would you do…? Natsuki, would you…stay with me…until I died?"

"Of course I would!"

I grabbed Yuki's arm and pulled her away from the ticket gate. Yuki's red, swollen eyes looked up at me, not quite able to maintain their focus.

"Of course I would. I'll stay with you forever… And I know. I know exactly how irresponsible those words are. I'm really disgusted with how easily I'm saying them."

"Then let me go." Yuki tugged on her trapped arm, putting up genuine resistance.

I resisted back, pulling her into a hug. "But this is the only way I can say it!"

Yuki's clenched left fist pounded my shoulder and neck. "I'm sorry," I said in her ear, over and over. Gradually, she stopped fighting so hard, and at last she went limp in my arms.

"This is the only way I can say it."

As if a dam had burst, a wail flooded out of her, and her warm breath seeped into the space between my shoulder and collarbone. The back of her skull was spasming. I gently covered it with a hand, then buried my head next to her ear, as fiercely as if I were going to bite it. "I'm sorry," I repeated, again and again, until the words had almost lost all meaning. For a little while, the only things with meaning that passed between us were our rough breathing and the warmth under our fingertips.

"It was pretty."

The words slipped out of me. I was irresistibly moved. Belatedly, the shock of that moment sparked in my mind.

Yuki had stepped back, out of my arms. Black eyes shining, she tilted her head, mystified. "Pretty?"

"The painting."

"Huh?"

"The one you made. On that huge canvas."

"Oh," Yuki murmured, nodding several times. Then her puffy eyelids blinked. "Did you maybe…see the back?"

Her cheeks had flushed faintly. I responded with an awkward smile, and just then, the 11:42 departure time disappeared from the electronic sign over our heads.

One week later, we left for Nagoya together. We invited Fuyumi to come with us, but she said she didn't want to deal with us flirting in front of her, so she left Tokyo two days later.

I always stayed in the storeroom. Every year, the dust had piled up again, but I felt cleaning it was the least I could do in exchange for being allowed to sleep there.

If you didn't sleep all winter, if your life were perfectly normal, would we even have met? Could I have entered your family home with you, held your hand as it grew colder?

It was still too early for me to know the answers to those questions. However, for two years now, I'd been given the role of holding your hand.

I asked Touko why that was. She said it was because, someday, family would go away. Yuki needed to gain something she could depend on with her own two hands.

"It might be you," she told me.

On November 1, 2020, the day after I saw you off, the Meteorological Agency recorded the year's first snow in Nagano.

Alone once again, I walked into another winter.

In my heart, I carried one unchanging promise.

That winter, Japan recorded its lowest temperatures and greatest snowfall in 145 years.

A long road lies in front of me.
The night wants to forget about the dawn,
wants to keep me alone forever.
But someone has cut the threads that kept me sewn to
the ground. Someone has lit my small lantern.
You'll never walk with me. This is my journey, time that's mine alone.
However, the light of this lantern you lit continues to shine
through the nights when you aren't here.

I can hear your breathing. The rise and fall of your chest as
you lie in bed is precious to me.
I can feel the heat of your body. The warmth wrapped in
that comforter still warms my skin.
I wave. I call out, quietly, that I'll be back soon.

I'm waiting for an awakening.
A journey of just eight hours may feel endless,
but the morning sun is bound to rise.
As always, I make fried eggs and toast, I brew coffee,
and I wait eagerly for you to wake up.

I opened my eyes to a gray, hazy world.

Beep, beep, beep. I heard an electronic noise at regular intervals, somewhere near my head.

I felt as if I'd been having an impossibly long dream.

I wanted to see him…to see Natsuki. Focused on that thought, I tried to get up, but I felt weaker than usual. My vision was blurred. Sounds seemed warped. Not only that, but I couldn't speak.

No one had noticed I was awake. Where was Mom? Fuyumi? One of them was always home. I wanted to call Natsuki right away.

With effort, I dragged my feet over the edge of the bed and managed to sit up. My eyes were still blurry, but the reason it had been hard to move was immediately clear.

Things that looked like black bandages were wound around both my arms and legs. They'd been put on over my hospital gown, which closed at the front, and they tightly squeezed my upper arms and forearms, my thighs and lower legs. Every so often, the bandages twitched, sending something that felt like a mild electrical shock through me. The shocks repeated at regular intervals, and as soon as I noticed them, the sensation turned into an almost unbearable itchiness.

"Wha…? It…i-itches!"

My voice was starting to work again, and I was so glad about it that I could have jumped for joy. Groping for the closures on the bandages, I pushed my opposite hand in. The side in contact with my arm was coated with a gel of some sort; the outside was fastened to itself with Velcro, like a blood pressure cuff, and I slowly ripped it open.

When I looked up, I saw an unfamiliar ceiling. Looking down brought an unfamiliar window into view. I didn't recognize the door, either.

Still sitting up, I shifted over, pulled out the needle stuck in my right arm, grabbed some gauze from the box by my pillow, and held it against the spot where the needle had been. A little red seeped into the gauze, and I kept pressing on it for a minute or so.

"O…kay…"

Getting my breathing under control, I counted to three, then shifted my weight onto my knees.

Strangely, I managed to stand without collapsing. I reached for the curtain and slowly pulled it aside. There was a *swish*, and pale light lanced in.

At first, I didn't know what it was. A white powdery substance was falling from the sky, all over the place. It fell in little clumps of all different sizes, and I could tell how strong the wind must be by the way it whirred down to the right and out of sight in an instant.

Maybe Dad or Natsuki had set up some sort of surprise for me. The white powder kept falling steadily, though, and no one knocked at the door.

"Oh, right. My smartphone."

I didn't see my favorite turtle smartphone stand. When I took another look out the long rectangular window, I saw streets far below where the neon was just beginning to come on.

I knew Natsuki had seen me off on my journey. I could still hear his voice saying, *Okay. I'll see you next spring.*

"Natsuki, where are you…?"

In our second spring together, he'd been holding my hand when I woke up. Just having him there had made that awakening special for me.

Glaring at the natural wood door, I pushed myself away from the edge of the bed. Staying as low as I could, poised to catch myself with my hands in case my knees buckled under me, I took one step, then another.

When I pushed the door, it opened easily. The moment it did, air colder than anything I'd ever felt blew in.

I shivered, flung open the closet, and grabbed white underwear, a long skirt, and a random turtleneck sweater. After returning to the bed, I got dressed, then made my way along the wall again.

At some point, I found the start of a wooden handrail, so I leaned on that until I'd made it to the front door.

I found a crutch in the umbrella stand and a coat and sheepskin cap on the hat rack. The coat was a little too big. One of the doors of the shoe cupboard was a mirror.

I gazed at my full-length reflection. There I was, almost twenty-five, a third-year in college.

I wasn't satisfied with the outfit I'd thrown together, but I pulled my sneakers on and left through the front door.

"Where am I?"

A strange town spread out below me.

I could see the setting sun on the horizon. The pale-pink sky was gradually turning blue.

"I have to find somebody... Right, I'll go to the police station."

I tried to press the button for the elevator, but it had a touch panel instead.

When I got to the building entrance, an automatic door opened for me. A man and woman came walking my way, arm in arm, holding several paper bags. As they passed, they nodded to me. I tried to speak, but a bow was all I could manage. I went outside, hurrying a little to get through the door before it closed.

The cold air crept up under the hem of my skirt, chilling me to the waist. I buttoned my coat.

White powder fluttered down from the purple sky and landed on my nose. It was cold. It hadn't seemed real when I looked at it from my room, but things were different now.

I spread my arms wide and stood still for a little while. I cupped my hands together, trying to gather the cold substance as it fell. The flakes looked large, but they vanished the moment they touched my hands, melting into droplets of water that looked like tears. Just as I gave up on catching them, another couple walked past me, and then—

"Excuse me. Are you the tenant from room 1405? You're awake."

The kind voice came from quite a ways below me. When I looked down, a woman the size of a small child was looking up at me, holding the hand of a tall man. At first glance, she really did seem like a child, but the timbre of her voice and the cast of her features made it clear she was an adult. The man frowned, looking troubled; he watched me but kept his head low.

"You mean…you know me?"

"Yes, I believe so." The woman smiled, revealing crooked teeth. "Only on paper, of course. This is the Hometown Building, you see."

"The Hometown Building…?"

"It's a privacy-free building, a good old-fashioned place that supports a neighborly spirit of cooperation." At that point, the woman got a little flustered and waved her hands in front of her chest dismissively. "I don't mean everybody knows everything, of course. We just know one another's lines of work, ages, and any major diseases or disorders we might need to be aware of."

"Diseases…"

"They're obvious with some people, like me, but that's not true of everybody." The woman scratched her head and smiled, looking a little abashed.

"Wait," I broke in, although the woman had seemed like she wanted to say more. "What disease was put down for me?"

"I'm pretty sure you were…"

As the woman racked her brain, the man crouched down, squeezing her small hand. I heard him say "It's cold. We should go soon" in a low voice. The woman nodded, then looked up at me again.

"I think it was Snow Sleep Syndrome. It's a type of designated intractable illness. When your surroundings reach a certain temperature, you fall into a long sleep, and your metabolism and aging slow down significantly."

The town was decked out with ornamental lights, and the streets teemed with people. It was the bustle of a town in winter, something I'd never seen. That wasn't the strangest thing about it, though. For one thing, the glass of the buildings occasionally displayed images, and driverless cars sped through the streets.

I walked around searching for a police station but couldn't find one. I tried to stop someone on the street and borrow their smartphone, but everyone wore a glowing device on their ear, and none of them had phones.

There wasn't a single thing here that I knew.

The clothes people wore, the way they walked, even the gestures they used while they ate seemed different from the world I knew.

Finally, I stopped walking. Beside a beverage store with a sign that said PERFECT NUTRITION JUICE, I found a row of vending machines. Crouching down on the stone paving between two of them, I stuck my cane under my knees and gazed at the white powder as it drifted down.

"I'll take a little break."

It would be fine. I was particularly good at killing time.

I watched the town. It kept on moving, all by itself; I didn't have to do a thing.

How long had I been there? The blanket of people that had buried the town had thinned out and only driverless taxis were on the streets when, out of nowhere, a shadow fell over me.

"Are you all right?"

The voice made a hard shiver run through my shoulders, and they bumped into the vending machines on either side, shaking them.

"Y-yes." I looked up and saw a man deep in shadow. The light was behind him, so I couldn't make out his expression. I retrieved my crutch from beneath my knees and tried to get to my feet, but my thighs were numb, and I couldn't get them to hold me. I nearly fell.

"Careful." The man put his arm below my shoulders, supporting me. Thanks to that, I managed to avoid a fall. As I used my crutch to compensate for my lack of strength, the numbness faded, and I gently stepped away from the man's arm.

"I-I'm sorry."

"It's fine." The man seemed to be trembling slightly. When I saw that, I remembered how cold the world was, and that I'd forgotten even to shiver.

"I was working over there. You'd been here for two hours, and you hadn't moved, so…I thought maybe…"

"Maybe?"

For a moment, the man's eyebrows drew together as if he was troubled. Then he exhaled a white puff of breath and went on. "I thought maybe you weren't feeling well, and I got worried."

The man was in his fifties, with round glasses and a beard. He wore a flat-topped cap with a brim and a navy-blue Chester coat over a suit. He held his umbrella out to me. "I work at a publishing house, you see." He shifted his bag to his free hand. "I used to want to be a novelist, way back when, but it just wasn't working out. I ended up taking this job instead."

"I…see."

"My boss was a couple of years ahead of me at my university. She's an eccentric and lethally strict, so I fled to a coworking space… Oops. That was too much information too soon, wasn't it? I'm sorry. In other words, we're—"

For a moment, the man's eyes gazed at something in the distance.

He was a complete stranger, and yet, oddly, I didn't feel afraid. That in itself was a bit creepy, and I wasn't sure how to respond to him.

When the man spoke again, he sounded as if he'd finally managed to find the right words to say. "What I mean is, we're probably going to catch colds if we stand out here talking. I'm a regular at a restaurant nearby. Let me buy you a drink… No, a meal."

Timidly, I accepted the umbrella he offered me.

"I became a certain new writer's supervising editor one year ago," the man said as he walked along to my right. The black umbrella he'd handed me was wider than I needed. On top of that, the man had taken a smaller collapsible umbrella from his bag, so there was quite a lot of space between us. However, the distance was made more obvious by the odd way the man walked: He kept his eyes on the ground the whole time.

"I'm told he's been writing since he was in college. He achieved his dream in style. But he wanted more than just to be published. He's struck out on an uncommon path. He's the type who can pull off what I couldn't. That's why I want to support him with everything I've got."

"I see."

"After our meetings, he and I often go drinking at the place we're headed to now."

Nothing the man told me mattered. The umbrella I was clinging to was his, though, and he was the only person I could have a proper conversation with. No matter what sort of place he took me to, I couldn't complain.

As we entered an area where more buildings had window glass doubling as video screens, the man turned up an alley. I kept walking with a lack of resistance that struck me as odd. For a total stranger, this man was easy to talk to. My curiosity about him was pretty much the only thing that carried me along.

"Do you think I'm strange?" he asked. "...It's all right. I get that a lot."

I'd been stealing frequent glances at the man's face for a while now, and apparently, he'd misinterpreted them. I shook my head, but the man gave a self-deprecating smile and kept his eyes on the ground. "Blame it on the season."

On the first floor of a sooty commercial building, a set of stairs had been filled in and smoothed out into a ramp. There was nothing resembling a shop sign out front, just a small emblem composed of a cross in a red circle.

It was a casual pub, its interior decorated in red and green. There was no shop curtain at the door and no sign set outside. Even so, the salt, pepper, and spice-mix bottles set out on the tables convinced me it wasn't some high-class club or bar.

The faint spicy aroma drifting through the air woke up my appetite, but right now, that only caused me pain. Holding my stomach, I bent over and hurried to the nearest chair.

We were the only customers, and there was just one employee. The man hung his coat on a hook, set his leather bag down on one chair, then sat down in the seat next to it. "This place has a nice atmosphere, doesn't it? It's a pub; it used to be near my house, but they moved. Basically, I followed them over here."

The employee brought us water, and the man briskly opened the menu. Slowly, drinking in little sips, I drained my glass.

The man ordered his own food, then glanced at me and made some sort of addition to his order.

"Right now, I'm not...," I began.

"It's fine."

Before long, a dish of cucumbers sprinkled with black powder and a bowl of clear soup arrived at our table.

"This place had the Universal mark outside, didn't it? Lots of places are significantly more accommodating than they used to be. Muslims and people with Crohn's disease have plenty of options now, too. That's a low-residue, highly nutritious spiced onion soup. Mine are numbing cucumbers."

The translucent brown soup was in a shallow bowl. I scooped up a big silver spoonful and brought it to my lips. It was hot enough to burn my tongue, and when I swallowed, I felt its warmth spread through my chest.

When I was a child, every time I had just woken up, my mother would caution me over and over: *Drink slowly. You may be awake, but your stomach is still asleep.* I knew I should eat more carefully, slow my spoon down, but I couldn't.

"Take it slow."

The back of my spoon kept hitting the bottom of my bowl with a repetitive *tnk, tnk.* I couldn't stop. I remembered the Ensures I'd forced down, holding my nose. The brown sugar kind was all right, but chocolate was awful. This, though. This was almost like...

"Slowly. That's right. Go slowly."

For some reason, even though its register, depth, and volume were completely different, the man's voice reminded me of my mother's. Around the time the pain in my stomach disappeared—not completely, but almost—the server cleared away my bowl.

"Was it good?" the man asked.

"Yes, very."

"I'm glad." The man shifted his cap back and smiled, massaging his beard.

The loud hum of the ceiling fan hurt my ears. Along the pillars set into the counter, I could see something that looked like jars of cayenne peppers. My memories felt scrambled. I thought I'd seen this somewhere before, but I couldn't remember where.

"This can't be right."

The warmth that had filled my stomach was gradually thawing me.

"There's something strange about you… I mean, you brought me here because you knew about my condition, didn't you? What am I doing here?"

The man only nodded silently. There was a gentle smile on his lips.

"Tell me…what you know. Why do you look as if you're seeing right through me…? This isn't— It can't be right. Even I don't know these things, so why do you know so much…? What do you know?"

This was crazy.

No, it had been crazy right from the start.

From the moment I was born, everything had been predetermined. No matter how hard I tried, no matter what road I took, the fact that it would all fall apart was clear. The hands in my lap clenched into fists, then turned to stone. My vision blurred, and my ears rang.

"I don't know everything about you, but I do know some things.'"

"You know that can't be true!"

"The thing is…" The man took his cap off and gently set it on the table. His hair, which had been clipped short, fluffed up slightly. "I stumble a lot. After a certain point, I stopped being able to look at the sky. Especially in winter. That white stuff coming down—I can't deal with it. I started taking a black umbrella with me whenever I went outside so I wouldn't see it. The umbrella doesn't keep me from stumbling. Sometimes, though, it comes in handy."

He removed his glasses and looked me steadily in the eye.

"Why is that…?" I asked.

"I promised someone I'd stay with her forever. Then she went far away, and she just wouldn't come back. The only thing I could do was hold her hand."

The black and white areas of his eyes were very clearly delineated. I didn't just recognize them—I'd seen them constantly, right up to the very last moment I remembered.

"But that's… If that's true… This can't be right; I mean…"

"It really is crazy, isn't it? I just couldn't take it, though… I couldn't stand to see the snow."

His sagging cheeks and eyes, the smile lines around his mouth, the mild set of his lips. There were plenty of age spots on his skin and several deep wrinkles on his forehead. His hair had grown coarser, and I wasn't sure he was taking proper care of it. However, if I stripped away all the traces of time clinging to his face, the expression that remained matched his and his alone— that special person dwelling in my memories.

The man—no, *he* slowly got to his feet. I remembered the way he stood. He came around to the side of my chair and knelt there, looking up at me.

"I didn't want to see it unless I was with you."

His voice was very sweet.

Somewhere along the way, my words had deserted me. The tens of thousands of things I should say to him flew off in all directions, and in the end, I didn't even make a sound. The violent pounding of my heart, the breath that skimmed my throat, even the sound of my fingernails raking the tablecloth— in that instant, all noise vanished, and I became nothing more than an eye that gazed at him.

Hesitantly, his hand reached up to my lap. With tears in his eyes, he extended it like Kandata reaching toward the spider's thread. I caught it, pulled it to my chest, brushed my long hair out of the way, and pressed it to my forehead.

His hand was warmer.

"Good morning, Yuki."

On the counter, I saw a digital clock. It was after 12:44. There was a dirty-looking piece of wood propped up next to it. It was painted dark red, and its barely legible letters spelled out TANGIER. The man's eyes scrunched up, and amid his bristly whiskers, his lips trembled as if he couldn't take it. This fully grown man, covered with the signs of aging, now looked far younger than he had when we first met.

Tears were streaming down my face, but I didn't sob. On a quiet night, a night on which everything had been washed away, I stared, captivated by this kneeling, sniffling man.

According to the time on the digital clock, we'd just missed the last train.

From that day on, my disease never came back.

About six years ago, I wrote a novel. I worked on it in an armchair at the end of an eighth-floor corridor in the east building of the Red Cross Nagoya First Hospital. There was a little round table there, but mostly I wedged a cushion into my lap and wrote on that. I remember there was a rectangular window that gave me a great view of Nakamura Ward at night, and that the river of headlights along the highway was pretty.

In the hospital at night, I could hear the faint undulating noise of the EKG machines, and the low lights of the nurses' station illuminated the corridor. People say hospitals are scary, but this one wasn't. I sat in the armchair with my MacBook open, said hello to the nurses who occasionally came by on their rounds, and wrote. It was a story about a girl who came from outer space, a modern-day Princess Kaguya story I'd titled *Bamboo Girl*.

Writing helped me stay strong.

Having something that would stick around even if I didn't make it was sort of… I'm not sure how to put it. It was like a save point in a game. I was still planning to return to my regular life, though. I had two faces: I'd feel down, but in the pit of my stomach, I was squaring up for a fight.

In October, I got through the toughest part of my treatment, and I felt as if I'd gained a little time. Since I had the chance, I decided to go to a university where I could study writing. My school was a place where aspiring creative types gathered. There were lots of weirdos. When I asked later on, they told me I was pretty weird, too. Looking back, I think I put up walls because I was uneasy. In my first year, though, a certain teacher told me, "You've got a reason to write, so you'll keep writing. That means you'll be fine." Even now, that "You'll be fine" still keeps me warm.

I've got a crowd of people I want to thank: the teacher who liked *Uma Musume Pretty Derby*, the people who've stayed friends with me through this and that, the staff of the Mie University Gastrointestinal and Pediatric Surgery Department, the underclassmen who read this book before I submitted it to the contest, the "back numbers" who read it again and again like complete fiends during my revisions, and countless others.

That said, I think my mom is the reason I survived to write this book. She cared for me more devotedly than anyone else for four years, so please allow me to take this opportunity to set down an expression of gratitude, one I'm usually too embarrassed to tell her: thank you.

I wonder if Yuki told Touko the same thing. I hope she did.

After all, we can't believe anything except what we see and hear. That's true for me, and for everybody else. I think it's important to put things into words, so that's what I'm going to do.

Thank you very much for picking up this book. You've made me really happy. I hope you'll take a look at the next one as well.

Rokudo Ningen